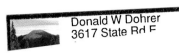

TUTT AND MR. TUTT

ARTHUR TRAIN

TUTT AND MR. TUTT

BIBLIOBAZAAR

TUTT AND MR. TUTT

CONTENTS

THE HUMAN ELEMENT

Although men flatter themselves with their great actions, they are not so often the result of great design as of chance.—LA ROCHEFOUCAULD.

"He says he killed him, and that's all there is about it!" said Tutt to Mr. Tutt. "What are you going to do with a fellow like that?" The junior partner of the celebrated firm of Tutt & Tutt, attorneys and counselors at law, thrust his hands deep into the pockets of his yellow checked breeches and, balancing himself upon the heels of his patent-leather boots, gazed in a distressed, respectfully inquiring manner at his distinguished associate.

"Yes," he repeated plaintively. "He don't make any bones about it at all. 'Sure, I killed him!' says he. 'And I'd kill him again, the—!' I prefer not to quote his exact language. I've just come from the Tombs and had quite a talk with Serafino in the counsel room, with a gum-chewing keeper sitting in the corner watching me for fear I'd slip his prisoner a saw file or a shotgun or a barrel of poison. I'm all in! These murder cases drive me to drink, Mr. Tutt. I don't mind grand larceny, forgery, assault or even manslaughter—but murder gets my goat! And when you have a crazy Italian for a client who says he's glad he did it and would like to do it again—please excuse me! It isn't law; it's suicide!"

He drew out a silk handkerchief ornamented with the colors of the Allies, and wiped his forehead despairingly.

"Oh," remarked Mr. Tutt with entire good nature. "He's glad he did it and he's quite willing to be hanged!"

"That's it in a nutshell!" replied Tutt.

The senior partner of Tutt & Tutt ran his bony fingers through the lank gray locks over his left eye and tilted ceilingward the stogy between his thin lips. Then he leaned back in his antique swivel chair, locked his hands behind his head, elevated his long legs luxuriously, and crossed his feet upon the fourth volume of the American and English Encyclopedia of Law, which lay open upon the desk at Champerty and Maintenance. Even in this inelegant and relaxed posture he somehow managed to maintain the air of picturesque dignity which always made his tall, ungainly figure noticeable in any courtroom. Indubitably Mr. Ephraim Tutt suggested a past generation, the suggestion being accentuated by a slight pedantry of diction a trifle out of character with the rushing age in which he saw fit to practise his time-honored profession. "Cheer up, Tutt," said he, pushing a box of stogies toward his partner with the toe of his congress boot. "Have a weed?"

Since in the office of Tutt & Tutt such an invitation like those of royalty, was equivalent to a command, Tutt acquiesced.

"Thank you, Mr. Tutt," said Tutt, looking about vaguely for a match.

"That conscienceless brat of a Willie steals 'em all," growled Mr. Tutt. "Ring the bell."

Tutt obeyed. He was a short, brisk little man with a pronounced abdominal convexity, and he maintained toward his superior, though but a few years his junior, a mingled attitude of awe, admiration and affection such as a dickey bird might adopt toward a distinguished owl.

This attitude was shared by the entire office force. Inside the ground glass of the outer door Ephraim Tutt was king. To Tutt the opinion of Mr. Tutt upon any subject whatsoever was law, even if the courts might have held to the contrary. To Tutt he was the eternal fount of wisdom, culture and morality. Yet until Mr. Tutt finally elucidated his views Tutt did not hesitate to hold conditional if temporary opinions of his own. Briefly their relations were symbolized by the circumstance that while Tutt always addressed his senior partner as "Mr. Tutt," the latter accosted him simply as "Tutt." In a word there was only one Mr. Tutt in the firm of Tutt & Tutt.

But so far as that went there was only one Tutt. On the theory that a lily cannot be painted, the estate of one seemingly was as dignified as that of the other. At any rate there never was and never had been any confusion or ambiguity arising out of the matter since the day, twenty years before, when Tutt had visited Mr. Tutt's law office in search of employment. Mr. Tutt was just rising into fame as a police-court lawyer. Tutt had only recently been admitted to the bar, having abandoned his native city of Bangor, Maine, for the metropolis.

"And may I ask why you should come to me?" Mr. Tutt had demanded severely from behind the stogy, which even at that early date had been as much a part of his facial anatomy as his long ruminative nose. "Why the devil should you come to me? I am nobody, sir—nobody! In this great city certainly there are thousands far more qualified than I to further your professional and financial advancement."

"Because," answered the inspired Tutt with modesty, "I feel that with you I should be associated with a good name."

That had settled the matter. They bore no relationship to one another, but they were the only Tutts in the city and there seemed to be a certain propriety in their hanging together. Neither had regretted it for a moment, and as the years passed they became indispensable to each other. They were the necessary component parts of a harmonious legal whole. Mr. Tutt was the brains and the voice, while Tutt was the eyes and legs of a combination that at intervals—rare ones, it must be confessed—made the law tremble, sometimes in fear and more often with joy.

At first, speaking figuratively, Tutt merely carried Mr. Tutt's bag—rode on his coat tails, as it were; but as time went on his activity, ingenuity and industry made him indispensable and led to a junior partnership. Tutt prepared the cases for Mr. Tutt to try. Both were well versed in the law if they were not profound lawyers, but as the origin of the firm was humble, their practise was of a miscellaneous character.

"Never turn down a case," was Tutt's motto.

"Our duty as sworn officers of the judicial branch of the Government renders it incumbent upon us to perform whatever services our clients' exigencies demand," was Mr. Tutt's way of putting it.

In the end it amounted to exactly the same thing. As a result, in addition to their own clientele, other members of the bar who found themselves encumbered with matters which for one reason or another they preferred not to handle formed the habit of turning them over to Tutt & Tutt. A never-ending stream of peculiar cases flowed through the office, each leaving behind it some residuum of golden dust, however small. The stately or, as an unkind observer might have put it, the ramshackly form of the senior partner was a constant figure in all the courts, from that of the coroner on the one hand to the appellate tribunals upon the other. It was immaterial to him what the case was about—whether it dealt with the "next eventual estate" or the damages for a dog bite—so long as he was paid and Tutt prepared it. Hence Tutt & Tutt prospered. And as the law, like any other profession requires jacks-of-all-trades, the firm acquired a certain peculiar professional standing of its own, and enjoyed the good will of the bar as a whole.

They had the reputation of being sound lawyers if not overafflicted with a sense of professional dignity, whose word was better than their bond, yet who, faithful to their clients' interests knew no mercy and gave no quarter. They took and pressed cases which other lawyers dared not touch lest they should be defiled—and nobody seemed to think any the less of them for so doing. They raised points that made the refinements of the ancient schoolmen seem blunt in comparison. No respecters of persons, they harried the rich and taunted the powerful, and would have as soon jailed a bishop or a judge as a pickpocket if he deserved it. Between them they knew more kinds of law than most of their professional brethren, and as Mr. Tutt was a bookworm and a seeker after legal and other lore their dusty old library was full of hidden treasures, which on frequent occasions were unearthed to entertain the jury or delight the bench. They were loyal friends, fearsome enemies, high chargers, and maintained their unique position in spite of the fact that at one time or another they had run close to the shadowy line which divides the ethical from that which is not. Yet Mr. Tutt had brought disbarment proceedings against many lawyers in his time and—what is more—had them disbarred.

"Leave old Tutt alone," was held sage advice, and when other lawyers desired to entertain the judiciary they were apt to invite Mr. Tutt to be of the party. And Tutt gloried in the glories of Mr. Tutt.

"That's it!" repeated Tutt as he lit his stogy, which flared up like a burning bush, the cub of a Willie having foraged successfully in the outer office for a match. "He's willing to be hanged or damned or anything else just for the sake of putting a bullet through the other fellow!"

"What was the name of the unfortunate deceased?"

"Tomasso Crocedoro—a barber."

"That is almost a defense in itself," mused Mr. Tutt. "Anyhow, if I've got to defend Angelo for shooting Tomasso you might as well give me a short scenario of the melodrama. By the way, are we retained or assigned by the court?"

"Assigned," chirped Tutt.

"So that all we'll get out of it is about enough to keep me in stogies for a couple of months!"

"And—if he's convicted, as of course he will be—a good chance of losing our reputation as successful trial counsel. Why not beg off?"

"Let me hear the story first," answered Mr. Tutt. "Angelo sounds like a good sport. I have a mild affection for him already."

He reached into the lower compartment of his desk and lifted out a tumbler and a bottle of malt extract, which he placed carefully at his elbow. Then he leaned back again expectantly.

"It is a simple and naive story," began Tutt, seating himself in the chair reserved for paying clients—that is to say, one which did not have the two front legs sawed off an inch or so in order to make lingering uncomfortable. "A plain, unvarnished tale. Our client is one who makes an honest living by blacking shoes near the entrance to the Brooklyn Bridge. He is one of several hundred original Tonys who conduct shoe-shining emporiums."

"Emporia," corrected his partner, pouring out a tumbler of malt extract.

"He formed an attachment for a certain young lady," went on Tutt, undisturbed, "who had previously had some sort of love affair with Crocedoro, as a result of which her social standing had become slightly impaired. In a word Tomasso jilted her. Angelo saw, pitied and loved her, took her for better or for worse, and married her."

"For which," interjected Mr. Tutt, "he is entitled to everyone's respect."

"Quite so!" agreed Tutt. "Now Tomasso, though not willing to marry the girl himself, seems to have resented the idea of having anyone else do so, and accordingly seized every opportunity which presented itself to twit Angelo about the matter."

"Dog in the manger, so to speak," nodded Mr. Tutt.

"He not only jeered at Angelo for marrying Rosalina but he began to hang about his discarded mistress again and scoff at her choice of a husband. But Rosalina gave him the cold shoulder, with the result that he became more and more insulting to Angelo. Finally one day our client made up his mind not to stand it any longer, secured a revolver, sought out Tomasso in his barber shop and put a bullet through his head. Now however much you may sympathize with Angelo as a man and a husband there isn't the slightest doubt that he killed Tomasso with every kind of deliberation and premeditation."

"If the case is as you say," replied Mr. Tutt, replacing the bottle and tumbler within the lower drawer and flicking a stogy ash from his waistcoat, "the honorable justice who handed it to us is no friend of ours."

"He isn't," assented his partner. "It was Babson and he hates Italians. Moreover, he stated in open court that he proposed to try the case himself next Monday and that we must be ready without fail."

"So Babson did that to us!" growled Mr. Tutt. "Just like him. He'll pack the jury and charge our innocent Angelo into the middle of hades."

"And O'Brien is the assistant district attorney in charge of the prosecution," mildly added Tutt. "But what can we do? We're assigned, we've got a guilty client, and we've got to defend him."

"Have you set Bonnie Doon looking up witnesses?" asked Mr. Tutt. "I thought I saw him outside during the forenoon."

"Yes," replied Tutt. "But Bonnie says it's the toughest case he ever had to handle in which to find any witnesses for the defense. There aren't any. Besides, the girl bought the gun and gave it to Angelo the same day."

"How do you know that?" demanded Mr. Tutt, frowning.

"Because she told me so herself," said Tutt. "She's outside if you want to see her."

"I might as well give her what you call 'the once over,'" replied the senior partner.

Tutt retired and presently returned half leading, half pushing a shrinking young Italian woman, shabbily dressed but with the features of one of Raphael's madonnas. She wore no hat and her hands and finger nails were far from clean, but from the folds of her black shawl her neck rose like a column of slightly discolored Carrara marble, upon which her head with its coils of heavy hair was poised with the grace of a sulky empress.

"Come in, my child, and sit down," said Mr. Tutt kindly. "No, not in that one; in that one." He indicated the chair previously occupied by his junior. "You can leave us, Tutt. I want to talk to this young lady alone."

The girl sat sullenly with averted face, showing in her attitude her instinctive feeling that all officers of the law, no matter upon which side they were supposed to be, were one and all engaged in a mysterious conspiracy of which she and her unfortunate Angelo were the victims. A few words from the old lawyer and she began to feel more confidence, however. No one, in fact, could help but realize at first glance Mr. Tutt's warmth of heart. The lines of his sunken cheeks if left to themselves automatically tended to draw together into a whimsical smile, and it required a positive act of will upon his part to adopt the stern and relentless look with which he was wont to glower down upon some unfortunate witness in cross-examination.

Inside Mr. Tutt was a benign and rather mellow old fellow, with a dry sense of humor and a very keen knowledge of his fellow men. He made a good deal of money, but not having any wife or child upon which to lavish it he spent it all either on books or surreptitiously in quixotic gifts to friends or strangers whom he either secretly admired or whom he believed to be in need of money. There were vague traditions in the office of presents of bizarre and quite impossible clothes made to office boys and stenographers; of ex-convicts reoutfitted and sent rejoicing to foreign parts; of tramps gorged to repletion and then pumped dry of their adventures in Mr. Tutt's comfortable, dingy old library; of a fur coat suddenly clapped upon the rounded shoulders of old Scraggs, the antiquated scrivener in the accountant's cage in the outer office, whose alcoholic career, his employer alleged, was marked by a trail of empty rum kegs, each one flying the white flag of surrender.

And yet old Ephraim Tutt could on occasion be cold as chiseled steel, and as hard. Any appeal from a child, a woman or an outcast always met with his ready response; but for the rich, successful and those in power he seemed to entertain a deep and enduring grudge. He would burn the midnight oil with equal zest to block a crooked deal on the part of a wealthy corporation or to devise a means to extricate some no less crooked rascal from the clutches of the law, provided that the rascal seemed the victim of hard luck, inheritance or environment. His weather-beaten conscience was as elastic as his heart. Indeed when under the expansive influence of a sufficient quantity of malt extract or ancient brandy from the cellaret on his library desk he had sometimes been heard to enunciate the theory that there was very little difference between the people in jail and those who were not.

He would work weeks without compensation to argue the case of some guilty rogue before the Court of Appeals, in order, as he said, to "settle the law," when his only real object was to get the miserable fellow out of jail and send him back to his wife and children. He went through life with a twinkling eye and a quizzical smile, and when he did wrong he did it—if such a thing is possible—in a way to make people better. He was a dangerous adversary and judges were afraid of him, not because he ever tricked or deceived them but because of the audacity and novelty of his arguments which left them speechless. He had the assurance that usually comes with age and with a lifelong knowledge of human nature, yet apparently he had always been possessed of it.

Once a judge having assigned him to look out for the interests of a lawyerless prisoner suggested that he take his new client into the adjoining jury room and give him the best advice he could. Mr. Tutt was gone so long that the judge became weary, and to find out what had become of him sent an officer, who found the lawyer reading a newspaper beside an open window, but no sign of the prisoner. In great excitement the officer reported the situation to the judge, who ordered Mr. Tutt to the bar.

"What has become of the prisoner?" demanded His Honor.

"I do not know," replied the lawyer calmly. "The window was open and I suspect that he used it as a means of exit."

"Are you not aware that you are a party to an escape—a crime?" hotly challenged the judge.

"I most respectfully deny the charge," returned Mr. Tutt.

"I told you to take the prisoner into that room and give him the best advice you could."

"I did!" interjected the lawyer.

"Ah!" exclaimed the judge. "You admit it! What advice did you give him?"

"The law does not permit me to state that," answered Mr. Tutt in his most dignified tones. "That is a privileged communication from the inviolate obligation to preserve which only my client can release me—I cannot betray a sacred trust. Yet I might quote Cervantes and remind Your Honor that 'Fortune leaves always some door open to come at a remedy!'"

Now as he gazed at the tear-stained cheeks of the girl-wife whose husband had committed murder in defense of her self-respect, he vowed that so far as he was able he would fight to save him. The more desperate the case the more desperate her need of him—the greater the duty and the greater his honor if successful.

"Believe that I am your friend, my dear!" he assured her. "You and I must work together to set Angelo free."

"It's no use," she returned less defiantly. "He done it. He won't deny it."

"But he is entitled to his defense," urged Mr. Tutt quietly.

"He won't make no defense."

"We must make one for him."

"There ain't none. He just went and killed him."

Mr. Tutt shrugged his shoulders.

"There is always a defense," he answered with conviction. "Anyhow we can't let him be convicted without making an effort. Will they be able to prove where he got the pistol?"

"He didn't get the pistol," retorted the girl with a glint in her black eyes. "I got it. I'd ha' shot him myself if he hadn't. I said I was goin' to, but he wouldn't let me."

"Dear, dear!" sighed Mr. Tutt. "What a case! Both of you trying to see which could get hanged first!"

The inevitable day of Angelo's trial came. Upon the bench the Honorable Mr. Justice Babson glowered down upon the cowering defendant flanked by his distinguished counsel, Tutt & Tutt, and upon the two hundred good and true talesmen who, "all other business laid aside," had been dragged from the comfort of their homes and the important affairs of their various livelihoods to pass upon the merits of the issue duly joined between The People of the State of New York and Angelo Serafino, charged with murder.

One by one as his name was called each took his seat in the witness chair upon the *voir dire* and perjured himself like a gentleman in order to escape from service, shyly confessing to an ineradicable prejudice against the entire Italian race and this defendant in particular, and to an antipathy against capital punishment which, so each unhesitatingly averred, would render him utterly incapable of satisfactorily performing his functions if selected as a juryman. Hardly one, however, but was routed by the Machiavellian Babson. Hardly one, however ingenious his excuse— whether about to be married or immediately become a father, whether engaged in a business deal involving millions which required his instant and personal attention whether in the last stages of illness or obligated to be present at the bedside of a dying wife—but was browbeaten into helplessness and ordered back to take his place amidst the waiting throng of recalcitrant citizens so disinclined to do their part in elevating that system of trial by jury the failure of which at other times they so loudly condemned.

This trifling preliminary having been concluded, the few jurymen who had managed to wriggle through the judicial sieve were allowed to withdraw, the balance of the calendar was adjourned, those spectators who were standing up were ordered to sit down and those already sitting down were ordered to sit somewhere else, the prisoners in the rear of the room were sent back to the Tombs to await their fate upon some later day, the reporters gathered rapaciously about the table just behind the defendant, a corpulent Ganymede in the person of an aged court officer bore tremblingly an opaque glass of yellow drinking water to the bench, O'Brien the prosecutor blew his nose with a fanfare of trumpets, Mr. Tutt smiled an ingratiating smile which seemed to clasp the whole world to his bosom—and the real battle commenced; a game in which every card in the pack had been stacked against the prisoner by an unscrupulous pair of officials whose only aim was to maintain their record of convictions of "murder in the first" and who laid their plans with ingenuity and carried them out with skill and enthusiasm to habitual success.

They were a grand little pair of convictors, were Babson and O'Brien, and woe unto that man who was brought before them. It was even alleged by the impious that when Babson was in doubt what to do or what O'Brien wanted him to do the latter communicated the information to his conspirator upon the bench by a system of preconcerted signals. But indeed no such system was necessary, for the judge's part in the drama was merely to sustain his colleague's objections and overrule those of his opponent, after which he himself delivered the *coup de grace* with unerring insight and accuracy. When Babson got through charging a jury the latter had always in fact been instructed in brutal and sneering tones to convict the defendant or forever after to regard themselves as disloyal citizens, oath violators and outcasts though the stenographic record of his remarks would have led the reader thereof to suppose that this same judge was a conscientious, tender-hearted merciful lover of humanity, whose sensitive soul quivered at the mere thought of a prison cell, and who meticulously sought to surround the defendant with every protection the law could interpose against the imputation of guilt.

He was, as Tutt put it, "a dangerous old cuss." O'Brien was even worse. He was a bull-necked, bullet-headed, pugnosed young ruffian with beery eyes, who had an insatiable ambition and a still greater conceit, but who had devised a blundering, innocent, helpless way of conducting himself before a jury that deceived them into believing that his inexperience required their help and his disinterestedness their loyal support. Both of them were apparently fair-minded, honest public servants; both in reality were subtly disingenuous to a degree beyond ordinary comprehension, for years of practise had made them sensitive to every whimsy of emotion and taught them how to play upon the psychology of the jury as the careless zephyr softly draws its melody from the aeolian harp. In a word

20

they were a precious pair of crooks, who for their own petty selfish ends played fast and loose with liberty, life and death.

Both of them hated Mr. Tutt, who had more than once made them ridiculous before the jury and shown them up before the Court of Appeals, and the old lawyer recognized well the fact that these two legal wolves were in revenge planning to tear him and his helpless client to pieces, having first deliberately selected him as a victim and assigned him to officiate at a ceremony which, however just so far as its consummation might be concerned, was nothing less in its conduct than judicial murder. Now they were laughing at him in their sleeves, for Mr. Tutt enjoyed the reputation of never having defended a client who had been convicted of murder, and that spotless reputation was about to be annihilated forever.

Though the defense had thirty peremptory challenges Mr. Tutt well knew that Babson would sustain the prosecutor's objections for bias until the jury box would contain the twelve automata personally selected by O'Brien in advance from what Tutt called "the army of the gibbet." Yet the old war horse outwardly maintained a calm and genial exterior, betraying none of the apprehension which in fact existed beneath his mask of professional composure. The court officer rapped sharply for silence.

"Are you quite ready to proceed with the case?" inquired the judge with a courtesy in which was ill concealed a leer of triumph.

"Yes, Your Honor," responded Mr. Tutt in velvet tones.

"Call the first talesman!"

The fight was on, the professional duel between traditional enemies, in which the stake—a human life—was in truth the thing of least concern, had begun. Yet no casual observer would have suspected the actual significance of what was going on or the part that envy, malice, uncharitableness, greed, selfishness and ambition were playing in it. He would have seen merely a partially filled courtroom flooded with sunshine from high windows, an attentive and dignified judge in a black silk robe sitting upon a dais below which a white-haired clerk drew little slips of paper from a wheel and summoned jurymen to a service which outwardly bore no suggestion of a tragedy.

He would have seen a somewhat unprepossessing assistant district attorney lounging in front of the jury box, taking apparently no great interest in the proceedings, and a worried-looking young Italian sitting at the prisoner's table between a rubicund little man with a round red face and a tall, grave, longish-haired lawyer with a frame not unlike that of Abraham Lincoln, over whose wrinkled face played from time to time the suggestion of a smile. Behind a balustrade were the reporters, scribbling on rough sheets of yellow paper. Then came rows of benches, upon the first of which, as near the jury box as possible, sat Rosalina in a new bombazine dress and wearing a large imitation gold cross furnished for the occasion out of the legal property room of Tutt & Tutt. Occasionally she sobbed softly. The bulk of the spectators consisted of rejected talesmen, witnesses, law clerks, professional court loafers and women seeking emotional sensations which they had not the courage or the means to satisfy otherwise. The courtroom was comparatively quiet, the silence broken only by the droning voice of the clerk and the lazy interplay of question and answer between talesman and lawyer.

Yet beneath the humdrum, casual, almost indifferent manner in which the proceedings seemed to be conducted each side was watching every move made by the other with the tension of a tiger ready to spring upon its prey. Babson and O'Brien were engaged in forcing upon the defense a jury composed entirely of case-hardened convictors, while Tutt & Tutt were fighting desperately to secure one so heterogeneous in character that they could hope for a disagreement.

By recess thirty-seven talesmen had been examined without a foreman having been selected, and Mr. Tutt had exhausted twenty-nine of his thirty challenges, as against three for the prosecution. The court reconvened and a new talesman was called, resembling in appearance a professional hangman who for relaxation leaned toward the execution of Italians. Mr.

Tutt examined him for bias and every known form of incompetency, but in vain—then challenged peremptorily. Thirty challenges! He looked on Tutt with slightly raised eyebrows.

"Patrick Henry Walsh—to the witness chair, please, Mr. Walsh!" called the clerk, drawing another slip from the box.

Mr. Walsh rose and came forward heavily, while Tutt & Tutt trembled. He was the one man they were afraid of—an old-timer celebrated as a bulwark of the prosecution, who could always be safely counted upon to uphold the arms of the law, who regarded with reverence all officials connected with the administration of justice, and from whose composition all human emotions had been carefully excluded by the Creator. He was a square-jawed, severe, heavily built person, with a long relentless upper lip, cheeks ruddy from the open air; engaged in the contracting business; and he had a brogue that would have charmed a mavis off a tree. Mr. Tutt looked hopelessly at Tutt.

Babson and O'Brien had won.

Once more Mr. Tutt struggled against his fate. Was Mr. Walsh sure he had no prejudices against Italians or foreigners generally? Quite. Did he know anyone connected with the case? No. Had he any objection to the infliction of capital punishment? None whatever. The defense had exhausted all its challenges. Mr. Tutt turned to the prospective foreman with an endearing smile.

"Mr. Walsh," said he in caressing tones, "you are precisely the type of man in whom I feel the utmost confidence in submitting the fate of my client. I believe that you will make an ideal foreman I hardly need to ask you whether you will accord the defendant the benefit of every reasonable doubt, and if you have such a doubt will acquit him."

Mr. Walsh gazed suspiciously at Mr. Tutt.

"Sure," he responded dryly, "Oi'll give him the benefit o' the doubt, but if Oi think he's guilty Oi'll convict him."

Mr. Tutt shivered.

"Of course! Of course! That would be your duty! You are entirely satisfactory, Mr. Walsh!"

"Mr. Walsh is more than satisfactory to the prosecution!" intoned O'Brien.

"Be sworn, Mr. Walsh," directed the clerk; and the filling of the jury box in the memorable case of People versus Serafino was begun.

"That chap doesn't like us," whispered Mr. Tutt to Tutt. "I laid it on a bit too thick."

In fact, Mr. Walsh had already entered upon friendly relations with Mr. O'Brien, and as the latter helped him arrange a place for his hat and coat the foreman cast a look tinged with malevolence at the defendant and his counsel, as if to say "You can't fool me. I know the kind of tricks you fellows are all up to."

O'Brien could not repress a grin. The clerk drew forth another name.

"Mr. Tompkins—will you take the chair?"

Swiftly the jury was impaneled. O'Brien challenged everybody who did not suit his fancy, while Tutt & Tutt sat helpless.

Ten minutes and the clerk called the roll, beginning with Mr. Walsh, and they were solemnly sworn a true verdict to find, and settled themselves to the task.

The mills of the gods had begun to grind, and Angelo was being dragged to his fate as inexorably and as surely, with about as much chance of escape, as a log that is being drawn slowly toward a buzz saw.

"You may open the case, Mr. O'Brien," announced Judge Babson, leaning back and wiping his glasses.

Then surreptitiously he began to read his mail as his fellow conspirator undertook to tell the jury what it was all about. One by one the witnesses were called—the coroner's physician, the policeman who had arrested Angelo outside the barber shop with the smoking pistol in his hand, the assistant barber who had seen the shooting, the customer who was being shaved. Each drove a spike into poor Angelo's legal coffin. Mr. Tutt could not shake them. This evidence was plain. He had come into the shop, accused Crocedoro of making his wife's life unbearable and—shot him.

Yet Mr. Tutt did not lose any of his equanimity. With the tips of his long fingers held lightly together in front of him, and swaying slightly backward and forward upon the balls of his feet, he smiled benignly down upon the customer and the barber's assistant as if these witnesses were merely unfortunate in not being able to disclose to the jury all the facts. His manner indicated that a mysterious and untold tragedy lay behind what they had heard, a tragedy pregnant with primordial vital passions, involving the most sacred of human relationships, which when known would rouse the spirit of chivalry of the entire panel.

On cross-examination the barber testified that Angelo had said: "You maka small of my wife long enough!"

"Ah!" murmured Mr. Tutt, waving an arm in the direction of Rosalina. Did the witness recognize the defendant's young wife? The jury showed interest and examined the sobbing Rosalina with approval. Yes, the witness recognized her. Did the witness know to what incident or incidents the defendant had referred by his remark—what the deceased Crocedoro had done to Rosalina—if anything? No, the witness did not. Mr. Tutt looked significantly at the row of faces in the jury box.

Then leaning forward he asked significantly: "Did you see Crocedoro threaten the defendant with his razor?"

"I object!" shouted O'Brien, springing to his feet. "The question is improper. There is no suggestion that Crocedoro did anything. The defendant can testify to that if he wants to!"

"Oh, let him answer!" drawled the judge.

"No—" began the witness.

"Ah!" cried Mr. Tutt. "You did not see Crocedoro threaten the defendant with his razor! That will do!"

But forewarned by this trifling experience, Mr. O'Brien induced the customer, the next witness, to swear that Crocedoro had not in fact made any move whatever with his razor toward Angelo, who had deliberately raised his pistol and shot him.

Mr. Tutt rose to the cross-examination with the same urbanity as before. Where was the witness standing? The witness said he wasn't standing. Well, where was he sitting, then? In the chair.

"Ah!" exclaimed Mr. Tutt triumphantly. "Then you had your back to the shooting!"

In a moment O'Brien had the witness practically rescued by the explanation that he had seen the whole thing in the glass in front of him. The firm of Tutt & Tutt uttered in chorus a groan of outraged incredulity. Several jurymen were seen to wrinkle their foreheads in meditation. Mr. Tutt had sown a tiny—infinitesimally tiny, to be sure—seed of doubt, not as to the killing at all but as to the complete veracity of the witness.

And then O'Brien made his coup.

"Rosalina Serafino—take the witness stand!" he ordered.

He would get from her own lips the admission that she bought the pistol and gave it to Angelo!

But with an outburst of indignation that would have done credit to the elder Booth Mr. Tutt was immediately on his feet protesting against the outrage, the barbarity, the heartlessness, the illegality of making a wife testify against her husband! His eyes flashed, his disordered locks waved in picturesque synchronization with his impassioned gestures Rosalina, her beautiful golden cross rising and falling hysterically upon her bosom, took her seat in the witness chair like a frightened, furtive creature of the woods, gazed for one brief instant upon the twelve men in the jury box with those great black eyes of hers, and then with burning cheeks buried her face in her handkerchief.

"I protest against this piece of cruelty!" cried Mr. Tutt in a voice vibrating with indignation. "This is worthy of the Inquisition. Will not even the cross upon her breast protect her from being compelled to reveal those secrets that are sacred to wife and motherhood? Can the law thus indirectly tear the seal of confidence from the Confessional? Mr.

26

O'Brien, you go too far! There are some things that even you—brilliant as you are—may not trifle with."

A juryman nodded. The eleven others, being more intelligent, failed to understand what he was talking about.

"Mr. Tutt's objection is sound—if he wishes to press it," remarked the judge satirically. "You may step down, madam. The law will not compel a wife to testify against her husband. Have you any more witnesses, Mister District Attorney?"

"The People rest," said Mr. O'Brien. "The case is with the defense."

Mr. Tutt rose with solemnity.

"The court will, I suppose, grant me a moment or two to confer with my client?" he inquired. Babson bowed and the jury saw the lawyer lean across the defendant and engage his partner in what seemed to be a weighty deliberation.

"I killa him! I say so!" muttered Angelo feebly to Mr. Tutt.

"Shut up, you fool!" hissed Tutt, grabbing him by the leg. "Keep still or I'll wring your neck."

"If I could reach that old crook up on the bench I would twist his nose," remarked Mr. Tutt to Tutt with an air of consulting him about the Year Books. "And as for that criminal O'Brien, I'll get him yet!"

With great dignity Mr. Tutt then rose and again addressed the court:

"We have decided under all the circumstances of this most extraordinary case, Your Honor, not to put in any defense. I shall not call the defendant—"

"I killa him—" began Angelo, breaking loose from Tutt and struggling to his feet. It was a horrible movement. But Tutt clapped his hand over Angelo's mouth and forced him back into his seat.

"The defense rests," said Mr. Tutt, ignoring the interruption. "So far as we are concerned the case is closed."

"Both sides rest!" snapped Babson. "How long do you want to sum up?"

27

Mr. Tutt looked at the clock, which pointed to three. The regular hour of adjournment was at four. Delay was everything in a case like this. A juryman might die suddenly overnight or fall grievously ill; or some legal accident might occur which would necessitate declaring a mistrial. There is, always hope in a criminal case so long as the verdict has not actually been returned and the jury polled and discharged. If possible he must drag his summing up over until the following day. Something might happen.

"About two hours, Your Honor," he replied.

The jury stirred impatiently. It was clear that they regarded a two-hour speech from him under the circumstances as an imposition. But Babson wished to preserve the fiction of impartiality.

"Very well," said he. "You may sum up until four-thirty, and have half an hour more to-morrow morning. See that the doors are closed, Captain Phelan. We do not want any interruption while the summations are going on."

"All out that's goin' out! Everybody out that's got no business, with the court!" bellowed Captain Phelan.

Mr. Tutt with an ominous heightening of the pulse realized that the real ordeal was at last at hand, for the closing of the case had wrought in the old lawyer an instant metamorphosis. With the words "The defense rests" every suggestion of the mountebank, the actor or the shyster had vanished. The awful responsibility under which he labored; the overwhelming and damning evidence against his client; the terrible consequences of the least mistake that he might make; the fact that only the sword of his ability, and his alone, stood between Angelo and a hideous death by fire in the electric chair—sobered and chastened him. Had he been a praying man in that moment he would have prayed—but he was not.

For his client was foredoomed—foredoomed not only by justice but also by trickery and guile—and was being driven slowly but surely towards the judicial shambles. For what had he succeeded in adducing in his behalf? Nothing but the purely apocryphal speculation that the dead barber might have threatened Angelo with his razor and that the witnesses might possibly have drawn somewhat upon their imaginations in giving the details of their testimony. A sorry defense! Indeed, no defense at all. All the sorrier in that he had not even been able to get before the jury the purely sentimental excuses for the homicide, for he could only do this by calling Rosalina to the stand, which would have enabled the prosecution to cross-examine her in regard to the purchase of the pistol and the delivery of it to her husband—the strongest evidence of premeditation. Yet he must find some argument, some plea, some thread of reason upon which the jury might hang a disagreement or a verdict in a lesser degree.

With a shuffling of feet the last of the crowd pushed through the big oak doors and they were closed and locked. An officer brought a corroded tumbler of brackish water and placed it in front of Mr. Tutt. The judge leaned forward with malicious courtesy. The jury settled themselves and turned toward the lawyer attentively yet defiantly, hardening their hearts already against his expected appeals to sentiment. O'Brien, ostentatiously producing a cigarette, lounged out through the side door leading to the jury room and prison cells. The clerk began copying his records. The clock ticked loudly.

And Mr. Tutt rose and began going through the empty formality of attempting to discuss the evidence in such a way as to excuse or palliate Angelo's crime. For Angelo's guilt of murder in the first degree was so plain that it had never for one moment been in the slightest doubt. Whatever might be said for his act from the point of view of human emotion only made his motive and responsibility under the statues all the clearer. There was not even the unwritten law to appeal to. Yet there was fundamentally a genuine defense, a defense that could not be urged even by innuendo: the defense that no accused ought to be convicted upon any evidence whatever, no matter how conclusive in a trial conducted with essential though wholly concealed unfairness.

Such was the case of Angelo. No one could demonstrate it, no one could with safety even hint at it; any charge that the court was anything but impartial would prove a boomerang to the defense; and yet the facts remained that the whole proceeding from start to finish had been conducted unfairly and with illegality, that the jury had been duped and deceived, and that the pretense that the guilty Angelo had been given an impartial trial was a farce. Every word of the court had been an accusation, a sneer, an acceptance of the defendant's guilt as a matter of course, an abuse far more subversive of our theory of government than the mere acquittal of a single criminal, for it struck at the very foundations of that liberty which the fathers had sought the shores of the unknown continent to gain.

Unmistakably the proceedings had been conducted throughout upon the theory that the defendant must prove his innocence and that presumably he was a guilty man; and this as well as his own impression that the evidence was conclusive the judge had subtly conveyed to the jury in his tone of speaking, his ironical manner and his facial expression. Guilty or not Angelo was being railroaded. That was the real defense— the defense that could never be established even in any higher court, except perhaps in the highest court of all, which is not of earth.

And so Mr. Tutt, boiling with suppressed indignation weighed down with the sense of his responsibility, fully realizing his inability to say anything based on the evidence in behalf of his client, feeling twenty years older than he had during the verbal duel of the actual cross-examination, rose with a genial smile upon his puckered old face and with a careless air almost of gaiety, which seemed to indicate the utmost confidence and determination, and with a graceful compliment to his arch enemy upon the bench and the yellow dog who had hunted with him, assured the jury that the defendant had had the fairest of fair trials and that he, Mr. Tutt, would now proceed to demonstrate to their satisfaction his client's entire innocence; nay, would show them that he was a man not only guiltless of any wrong-doing but worthy of their hearty commendation.

With jokes not too unseemly for the occasion he overcame their preliminary distrust and put them in a good humor. He gave a historical dissertation upon the law governing homicide, on the constitutional rights of American citizens, on the laws of naturalization, marriage, and the domestic relations; waxed eloquent over Italy and the Italian character, mentioned Cavour, Garibaldi and Mazzini in a way to imply that Angelo was their lineal descendant; and quoted from D'Annunzio back to Horace, Cicero and Plautus.

"Bunk! Nothing but bunk!" muttered Tutt, studying the twelve faces before him. "And they all know it!"

But Mr. Tutt was nothing if not interesting. These prosaic citizens of New York County, these saloon and hotel keepers, these contractors, insurance agents and salesmen were learning something of history, of philosophy, of art and beauty. They liked it. They felt they were hearing something worth while, as indeed they were, and they forgot all about Angelo and the unfortunate Crocedoro in their admiration for Mr. Tutt, who had lifted them out of the dingy sordid courtroom into the sunlight of the Golden Age. And as he led them through Greek and Roman literature, through the early English poets, through Shakespeare and the King James version, down to John Galsworthy and Rupert Brooke, he brought something that was noble, fine and sweet into their grubby materialistic lives; and at the same time the hand of the clock crept steadily on until he and it reached Château-Thierry and half past four together.

"Bang!" went Babson's gavel just as Mr. Tutt was leading Mr. Walsh, Mr. Tompkins and the others through the winding paths of the Argonne forests with tin helmets on their heads in the struggle for liberty.

"You may conclude your address in the morning, Mr. Tutt," said the judge with supreme unction. "Adjourn court!"

* * * * *

31

Gray depression weighed down Mr. Tutt's soul as he trudged homeward. He had made a good speech, but it had had absolutely nothing to do with the case, which the jury would perceive as soon as they thought it over. It was a confession of defeat. Angelo would be convicted of murder in the first degree and electrocuted, Rosalina would be a widow, and somehow he would be in a measure responsible for it. The tragedy of human life appalled him. He felt very old, as old as the dead-and-gone authors from whom he had quoted with such remarkable facility. He belonged with them; he was too old to practise his profession.

"Law, Mis' Tutt," expostulated Miranda, his ancient negro handmaiden, as he pushed away the chop and mashed potato, and even his glass of claret, untasted, in his old-fashioned dining room on West Twenty-third Street, "you ain't got no appetite at all! You's sick, Mis' Tutt."

"No, no, Miranda!" he replied weakly. "I'm just getting old."

"You's mighty spry for an old man yit," she protested. "You kin make dem lawyer men hop mighty high when you tries. Heh, heh! I reckon dey ain't got nuffin' on my Mistah Tutt!"

Upstairs in his library Mr. Tutt strode up and down before the empty grate, smoking stogy after stogy, trying to collect his thoughts and devise something to say upon the morrow, but all his ideas had flown. There wasn't anything to say. Yet he swore Angelo should not be offered up as a victim upon the altar of unscrupulous ambition. The hours passed and the old banjo clock above the mantel wheezed eleven, twelve; then one, two. Still he paced up and down, up and down in a sort of trance. The air of the library, blue with the smoke of countless stogies, stifled and suffocated him. Moreover he discovered that he was hungry. He descended to the pantry and salvaged a piece of pie, then unchained the front door and stepped forth into the soft October night.

A full moon hung over the deserted streets of the sleeping city. In divers places, widely scattered, the twelve good and true men were snoring snugly in bed. To-morrow they would send Angelo to his death without a quiver. He shuddered, striding on, he knew not whither, into the night.

His brain no longer worked. He had become a peripatetic automaton self-dedicated to nocturnal perambulation.

With his pockets bulging with stogies and one glowing like a headlight in advance of him he wandered in a sort of coma up Tenth Avenue, crossed to the Riverside Drive, mounted Morningside Heights, descended again through the rustling alleys of Central Park, and found himself at Fifth Avenue and Fifty-ninth Street just as the dawn was paling the electric lamps to a sickly yellow and the trees were casting strange unwonted shadows in the wrong direction. He was utterly exhausted. He looked eagerly for some place to sit down, but the doors of the hotels were dark and tightly closed and it was too cold to remain without moving in the open air.

Down Fifth Avenue he trudged, intending to go home and snatch a few hours' sleep before court should open, but each block seemed miles in length. Presently he approached the cathedral, whose twin spires were tinted with reddish gold. The sky had become a bright blue. Suddenly all the street lamps went out. He told himself that he had never realized before the beauty of those two towers reaching up toward eternity, typifying man's aspiration for the spiritual. He remembered having heard that a cathedral was never closed, and looking toward the door he perceived that it was open. With utmost difficulty he climbed the steps and entered its dark shadows. A faint light emanated from the tops of the stained-glass windows. Down below a candle burned on either side of the altar while a flickering gleam shone from the red cup in the sanctuary lamp. Worn out, drugged for lack of sleep, faint for want of food, old Mr. Tutt sank down upon one of the rear seats by the door, and resting his head upon his arms on the back of the bench in front of him fell fast asleep.

He dreamed of a legal heaven, of a great wooden throne upon which sat Babson in a black robe and below him twelve red-faced angels in a double row with harps in their hands, chanting: "Guilty! Guilty! Guilty!" An organ was playing somewhere, and there was a great noise of footsteps. Then a bell twinkled and he raised his head and saw that the chancel was full of lights and white-robed priests. It was broad daylight. Horrified he looked at his watch, to find that it was ten minutes after ten. His joints creaked as he pulled himself to his feet and his eyes were half closed as he staggered down the steps and hailed a taxi.

"Criminal Courts Building—side door. And drive like hell!" he muttered to the driver.

He reached it just as Judge Babson and his attendant were coming into the courtroom and the crowd were making obeisance. Everybody else was in his proper place.

"You may proceed, Mr. Tutt," said the judge after the roll of the jury had been called.

But Mr. Tutt was in a daze, in no condition to think or speak. There was a curious rustling in his ears and his sight was somewhat blurred. The atmosphere of the courtroom seemed to him cold and hostile; the jury sat with averted faces. He rose feebly and cleared his throat.

"Gentlemen of the jury," he began, "I—I think I covered everything I had to say yesterday afternoon. I can only beseech you to realize the full extent of your great responsibility and remind you that if you entertain a reasonable doubt upon the evidence you are sworn to give the benefit of it to the defendant."

He sank back in his chair and covered his eyes with his hands, while a murmur ran along the benches of the courtroom. The old man had collapsed—tough luck—the defendant was cooked! Swiftly O'Brien leaped to his feet. There had been no defense. The case was as plain as a pike-staff. There was only one thing for the jury to do—return a verdict of murder in the first. It would not be pleasant, but that made no difference! He read them the statute, applied it to the facts, and shook his fist in their faces. They must convict—and convict of only one thing— and nothing else—murder in the first degree. They gazed at him like silly sheep, nodding their heads, doing everything but bleat.

Then Babson cleared his decks and rising in dignity expounded the law to the sheep in a rich mellow voice, in which he impressed upon them the necessity of preserving the integrity of the jury system and the sanctity of human life. He pronounced an obituary of great beauty upon the deceased barber—who could not, as he pointed out, speak for himself, owing to the fact that he was in his grave. He venomously excoriated the defendant who had deliberately planned to kill an unarmed man peacefully conducting himself in his place of business, and expressed the utmost confidence that he could rely upon the jury, whose character he well knew, to perform their full duty no matter how disagreeable that duty might be. The sheep nodded.

"You may retire, gentlemen."

Babson looked down at Mr. Tutt with a significant gleam in his eye. He had driven in the knife to the hilt and twisted it round and round. Angelo had almost as much chance as the proverbial celluloid cat. Mr. Tutt felt actually sick. He did not look at the jury as they went out. They would not be long—and he could hardly face the thought of their return. Never in his long experience had he found himself in such a desperate situation. Heretofore there had always been some argument, some construction of the facts upon which he could make an appeal, however fallacious or illogical.

He leaned back and closed his eyes. The judge was chatting with O'Brien, the court officers were betting with the reporters as to the length of time in which it would take the twelve to agree upon a verdict of murder in the first. The funeral rites were all concluded except for the final commitment of the corpse to mother earth.

And then without warning Angelo suddenly rose and addressed the court in a defiant shriek.

"I killa that man!" he cried wildly. "He maka small of my wife! He no good! He bad egg! I killa him once—I killa him again!"

"So!" exclaimed Babson with biting sarcasm. "You want to make a confession? You hope for mercy, do you? Well, Mr. Tutt, what do you wish to do under the circumstances? Shall I recall the jury and reopen the case by consent?"

Mr. Tutt rose trembling to his feet.

"The case is closed, Your Honor," he replied. "I will consent to a mistrial and offer a plea of guilty of manslaughter. I cannot agree to reopen the case. I cannot let the defendant go upon the stand."

The spectators and reporters were pressing forward to the bar, anxious lest they should lose a single word of the colloquy. Angelo remained standing, looking eagerly at O'Brien, who returned his gaze with a grin like that of a hyena.

"I killa him!" Angelo repeated. "You killa me if you want."

"Sit down!" thundered the judge. "Enough of this! The law does not permit me to accept a plea to murder in the first degree, and my conscience and my sense of duty to the public will permit me to accept no other. I will go to my chambers to await the verdict of the jury. Take the prisoner downstairs to the prison pen."

He swept from the bench in his silken robes. Angelo was led away. The crowd in the courtroom slowly dispersed. Mr. Tutt, escorted by Tutt, went out in the corridor to smoke.

"Ye got a raw deal, counselor," remarked Captain Phelan, amiably accepting a stogy. "Nothing but an act of Providence c'd save that Eyetalian from the chair. An' him guilty at that!"

An hour passed; then another. At half after four a rumor flew along the corridors that the jury in the Serafino case had reached a verdict and were coming in. A messenger scurried to the judge's chambers. Phelan descended the iron stairs to bring up the prisoner, while Tutt to prevent a scene invented an excuse by which he lured Rosalina to the first floor of the building. The crowd suddenly reassembled out of nowhere and poured into the courtroom. The reporters gathered expectantly round their table. The judge entered, his robes, gathered in one hand.

"Bring in the jury," he said sharply. "Arraign the prisoner at the bar."

Mr. Tutt took his place beside his client at the railing, while the jury, carrying their coats and hats, filed slowly in. Their faces were set and relentless. They looked neither to the right nor to the left. O'Brien sauntered over and seated himself nonchalantly with his back to the court, studying their faces. Yes, he told himself, they were a regular set of hangmen—he couldn't have picked a tougher bunch if he'd had his choice of the whole panel.

The clerk called the roll, and Messrs. Walsh, Tompkins, *et al.*, stated that they were all present.

"Gentlemen of the jury, have you agreed upon a verdict?" inquired the clerk.

"We have!" replied Mr. Walsh sternly.

"How say you? Do you find the defendant guilty or not guilty?"

Mr. Tutt gripped the balustrade in front of him with one hand and put his other arm round Angelo. He felt that now in truth murder was being done.

"We find the defendant not guilty," said Mr. Walsh defiantly.

There was a momentary silence of incredulity. Then Babson and O'Brien shouted simultaneously: "What!"

"We find the defendant not guilty," repeated Mr. Walsh stubbornly.

"I demand that the jury be polled!" cried the crestfallen O'Brien, his face crimson.

And then the twelve reiterated severally that that was their verdict and that they hearkened unto it as it stood recorded and that they were entirely satisfied with it.

"You are discharged!" said Babson in icy tones. "Strike the names of these men from the list of jurors—as incompetent. Haven't you any other charge on which you can try this defendant?"

"No, Your Honor," answered O'Brien grimly. "He didn't take the stand, so we can't try him for perjury; and there isn't any other indictment against him."

Judge Babson turned ferociously upon Mr. Tutt:

"This acquittal is a blot upon the administration of criminal justice; a disgrace to the city! It is an unconscionable verdict; a reflection upon the intelligence of the jury! The defendant is discharged. This court is adjourned."

The crowd surged round Angelo and bore him away, bewildered. The judge and prosecutor hurried from the room. Alone Mr. Tutt stood at the bar, trying to grasp the full meaning of what had occurred.

He no longer felt tired; he experienced an exultation such as he had never known before. Some miracle had happened! What was it?

Unexpectedly the lawyer felt a rough warm hand clasped over his own upon the rail and heard the voice of Mr. Walsh with its rich brogue saying: "At first we couldn't see that there was much to be said for your side of the case, Mr. Tutt; but when Oi stepped into the cathedral on me way down to court this morning and spied you prayin' there for guidance I knew you wouldn't be defendin' him unless he was innocent, and so we decided to give him the benefit of the doubt."

MOCK HEN AND MOCK TURTLE

"Oh, East is East and West is West, and never the twain shall meet."—BALLAD OF EAST AND WEST.

"But the law of the jungle is jungle law only, and the law of the pack is only for the pack."—OTHER SAYINGS OF SHERE KHAN.

A half turn from the clattering hubbub of Chatham Square and you are in Chinatown, slipping, within ten feet, through an invisible wall, from the glitter of the gin palace and the pawn-shop to the sinister shadows of irregular streets and blind alleys, where yellow men pad swiftly along greasy asphalt beneath windows glinting with ivory, bronze and lacquer; through which float the scents of aloes and of incense and all the subtle suggestion of the East.

No one better than the Chink himself realizes the commercial value of the taboo, the bizarre and the unclean. Nightly the rubber-neck car swinging gayly with lanterns stops before the imitation joss house, the spurious opium joint and tortuous passage to the fake fan-tan and faro game, with a farewell call at Hong Joy Fah's Oriental restaurant and the well-stocked novelty store of Wing, Hen & Co. The visitors see what they expect to see, for the Chinaman always gives his public exactly what it wants.

But a dollar does not show you Chinatown. To some the ivories will always be but crudely carven bone, the jades the potter's sham, the musk and aloes the product of a soap factory, the joss but a cigar-store Indian, and the Oriental dainties of Hong Fah the scrappings of a Yankee grocery store. Yet behind the shoddy tinsel of Doyers and Pell Streets, as behind Alice's looking-glass, there is another Chinatown—a strange, inhuman, Oriental world, not necessarily of trapdoors and stifled screams, but one moved by influences undreamed of in our banal philosophies. Hearken then to the story of the avenging of Wah Sing.

‘

> *Tis a tale was undoubtedly true*
> *In the reign of the Emperor Hwang.*

In the murky cellar of a Pell Street tenement seventeen Chinamen sat cross-legged in a circle round an octagonal teakwood table. To an Occidental they would have appeared to differ in no detail except that of a varying degree of fatness. An oil lamp flickered before a joss near by, and the place reeked with the odor of starch, sweat, tobacco, rice whisky and the incense that rose ceilingward in thin, shaking columns from two bowls of Tibetan soapstone. An obese Chinaman with a walnutlike countenance in which cunning and melancholy were equally commingled was speaking monotonously through long, rat-tailed mustaches, while the others listened with impassive decorum. It was a special meeting of the Hip Leong Tong, held in their private clubrooms at the Great Shanghai Tea Company, and conducted according to rule.

"Therefore," said Wong Get, "as a matter of honor it is necessary that our brother be avenged and that no chances be taken. A much too long time has already elapsed. I have written the letter and will read it."

He fumbled in his sleeve and drew forth a roll of brown paper covered with heavy Chinese characters unwinding it from a strip of bamboo.

To the Honorable Members of the On Gee Tong:
Whereas it has pleased you to take the life of our beloved friend and relative Wah Sing, it is with greatest courtesy and the utmost regret that we inform you that it is necessary for us likewise to

remove one of your esteemed society, and that we shall proceed thereto without delay.

Due warning being thus honorably given I subscribe myself with profound appreciation,

For the Hip Leong Tong,
WONG GET.

He ceased reading and there was a perfunctory grunt of approval from round the circle. Then he turned to the official soothsayer and directed him to ascertain whether the time were propitious. The latter tossed into the air a handful of painted ivory sticks, carefully studied their arrangement when fallen, and nodded gravely.

"The omens are favorable, O honorable one!"

"Then there is nothing left but the choice of our representatives," continued Wong Get. "Pass the fateful box, O Fong Hen."

Fong Hen, a slender young Chinaman, the official slipper, or messenger, of the society, rose and, lifting a lacquered gold box from the table, passed it solemnly to each member.

"This time there will be four," said Wong Get.

Each in turn averted his eyes and removed from the box a small sliver of ivory. At the conclusion of the ceremony the four who had drawn red tokens rose. Wong Get addressed them.

"Mock Hen, Mock Ding, Long Get, Sui Sing—to you it is confided to avenge the murder of our brother Wah Sing. Fail not in your purpose!"

And the four answered unemotionally: "Those to whom it is confided will not fail."

Then pivoting silently upon their heels they passed out of the cellar.

Wong Get glanced round the table.

"If there is no further business the society will disperse after the customary refreshment."

Fong Hen placed thirteen tiny glasses upon the table and filled them with rice whisky scented with aniseed and a dash of powdered ginger.

At a signal from Wong Get the thirteen Chinamen lifted the glasses and drank.

"The meeting is adjourned," said he.

* * * * *

Eighty years before, in a Cantonese rabbit warren two yellow men had fought over a white woman, and one had killed the other. They had belonged to different societies, or tongs. The associates of the murdered man had avenged his death by slitting the throat of one of the members of the other organization, and these in turn had retaliated thus establishing a vendetta which became part and parcel of the lives of certain families, as naturally and unavoidably as birth, love and death. As regularly as the solstice they alternated in picking each other off. Branches of the Hip Leong and On Gee tongs sprang up in San Francisco and New York—and the feud was transferred with them to Chatham Square, a feud imposing a sacred obligation rooted in blood, honor and religion upon every member, who rather than fail to carry it out would have knotted a yellow silken cord under his left ear and swung himself gently off a table into eternal sleep.

Young Mock Hen, one of the four avengers, had created a distinct place for himself in Chinatown by making a careful study of New York psychology. He was a good-looking Chink, smooth-faced, tall and supple; he knew very well how to capitalize his attractiveness. By day he attended Columbia University as a special student in applied electricity, keeping a convenient eye meanwhile on three coolies whom he employed to run The College Laundry on Morningside Heights. By night he vicariously operated a chop-suey palace on Seventh Avenue, where congregated the worst elements of the Tenderloin. But his heart was in the gambling den which he maintained in Doyers Street, and where anyone who knew the knock could have a shell of hop for the asking, once Mock had given him the once-over through the little sliding panel.

Mock was a Christian Chinaman. That is to say, purely for business reasons—for what he got out of it and the standing that it gave him—he attended the Rising Star Mission and also frequented Hudson House, the social settlement where Miss Fanny Duryea taught him to play ping-pong and other exciting parlor games, and read to him from books adapted to an American child of ten. He was a great favorite at both places, for he was sweet-tempered and wore an expression of heaven-born innocence. He had even been to church with Miss Duryea, temporarily absenting himself for that purpose of a Sunday morning from the steam-heated flat where—unknown to her, of course—he lived with his white wife, Emma Pratt, a lady of highly miscellaneous antecedents.

Except when engaged in transacting legal or oilier business with the municipal, sociologic or religious world—at which times his vocabulary consisted only of the most rudimentary pidgin—Mock spoke a fluent and even vernacular English learned at night school. Incidentally he was the head of the syndicate which controlled and dispensed the loo, faro, fan-tan and other gambling privileges of Chinatown.

Detective Mooney, of the Second, detailed to make good District Attorney Peckham's boast that there had never been so little trouble with the foreign element since the administration—of which he was an ornament—came into office, saw Quong Lee emerge from his doorway in Doyers Street just before four o'clock the following Thursday and slip silently along under the shadow of the eaves toward Ah Fong's grocery—and instantly sensed something peculiar in the Chink's walk.

"Hello, Quong!" he called, interposing himself. "Where you goin'?"

Quong paused with a deprecating gesture of widely spread open palms.

"'Lo yourself!" replied blandly. "Me go buy li'l' glocery."

Mooney ran his hands over the rotund body, frisking him for a possible forty-four.

"For the love of Mike!" he exclaimed, tearing open Quong's blouse. "What sort of an undershirt is that?" Quong grinned broadly as the detective lifted the suit of double-chain mail which swayed heavily under his blue blouse from his shoulders to his knees.

"So-ho!" continued the plain-clothes man. "Trouble brewin', eh?"

He knew already that something was doing in the tongs from his lobby-gow, Wing Foo.

"Must weigh eighty pounds!" he whistled. "I'd like to see the pill that would go through that!" It was, in fact, a medieval corselet of finest steel mesh, capable of turning an elephant bullet.

"Go'long!" ordered Mooney finally. "I guess you're safe!"

He turned back in the direction of Chatham Square, while Quong resumed his tortoiselike perambulation toward Ah Fong's. Pell and Doyers Streets were deserted save for an Italian woman carrying a baby, and were pervaded by an unnatural and suspicious silence. Most of the shutters on the lower windows were down. Ah Fong's subsequent story of what happened was simple, and briefly to the effect that Quong, having entered his shop and priced various litchi nuts and pickled starfruit, had purchased some powdered lizard and, with the package in his left hand, had opened the door to go out. As he stood there with his right hand upon the knob and facing the afternoon sun four shadows fell aslant the window and a man whom he positively identified as Sui Sing emptied a bag of powder—afterward proved to be red pepper—upon Quong's face; then another, Long Get, made a thrust at him with a knife, the effect of which he did not observe, as almost at the same instant Mock Hen felled him with a blow upon the head with an iron bar, while a fourth, Mock Ding, fired four shots at his crumpling body with a revolver one of which glanced off and fractured a very costly Chien Lung vase and ruined four boxes of mandarin-blossom tea. In his excitement he ducked behind the counter, and when sufficiently revived he crawled forth to find what had once been Quong lying across the threshold, the murderers gone, and the Italian woman prostrate and shrieking with a hip splintered by a stray bullet. On the sidewalk outside the window lay the remnants of the bag of pepper, a knife broken short off at the handle, a heavy bar of soft iron slightly bent, and a partially emptied forty-four-caliber revolver. Quong's suit of mail had effectually protected him from the knife thrust and the revolver shots, but his skull was crushed beyond repair. Thus was the murder of Wah Sing avenged in due and proper form.

Detective Mooney, distant not more than two hundred feet, rushed back to the corner at the sound of the first shot—just in time to catch a side glimpse of Mock Hen as he raced across Pell Street and disappeared into the cellar of the Great Shanghai Tea Company. The Italian woman was filling the air with her outcries, but the detective did not pause in his hurtling pursuit. He was too late, however. The cellar door withstood all his efforts to break it open.

Bull Neck Burke, the wrestler, who tied Zabisko once on the stage of the old Grand Opera House in 1913, had been promenading with Mollie Malone, of the Champagne Girls and Gay Burlesquers Company. Both heard the fusillade and saw Mock—a streak of flying blue—pass within a few feet of them.

"God!" ejaculated Mollie. "Sure as shootin', that's Mock Hen—and he's murdered somebody!"

"It's Mock all right!" agreed Bull Neck. "That puts us in as witnesses or strike me!" And he looked at his watch—four one.

"Here, Burke, put your shoulder to this!" shouted Mooney from the cellar steps. "Now then!"

The two of them threw their combined weight against it, the lock flew open and they fell forward into the darkness. Three doors leading in different directions met the glare of Mooney's match. But the fugitive had a start of at least four minutes, which was three and a half more than he required.

* * * * *

Mock Hen took the left-hand of the three doors and crept along a passage opening into an empty opium parlor back of the Hip Leong clubroom.

Diving beneath one of the bunks he inserted his body between the lower planking at the back and the cellar wall, wormed his way some twelve feet, raised a trap and emerged into a tunnel by means of which and others he eventually reached the end of the block and the rooms of his friend Hong Sue.

Here he changed from the Oriental costume according to Chinese etiquette necessary to the homicide, into a nobby suit of American clothes, put on a false mustache, and walked boldly down Park Row, while just behind him Doyers and Pell Streets swarmed with bluecoats and excited citizenry.

Hudson House, the social settlement presided over by Miss Fanny and affected for business reasons by Mock Hen, was a mile and a half away. But Mock took his time. Twenty-five full minutes elapsed before he leisurely climbed the steps and slipped into the big reading room. There was no one there and Mock deftly turned back the hand of the automatic clock over the platform to three-fifty-five. Then he began to whistle. Presently Miss Fanny entered from the rear room, her face lighting with pleasure at the sight of her pet convert.

"Good afternoon, Mock Hen! You are early to-day."

Mock took her hand and stroked it affectionately.

"I go Fulton Mark' buy li'l' terrapin. Stop in on way to see dear Miss Fan'."

They stood thus for a moment, and while they did so the clock struck four.

"I go now!" said Mock suddenly. "Four o'clock already."

"It's early," answered Miss Fanny. "Won't you stay a little while?"

"I go now," he repeated with resolution. "Good-by li'l' teacher!"

She watched until his lithe figure passed through the door, and presently returned to the back room. Mock waited outside until she had disappeared.

Then he changed back the clock.

* * * * *

"We've got you, you blarsted heathen!" cried Mooney hoarsely as he and two others from the Central Office threw themselves upon Mock Hen on the landing outside the door of his flat. "Look out, Murtha. Pipe that thing under his arm!"

"It's a bloody turtle!" gasped Murtha, shuddering

"What's the matter, boys?" inquired Mock. "Leggo my arm, can't yer? What'd yer want, anyway?"

"We want you, you yellow skunk!" retorted Mooney. "Open that door! Lively now!"

"Sure!" answered Mock amiably. "Come on in! What's bitin' yer?"

He unlocked the door and threw it open.

"Take a chair," he invited them. "Have a cigar? You there, Emma?"

Emma Pratt, clad in a wrapper and lying on the big double brass bedstead in the rear room, raised herself on one elbow.

"Yep!" she called through the passage. "Got the bird?"

Mock looked at Murtha, who was carrying the terrapin.

"Sure!" he called back. "Sit down, boys. What'd yer want? Can't yer tell a feller?"

"We want you for croaking Quong Lee!" snapped Mooney. "Where have you been?"

"Fulton Market—and Hudson House. I left here quarter of four. I haven't seen Quong Lee. Where was he killed?"

Mooney laughed sardonically.

"That'll do for you, Mock! Your alibi ain't worth a damn this time. I saw you myself."

"You saw someone else," Mock assured him politely. "I haven't been in Chinatown."

"Say, what yer doin' wit' my Chink?" demanded Emma, appearing in the doorway. "He was sittin' here wit' me all the afternoon, until about just before four I sent him over to Fulton Market to buy a bird. Who's been croaked, eh?"

"Aw, cut it out, Emma!" replied Mooney. "That old stuff won't go here. Your Chink's goin' to the chair. Murtha, look through the place while we put Mock in the wagon. Hell!" he added under his breath. "Won't this make Peckham sick!"

* * * * *

Mr. Ephraim Tutt just finished his morning mail when he was informed that Mr. Wong Get desired an interview. Though the old lawyer did not formally represent the Hip Leong Tong he was frequently retained by its individual members, who held him in high esteem, for they had always found him loyal to their interests and as much a stickler for honor as themselves. Moreover, between him and Wong Get there existed a curious sympathy as if in some previous state of existence Wong Get might have been Mr. Tutt, and Mr. Tutt Wong Get. Perhaps, however, it was merely because both were rather weary, sad and worldly wise.

Wong Get did not come alone. He was accompanied by two other Hip Leongs, the three forming the law committee appointed to retain the best available counsel to defend Mock Hen. In his expansive frock coat and bowler hat Wong might easily have excited mirth had it not been for the extreme dignity of his demeanor. They were there, he stated, to request Mr. Tutt to protect the interests of Mock Hen, and they were prepared to pay a cash retainer and sign a written contract binding themselves to a balance—so much if Mock should be convicted; so much if acquitted; so much if he should die in the course of the trial without having been either convicted or acquitted. It was, said Wong Get gently, a matter of grave importance and they would be glad to give Mr. Tutt time to think it over and decide upon his terms. Suppose, then, that they should return at noon? With this understanding, accordingly, they departed.

"There's no point in skinning a Chink just because he is a Chink," said the junior Tutt when his partner had explained the situation to him. "But it isn't the highest-class practise and they ought to pay well."

"What do you call well?" inquired Mr. Tutt.

"Oh, a thousand dollars down, a couple more if he's convicted, and five altogether if he's acquitted."

"Do you think they can raise that amount of money?"

"I think so," answered Tutt. "It might be a good deal for an individual Chink to cough up on his own account, but this is a coöperative affair. Mock Hen didn't kill Quong Lee to get anything out of it for himself, but to save the face of his society."

"He didn't kill him at all!" declared Mr. Tutt, hardly moving a muscle of his face.

"Well, you know what I mean!" said Tutt.

"He wasn't there," insisted Mr. Tutt. "He was way over in Fulton Market buying a terrapin."

"That is what, if I were district attorney, I should call a Mock Hen with a mockturtle defense!" grunted Tutt.

Mr. Tutt chuckled.

"I shall have to get that off myself at the beginning of the case, or it might convict him," he remarked. "But he wasn't there—unless the jury find that he was."

"In which case he will—or shall—have been there—whatever the verb is," agreed Tutt. "Anyhow they'll tax every laundry and chop-suey palace from the Bronx to the Battery to pay us."

"I'd hate to take our fee in bird's-nest soup, shark's fin, bamboo-shoots salad and ya ko main," mused Mr. Tutt.

"Or in ivory chopsticks, oolong tea, imitation jade, litchi nuts and preserved leeches!" groaned Tutt. "Be sure and get the thousand down; it may be all the cash we'll ever see!"

Promptly at twelve the law committee of the Hip Leong Tong returned to the office of Tutt & Tutt. With them came a venerable Chinaman in native costume, his wrinkled face as inscrutable as that of a snapping turtle. The others took chairs, but this high dignitary preferred to sit upon his heels on the floor, creating something of the impression of an ancient slant-eyed Buddha.

Wong Get translated for his benefit the arrangement proposed by Mr. Tutt, after which there was a long pause while His Eminence remained immovable, without even the flicker of an eyelid. Then he delivered himself in an interminable series of gargles and gurgles, supplemented by a few cough-like hisses, while Wong Get translated with rapid dexterity, running verbally in and out among his words like a carriage dog between the wheels of a vehicle.

It was, declared Buddha, an affair of great moment touching upon and appertaining to the private honor of the Duck, the Wong, the Fong, the Long, the Sui and various other families, both in America and China. The life of one of their members was at stake. Their face required that the proceedings should be as dignified as possible. The price named by Mr. Tutt was quite inadequate.

Mr. Tutt, repressing a smile, passed a box of stogies. What amount, he inquired through Wong Get, would satisfy the face of the Duck family? A somewhat lengthy discussion ensued. Then Buddha rendered his decision.

The honor of the Ducks, Longs and Fongs would not be satisfied unless Mr. Tutt received five thousand dollars down, five more if Mock Hen was convicted, three more if he died before the conclusion of the trial, and twenty thousand if he was acquitted.

Mr. Tutt, assuming an equal impassivity, pondered upon the matter for about an inch of stogy and then informed the committee that the terms were eminently satisfactory. Buddha thereupon removed from the folds of his tunic a gigantic roll of soiled bills of all denominations and carefully counting out five thousand dollars placed it upon the table.

"H'm!" remarked Tutt when he learned of the proceeding. "*His* face is *our* fortune!"

* * * * *

"Look here," expostulated District Attorney Peckham in his office to Mr. Tutt a month later. "What's the use of our both wasting a couple of weeks trying a Chinaman who is bound to be convicted? Your time's too valuable for that sort of thing, and so is mine. We've got three white witnesses that saw him do it, and a couple of dozen Chinks besides. He doesn't stand a chance; but just because he is a Chink, and to get the case out of the way, I'll let you plead him to murder in the second degree. What do you say?"

He tried to conceal his anxiety by nervously lighting a cigar. He would have given a year's salary to have Mock Hen safely up the river, even on a conviction for manslaughter in the third, for the newspapers were making his life a burden with their constant references to the seeming inability of the police department and district attorney's office to prevent the recurrence of feud killings in the Chinatown districts. What use was it, they demanded, to maintain the expensive machinery of criminal justice if the tongs went gayly on shooting each other up and incidentally taking the lives of innocent bystanders? Wasn't the law intended to cover Chinamen as much as Italians, Poles, Greeks and niggers? And now that one of these murdering Celestials had been caught red-handed it was up to the D.A. to go to it, convict him, and send him to the chair! They did not express themselves precisely that way, but that was the gist of it. But Peckham knew that it was one thing to catch a Chinaman, even red-handed, and another to convict him. And so did Mr. Tutt.

The old lawyer smiled blandly—after the fashion of the Hip Leong Tong. Of course, he admitted, it would be much simpler to dispose of the case as Mr. Peckham suggested, but his client was insistent upon his innocence and seemed to have an excellent alibi. He regretted, therefore, that he had no choice except to go to trial.

"Then," groaned Peckham, "we may as well take the winter for it. After this there's going to be a closed season on Chinamen in New York City!"

Now though it was true that Mock Hen insisted upon his innocence, he had not insisted upon it to Mr. Tutt, for the latter had not seen him. In fact, the old lawyer, recognizing what the law did not, namely that a system devised for the trial and punishment of Occidentals is totally inadequate to cope with the Oriental, calmly went about his affairs, intrusting to Mr. Bonnie Doon of his office the task of interviewing the witnesses furnished by Wong Get. There was but one issue for the jury to pass upon. Quong Lee was dead and his honorable soul was with his illustrious ancestors. He had died from a single blow upon the head, delivered with an iron bar, there present, to be in evidence, marked "Exhibit A." Mock Hen was alleged to have done the deed. Had he? There would be nothing for Mr. Tutt to do but to cross-examine the witnesses and then call such as could testify to Mock's alibi. So he made no preparation at all and dismissed the case from his mind. He had hardly seen a dozen Chinamen in his life—outside of a laundry.

* * * * *

On the morning set for the trial Mr. Tutt, having been delayed by an accident in the Subway, entered the Criminal Courts Building only a moment or two before the call of the calendar. Somewhat preoccupied, he did not notice the numerous Chinamen who dawdled about the entrance or the half dozen who crowded with him into the elevator, but when Pat the elevator man called, "Second floor!—Part One to your right!—Part

Two to the left!" and he stepped out into the marble-floored corridor that ran round the inside of the building, he was confronted with an unusual and somewhat ominous spectacle.

The entire hallway on two sides of the building was lined with Chinamen! They sat there motionless as blue-coated images, faces front, their hands in their laps, their legs crossed beneath them. If anyone appeared in the offing a couple of hundred pairs of glinting eyes shifted automatically and followed him until he disappeared, but otherwise no muscle quivered.

"Say," growled Hogan, Judge Bender's private attendant, who was the first to run the gantlet, "those Chinks are enough to give you the Willies! Their eyes scared me to death, sticking me through the back!"

Even dignified Judge Bender himself as he stalked along the hall, preceded by two police officers, was not immune from a slight feeling of uncanniness, and he instinctively drew his robe round his legs that it might not come into contact with those curious slippers with felt soles that protruded across the marble slabs.

"Eyes right!" They had picked him up the instant he stepped out of the private elevator—the four hundred of them. If he turned and looked they were seemingly not watching him, but if he dropped his glance they swung back in a single moment and focused themselves upon him. And every one of them probably had a gun hidden somewhere in his baggy pants! The judge confessed to not liking these foreign homicide cases. You never could tell what might happen or when somebody was going to get the death sign. There was Judge Deasy—he had the whole front of his house blown clean out by a bomb! That had been a close call! And these Chinks—with their secret oaths and rituals—they'd think nothing at all of jabbing a knife into you. He didn't fancy it at all and, as he hurried along, supremely conscious of the deadly cumulative effect of those beady eyes, he fancied it less and less. What was there to prevent one of them from getting right up in court and putting a bullet through you? He shivered, recalling the recent assassination of a judge upon the bench by a Hindu whom he had sentenced. When he reached his robing room he sent for Captain Phelan.

"See here, captain," he directed sharply, "I want you to keep all those Chinamen out in the corridor; understand?"

"I've got to let some of 'em in, judge," urged Phelan. "You've got to have an interpreter—and there's a Chinese lawyer associated with Tutt & Tutt—and of course Mr. O'Brien has to have a couple of 'em so's he'll know what's going on. Y' see, judge, the On Gee Tong is helping the prosecution against the Hip Leongs, so both sides has to be more or less represented."

"Well, make sure none of 'em is armed," ordered Judge Bender. "I don't like these cases."

Now the judge, being recently elected and unfamiliar with the situation, did not realize that nothing could have been farther from the Oriental mind or intention than an attack upon the officers engaged in the administration of local justice, whom they regarded merely as nuisances. What these Chinamen supremely desired was to be allowed to settle their own affairs in their own historic and traditional way—the way of the revolver, the silken cord, the knife and the iron bar. Once enmeshed in Anglo-Saxon juridical procedure, to be sure, they were not averse to letting it run its course on the bare chance that it might automatically accomplish their revenge. But they distrusted it, being brought up according to a much more effective system—one which when it wanted to punish anybody simply reached out, grabbed him by the pigtail, yanked him to his knees and sliced off his head. This so-called American justice was all talk—words, words, words! From their point of view judges, jurymen and prosecutors were useless pawns in life's game of chess. Perhaps they are! Who knows!

When Judge Bender entered the court room it was, in spite of his injunction, full of blue blouses. A special panel of two hundred talesmen filled the first half dozen rows of benches, the others being occupied by witnesses both Chinese and white, policemen and the miscellaneous

54

human flotsam and jetsam that always manages somehow or other to find its way to a murder trial. Inside the rail O'Brien, the assistant district attorney, was busy in conversation with three cueless Chinamen in American clothes. At the bar sat Mock Hen with Mr. Tutt beside him, flanked by Wong Get, Tutt, Bonnie Doon and Buddha.

The judge beckoned Mr. Tutt and O'Brien to the front of the bench.

"Is there any chance of disposing of this case by a plea?" he inquired.

O'Brien looked expectantly at Mr. Tutt, who shook his head. The judge shrugged his shoulders.

"Well, how long is it going to take?"

"About six weeks," answered the old lawyer quietly.

"What!" ejaculated judge and prosecutor in unison.

"A day or two less, perhaps," affirmed Mr. Tutt, "but, likely as not, considerably longer."

"I shall cut it down as much as I can," announced the judge, appalled at the prospect. "I shall not permit this trial to be dragged out indefinitely."

"Nothing would please me better, Your Honor," said Mr. Tutt with the shadow of a smile. "Shall we proceed to select the jury?"

The accuracy of Mr. Tutt's prophecy as to the probable length of the trial was partially demonstrated when it developed that most of the talesmen had a pronounced antipathy to Chinese murder cases, and a deep-rooted prejudice against the race as a whole. In fact, a certain subconscious influence affecting most of them was formulated by the thirty-ninth talesman to be rejected, who, in a moment of resentment, burst forth, "I don't mind trying decent American criminals, but I hold it isn't any part of a citizen's duty to try Chinamen!" and was promptly struck off the jury list.

"I say, chief," disgustedly declared O'Brien to Peckham at the noon recess as they clinked glasses over the bar at Pont's, "you've handed me a ripe, juicy Messina all right! I won't be able to get a jury. We've been at it since ten o'clock and we haven't lured a single sucker into the box!"

"What's the matter?" inquired the D.A. apprehensively.

"I can't quite make out," answered O'Brien. "But most of 'em seem to have a sort of idea that to kill a Chinaman ain't a crime but a virtue!"

"Well, don't tell anybody," whispered Peckham, "but I'm somewhat of that way of thinking myself. Set 'em up again, John!"

However, by invoking the utmost celerity a jury was at last selected and sworn at the end of the nineteenth day of the trial. As a jury O'Brien confidentially admitted to Peckham it wasn't much! But what could you expect of a bunch who were willing to swear that they hadn't any prejudice against a Chink and would as soon acquit him as a white man? The truth was that they were all gentlemen who, having lost their jobs, were willing to swear to anything that would bring them in two dollars a day. The more days the better! And it is historic fact that during the sixty-nine days of Mock Hen's prosecution not one of them protested at being kept away from his wife and children, his business or his pleasure. On the contrary they all slumbered peacefully from ten until four—and when the trial ended, on the whole they rather regretted that it was over, the only genuine opinion regarding the case being that the Chinks were all as funny as hell and that Mr. Tutt was a bully old boy.

The evidence respecting the death of the unfortunate Quong Lee made little impression upon them. Seemingly they regarded the story much as they did that of Elisha and the bears or Bel and the dragon— as a sort of apocryphal narrative which they were required to listen to, but in no wise bound to believe. They were much interested in Quong's suit of chain mail, however, and from time to time awoke to enjoy the various verbal encounters between the judge and Mr. Tutt. As factors in the proceedings they did not count, except to receive their two dollars per diem, board, lodging and hack fare.

The trial of Mock Hen being conducted in a foreign language, the first judicial step was the swearing of an interpreter. The On Gees had promptly produced one, whom O'Brien told the court was a very learned man; a graduate of the Imperial University at Peking, and a Son of the Sacred Dragon. Be that as it may, he was not prepossessing in his appearance and Mr. Tutt assured Judge Bender that far from being what the district attorney pretended, the man was a well-known gambler, who made his living largely by blackmail. He might be a son of a dragon or he might not; anyway he was a son of Belial. An interpreter was the conduit through which all the evidence must pass. If the official were biased or corrupt the testimony would be distorted, colored or suppressed.

Now he—Mr. Tutt—had an interpreter, the well-known Dr. Hong Su, against whom nothing could be said, and upon whose fat head rested no imputation of partiality; a graduate of Harvard, a writer of note, a—

O'Brien sprang to his feet: "My interpreter says your interpreter is an opium smuggler, that he murdered his aunt in Hong Kong, that he isn't a doctor at all, and that he never graduated from anything except a chop-suey joint," he interjected.

"This is outrageous!" cried Mr. Tutt, palpably shocked at such language.

"Gentlemen! Gentlemen!" groaned Judge Bender. "What am I to do? I don't know anything about these men. One looks to me about the same as the other. The court has no time to inquire into their antecedents. They may both be learned scholars or they may each be what the other says he is—I don't know. But we've got to begin to try this case sometime."

It was finally agreed that in order that there might be no possible question of partiality there should be two interpreters—one for the prosecution and one for the defense. Both accordingly were sworn and the first witness, Ah Fong, was called.

"Ask him if he understands the nature of an oath," directed O'Brien.

The interpreter for the state turned to Ah Fong and said something sweetly to him in multitudinous words.

Instantly Doctor Su rose indignantly. The other interpreter was not putting the question at all, but telling the witness what to say. Moreover, the other interpreter belonged to the On Gee Tong. He stood waving his arms and gobbling like an infuriated turkey while his adversary replied in similar fashion.

"This won't do!" snapped the judge. "This trial will degenerate into nothing but a cat fight if we are not careful." Then a bright idea suggested itself to his Occidental mind. "Suppose I appoint an official umpire to say which of the other two interpreters is correct—and let them decide who he shall be?"

This proposition was received with grunts of satisfaction by the two antagonists, who conferred together with astonishing amiability and almost immediately conducted into the court room a tall, emaciated Chinaman who they alleged was entirely satisfactory to both of them. He was accordingly sworn as a third interpreter, and the trial began again.

It was observed that thereafter there was no dispute whatever regarding the accuracy of the testimony, and as each interpreter was paid for his services at the rate of ten dollars a day it was rumored that the whole affair had been arranged by agreement between the two societies, which divided the money, amounting to some eighteen hundred dollars, between them. But, as O'Brien afterward asked Peckham, "How in thunder could you tell?"

The court's troubles had, however, only begun. Ah Fong was a whimsical-looking person, who gave an impression of desiring to make himself generally agreeable. He was, of course, the star witness—if a Chinaman can ever be a star witness—and presumably had been carefully schooled as to the manner in which he should give his testimony. He and he alone had seen the whole tragedy from beginning to end. He it was, if anybody, who would tuck Mock Hen comfortably into his coffin.

The problem of the interpreters having been solved Fong settled himself comfortably in the witness chair, crossed his hands upon his stomach and looked complacently at Mock Hen.

"Well, now let's get along," adjured His Honor. "Swear the witness."

Mr. Tutt immediately rose.

"If the court please," said he, "I object to the swearing of the witness unless it is made to appear that he will regard himself as bound by the oath as administered. Now this man is a Chinaman. I should like to ask him a preliminary question or two."

"That seems fair, Mr. O'Brien," agreed the court. "Do you see any reason why Mr. Tutt shouldn't interrogate the witness?"

"Oh, let me qualify my own witness!" retorted O'Brien fretfully. "Ah Fong, will you respect the oath to testify truthfully, about to be administered to you?"

The interpreter delivered a broadside of Chinese at Ah Fong, who listened attentively and replied at equal length. Then the interpreter went at him again, and again Ah Fong affably responded. It was interminable.

The two muttered and chortled at each other until O'Brien, losing patience, jumped up and called out: "What's all this? Can't you ask him a simple question and get a simple answer? This isn't a debating society."

The interpreter held up his hand, indicating that the prosecutor should have patience.

"*Ah-ya-ya-oo-aroo-yung-ung-loy-a-a-ya   oo-chu-a-oy-ah-ohay-tching!*" he concluded.

"*A-yah-oy-a-yoo-oy-ah-chuck-uh-ung-loy-oo-ayah-a-yoo-chung-chung-szt-oo-aha-oy-ou-ungaroo—yah-yah-yah!*" replied Ah Fong.

"Thank heaven, that's over!" sighed O'Brien.

The interpreter drew himself up to his full height.

"He says yes," he declared dramatically.

"It's the longest yes I ever heard!" audibly remarked the foreman, who was feeling his oats.

"Does not that satisfy you?" inquired the court of Mr. Tutt.

"I am sorry to say it does not!" replied the latter. "Mr. O'Brien has simply asked whether he will keep his oath. His reply sheds no light on whether his religious belief is such that it would obligate him to respect an oath."

"Well, ask him yourself!" snorted O'Brien.

"Ah Fong, do you believe in any god?" inquired Mr. Tutt.

"He says yes," answered the interpreter after the usual interchange.

"What god do you believe in?" persisted Mr. Tutt.

Suddenly Ah Fong made answer without the intervention of the interpreter.

"When I in this country," he replied complacently in English, "I b'lieve Gees Clist; when I in China I b'lieve Chinese god."

"Does Your Honor hold that an obliging acquiescence in local theology constitutes such a religious belief as to make this man's oath sacred?" inquired Mr. Tutt.

The judge smiled.

"I don't see why not!" he declared. "There isn't any precedent as far as I am aware. But he says he believes in the Deity. Isn't that enough?"

"Not unless he believes that the Deity will punish him if he breaks his oath," answered Mr. Tutt. "Let me try him on that?"

"Ah Fong, do you think God will punish you if you tell a lie?"

Fong looked blank. The interpreter fired a few salvos.

"He says it makes a difference the kind of oath."

"Suppose it is a promise to tell the truth?"

"He says what kind of a promise?"

"A promise on the Bible," answered Mr. Tutt patiently.

"He says what god you mean!" countered the interpreter.

"Oh, any god!" roared Mr. Tutt.

The interpreter, after a long parley, made reply.

"Ah Fong says there is no binding oath except on a chicken's head."

Judge Bender, O'Brien and Mr. Tutt gazed at one another helplessly.

"Well, there you are!" exclaimed the lawyer. "Mr. O'Brien's oath wasn't any oath at all! What kind of a chicken's head?"

"A white rooster."

"Quite so!" nodded Mr. Tutt. "Your Honor, I object to this witness being sworn by any oath or in any form except on the head of a white rooster!"

"Well, I don't happen to have a white rooster about me!" remarked O'Brien, while the jury rocked with glee. "Ask him if something else won't do. A big book for instance?"

The interpreter put the question and then shook his head. According to Ah Fong there was no virtue in books whatever, either large or small. On some occasions an oath could be properly taken on a broken plate—also white—but not in murder cases. It was chicken or nothing.

"Are you not willing to waive the formality of an oath, Mr. Tutt?" asked the judge in slight impatience.

"And wave my client into the chair?" demanded the lawyer. "No, sir!"

"I don't see what we can do except to adjourn court until you can procure the necessary poultry," announced Judge Bender. "Even then we can't slaughter them in court. We'll have to find some suitable place!"

"Why not kill one rooster and swear all the witnesses at once?" suggested Mr. Tutt in a moment of inspiration.

* * * * *

"My God, chief!" exclaimed O'Brien at four o'clock. "There ain't a white rooster to be had anywhere! Hens, yes! By the hundred! But roosters are extinct! Tomorrow will be the twenty-first day of this prosecution and not a witness sworn yet."

However, a poultryman was presently discovered who agreed simply for what advertising there was in it to furnish a crate of white roosters, a hatchet and a headsman's block, and to have them in the basement of the building promptly at ten o'clock.

Accordingly, at that hour Judge Bender convened Part IX of the General Sessions in the court room and then adjourned downstairs, where all the prospective witnesses for the prosecution were lined up in a body and told to raise their right hands.

Meantime Clerk McGuire was handed the hatchet, and approached the coop with obvious misgivings. Ah Fong had already given a dubious approval to the sex and quality of the fowls inside and naught remained but to submit the proper oath and remove the head of the unfortunate victim. A large crowd of policemen, witnesses, reporters, loafers, truckmen and others drawn by the unusual character of the proceedings had assembled and now proceeded without regard for the requirements of judicial dignity to encourage McGuire in his capacity of executioner, by profane shouts and jeers, to do his deadly deed.

But the clerk had had no experience with chickens and in bashfully groping for the selected rooster allowed several other occupants of the crate to escape. Instantly the air was filled with fluttering, squawking fowls while fifty frenzied police officers and Chinamen attempted vainly to reduce them to captivity again. In the midst of the mêlée McGuire caught his rooster, and fearful lest it should escape him managed somehow to decapitate it. The body, however, had been flopping around spasmodically several seconds upon the floor before he realized that the oath had not been administered, and his voice suddenly rose above the pandemonium in an excited brogue.

"Hold up your hands, you! You do solemnly swear that in the case of The People against Mock Hen you will tell the truth, the whole truth and nothing but the truth so help you God!"

But the interpreter was at that moment engaged in clasping to his bosom a struggling rooster and was totally unable to fulfill his functions. Meantime the jury, highly edified at this illustration of the administration of justice, gazed down upon the spectacle from the stairs.

"This farce has gone far enough!" declared Judge Bender disgustedly. "We will return to the court room. Put those roosters back where they belong!"

Once more the participants ascended to Part IX and Ah Fong took his seat in the witness chair. The interpreter's blouse was covered with pin-feathers and one of his thumbs was bleeding profusely.

"Ask the witness if the oath that he has now taken will bind his conscience?" directed the court.

Again the interpreter and Ah Fong held converse.

"He says," translated that official calmly, "that the chicken oath is all right in China, but that it is no good in United States, and that anyway the proper form of words was not used."

"Good Lord!" ejaculated O'Brien. "Where am I?"

"Me tell truth, all light," suddenly announced Ah Fong in English. "Go ahead! Shoot!" And he smiled an inscrutable age-long Oriental smile.

The jury burst into laughter.

"He's stringing you!" the foreman kindly informed O'Brien, who cursed silently.

"Go on, Mister District Attorney, examine the witness," directed the judge. "I shall permit no further variations upon the established forms of procedure."

Then at last and not until then—on the morning of the twenty-first day—did Ah Fong tell his simple story and the jury for the first time learn what it was all about. But by then they had entirely ceased to care, being engrossed in watching Mr. Tutt at his daily amusement of torturing O'Brien into a state of helpless exasperation.

Ah Fong gave his testimony with a clarity of detail that left nothing to be desired, and he was corroborated in most respects by the Italian woman, who identified Mock Hen as the Chinaman with the iron bar. Their evidence was supplemented by that of Bull Neck Burke and Miss Malone, who also were positive that they had seen Mock running from the scene of the murder at exactly four-one o'clock.

Mr. Tutt hardly cross-examined Fong at all, but with Mr. Burke he pursued very different tactics, speedily rousing the wrestler to such a condition of fury that he was hardly articulate, for the old lawyer gently hinted that Mr. Burke was inventing the whole story for the purpose of assisting his friends in the On Gee Tong.

"But I tell yer I don't know no Chinks!" bellowed Burke, looking more like a bull than ever. "This here Mock Hen run right by me. My goil saw him too. I looked at me ticker to get the time!"

"Ah! Then you expected to be a witness for the On Gee Tong!"

"Naw! I tell yer I was walkin' wit' me goil!"

"What is the lady's name?"

"Miss Malone."

"What is her occupation?"

"She's a gay burlesquer."

"A gay burlesquer?"

"Sure—champagne goil and gay burlesquer."

"A champagne girl!"

"Dat's what I said."

"You mean that she is upon the stage?"

"Sure—dat's it!"

"Oh!" Mr. Tutt looked relieved.

"What had you and Miss Malone been doing that afternoon?"

"I told yer—walkin'."

Mr. Tutt coughed slightly.

"Is that all?"

"Say, watcha drivin' at?"

Mr. Tutt elevated his bushy eyebrows.

"How do you earn your living?" he demanded, changing his method of attack.

Bull Neck allowed his head to sink still farther into the vast bulk of his immense torso, strangely resembling, in this position, the fabled anthropophagi whose heads are reputed thus to "grow beneath their shoulders."

Then throwing out his jaw he announced proudly between set teeth: "I'm a perfessor of physical sculture!"

The jury sniggered. Mr. Tutt appeared politely puzzled.

"A professor of what?"

"A perfessor of physical sculture!" repeated Bull Neck with great satisfaction.

"Oh! A professor of physical sculpture!" exclaimed Mr. Tutt, light breaking over his wrinkled countenance. "And what may that be?"

Bull Neck looked round disgustedly at the jury as if to say: "What ignorance!"

"Trainin' an' developin' prominent people!" he explained.

"Um!" remarked Mr. Tutt. "Who invited you to testify in this case?"

"Mr. Mooney."

"Oh, you're a friend of Mooney's! That is all!"

Now it is apparent from these questions and answers that Mr. Burke had testified to nothing to his discredit and had conducted himself as a gentleman and a sportsman according to his best lights. Yet owing to the subtle suggestions contained in Mr. Tutt's inflections and demeanor the jury leaped unhesitatingly to the conclusion that here was a man so ignorant and debased that if he were not deliberately lying he was being made a cat's-paw by the police in the interest of the On Gee Tong.

Miss Malone fared even worse, for after a preliminary skirmish she flatly refused to give Mr. Tutt or the jury any information whatever regarding her past life, while Mooney, of course, labored from the beginning to the end of his testimony under the curse of being a policeman, one of that class whom most jurymen take pride in saying they hold in natural distrust. In a word, the white witnesses to the dastardly murder of Quong Lee created a general impression of unreliability upon the minds of the jury, who wholly failed to realize the somewhat obvious truth that the witnesses to a crime in Chinatown will naturally if not inevitably be persons who either reside in or frequent that locality.

Twenty-four days had now been consumed in the trial, and as yet no Chinese witnesses except Ah Fong had been called. Now, however, they appeared in cohorts. Though Mooney had sworn that the streets were practically empty at the time of the homicide forty-one Chinese witnesses swore positively that they had been within easy view, claiming variously to have been behind doors, peeking through shutters, at upper windows and even on the roofs. All had identified Mock Hen as the murderer, and none of them had ever heard of either the On Gee or the Hip Leong Tong! Mr. Tutt could not shake them upon cross-examination, and O'Brien began to show signs of renewed confidence. Each testified to substantially the same story and they occupied seventeen full days in the telling, so that when the prosecution rested, forty-two days had been consumed since the first talesman had been called. The trial had sunk into a dull, unbroken monotony, as Mr. Tutt said, of the "vain repetitions of the heathen." Yet the police and the district attorney had done all that could reasonably have been expected of them. They were simply confronted by the very obvious fact—a condition and not a theory— that the legal processes of Anglo-Saxon jurisprudence are of slight avail in dealing with people of another race.

Now it is possible that even had Mr. Tutt put in no defense whatever the jury might have refused to convict, for there was a curious air of unreality surrounding the whole affair. It all seemed somehow as if— assuming that it had ever taken place at all—it had occurred in some other world and in some other age. Perhaps under what might have been practically a direction of the court a verdict of conviction might have been returned—but it is doubtful. The more witnesses testified to exactly the same thing in precisely the same words the less likely it appeared to be.

But Mr. Tutt was taking no chances and, upon the forty-third day of the trial, at a nod from the bench, he opened his case. Never had he been more serious; never more persuasive. Abandoning every suggestion of frivolity, he weighed the testimony of each white witness and pointed out its obvious lack of probative value. Not one, he said, except the Italian woman, had had more than a fleeting glance of the face of the man now accused of the crime. Such an identification was useless. The Chinamen were patently lying. They had not been there at all! Would any member of the jury hang a dog, even a yellow one, on such testimony? Of course not! Much less a human being. The people had called forty witnesses to prove that Mock Hen had killed Quong Lee. It made no difference. The On Gee could have just as easily produced four hundred. Moreover, Mr. Tutt did a very daring thing. He pronounced all Chinese testimony in an American court of justice as absolutely valueless, and boasted that for every Chinaman who swore Mock Hen was guilty he would bring forward two who would swear him innocent.

The thing was, as he had carefully explained to Bonnie Doon, to prove that Mock was a good Chinaman and, if the jury did not believe that there was any such animal, to convince them that it was possible. His first task, however, was to polish off the Chinese testimony by calling the witnesses who had been secured under the guidance of Wong Get. He admitted afterward that in view of the exclusion law he had not supposed there were so many Chinamen in the United States, for they crowded the corridors and staircases of the Criminal Courts Building, arriving in companies—the Wong family, the Mocks, the Fongs, the Lungs, the Sues, and others of the sacred Hip Sing Society from near at hand and from distant parts—from Brooklyn and Flatbush, from Flushing and Far Rockaway, from Hackensack and Hoboken, from Trenton and Scranton, from Buffalo and Saratoga, from Chicago and St. Louis, and each and every one of them swore positively upon the severed neck of the whitest rooster—the broken fragments of the whitest of porcelain plates—the holiest of books—that he had been present in person at Fulton Market in New York City at precisely four-fifteen o'clock in the afternoon and assisted Mock Hen, the defendant, in selecting and purchasing a terrapin for stew.

Mr. Tutt grinned at the jury and the jury grinned affectionately back at Mr. Tutt. Indeed, after the length of time they had all been together they had almost as much respect for him as for the judge upon the bench. The whole court seemed to be a sort of Tutt Club, of which even O'Brien was a member.

"Now," said Mr. Tutt, "I will call a few witnesses to show you what kind of a man this is whom these highbinders accuse of the crime of murder!"

Mock, rolling his eyes heavenward, assumed an expression of infantile helplessness and trust.

"Don't overdo it!" growled Tutt. "Just look kind of gentle."

So Mock looked as gentle as a suckling dove while two professors from Columbia University, three of his landlords in his more reputable business enterprises, the superintendent of the Rising Sun Mission, four ex-police officers, a fireman, and an investigator for the Society for the Suppression of Sin swore upon Holy Writ and with all sincerity that Mock Hen was not only a person of the most excellent character and reputation but a Christian and a gentleman.

And then Mr. Tutt played his trump card.

"I will call Miss Frances Duryea, of Hudson House," he announced. "Miss Duryea, will you kindly take the witness chair?"

Miss Fanny modestly rose from her seat in the rear of the room and came forward. No one could for an instant doubt the honesty and impartiality of this devoted middle-aged woman, who, surrendering the comforts and luxuries of her home uptown, to which she was well entitled by reason of her age, was devoting herself to a life of service. If a woman like that, thought the jury, was ready to vouch for Mock's good character, why waste any more time on the case? But Miss Fanny was to do much more.

"Miss Duryea," began Mr. Tutt, "do you know the defendant?"

"Yes, sir; I do," she answered quietly.

"How long have you known him?"

"Six years."

"Do you know his reputation for peace and quiet?"

Miss Fanny half turned to the judge and then faced the jury.

"He is one of the sweetest characters I have ever known," she replied, "and I have known many—"

"Oh, I object!" interrupted O'Brien. "This lady can't be permitted to testify to anything like that. She must be limited by the rules of evidence!"

With one movement the jury wheeled and glared at him.

"I guess this lady can say anything she wants!" declared the foreman chivalrously.

O'Brien sank down in his seat. What was the use!

"Go on, please," gently directed Mr. Tutt.

"As I was saying, Mr. Mock Hen is a very remarkable character," responded Miss Fanny. "He is devoted to the mission and to us at the settlement. I would trust him absolutely in regard to anything."

"Thank you," said Mr. Tutt, smiling benignly. "Now, Miss Duryea, did you see Mock Hen at any time on May sixth?"

Instantly the jury showed renewed signs of life. May sixth? That was the day of the murder.

"I did," answered Miss Fanny with conviction. "He came to see me at Hudson House in the afternoon and while we were talking the clock struck four."

The jury looked at one another and nodded.

"Well, I guess that settles this case!" announced the foreman.

"Right!" echoed a talesman behind him.

"I object!" wailed O'Brien. "This is entirely improper!"

"Quite so!" ruled Judge Bender sternly. "The jurymen will not make any remarks!"

"But, Your Honor—we all agreed at recess there was nothing in this case," announced the foreman. "And now this testimony simply clinches it. Why go on with it!"

"That's so!" ejaculated another. "Let us go, judge."

Mr. Tutt's weather-beaten face was wreathed in smiles.

"Easy, gentlemen!" he cautioned.

The judge shrugged his shoulders, frowning.

"This is very irregular!" he said.

Then he beckoned to O'Brien, and the two whispered together for several minutes, while all over the court room on the part of those who had sat there so patiently for sixty-nine days there was a prolonged and ecstatic wriggling of arms and legs. Instinctively they all knew that the farce was over.

The assistant district attorney returned to his table but did not sit down.

"If the court please," he said rather wearily, "the last witness, Miss Duryea, by her testimony, which I personally am quite ready to accept as truthful, has interjected a reasonable doubt of the defendant's guilt into what otherwise would in my opinion be a case for the jury. If Mock Hen was at Hudson House, nearly two miles from Pell and Doyers Streets, at four o'clock on the afternoon of the homicide, manifestly he could not have been one of the assailants of Quong Lee at one minute past four. I am satisfied that no jury would convict—"

"Not on your life!" snorted the foreman airily.

"—and I therefore," went on O'Brien, "ask the court to direct an acquittal."

* * * * *

In the grand banquet hall of the Shanghai and Hongkong American-Chinese Restaurant, Ephraim Tutt, draped in a blue mandarin coat with a tasseled pill box rakishly upon his old gray head, sat beside Wong Get and Buddha at the head of a long table surrounded by three hundred Chinamen in their richest robes of ceremony. Lanterns of party-colored glass swaying from gilded rafters shed a strange light upon a silken cloth marvelously embroidered and laden with the choicest of Oriental dishes, and upon the pale faces of the Hip Leong Tong—the Mocks, the Wongs, the Fongs and the rest—both those who had testified and also those who had merely been ready if duty called to do so, all of whom were now gathered together to pay honor where they felt honor to be due; namely, at the shrine of Mr. Tutt.

Deft Chinese waiters slipped silently from guest to guest with bird's-nest soup, guy soo main, mon goo guy pan, shark's fin and lung har made of shreds of lobster, water chestnuts, rice and the succulent shoots of the young bamboo, while three musicians in a corner sang through their nose a syncopated dirge. "Wang-ang-ang-ang!" it rose and fell as Mr. Tutt, his neck encircled by a wreath of lilies, essayed to manipulate a pair of long black chop-sticks. "Wang-ang-ang-ang!" About him were golden limes, ginger in syrup, litchi nuts, pickled leeches.

Then he felt a touch upon his shoulder and turned to see Fong Hen, the slipper, standing beside him. It was the duty of Fong Hen to drink with each guest—more than that, to drink as much as each guest drank! He gravely offered Mr. Tutt a pony of rice brandy. It was not the fiery lava he had anticipated, but a soft, caressing nectar, fragrant as if distilled from celestial flowers of the time of Confucius. The slipper swallowed the same quantity at a gulp, bowed and passed along.

Mr. Tutt vainly tried to grasp the fact that he was in his own native city of New York. Long sleeves covered with red and purple dragons hid his arms and hands, and below the collar a smooth tight surface of silk across his breast made access to his pockets quite impossible. In one of them reposed twenty one-thousand-dollar bills—his fee for securing the acquittal of Mock Hen. Yes, he was in New York!

The monotonous wail of the instruments, the pungency of the incense, the subdued light, the humid breath of the roses carried the thoughts of Mr. Tutt far away. Before him, against the blue misty sunshine, rose the yellow temples of Peking. He could hear the faint tintinnabulation of bells. He was wandering in a garden fragrant with jasmine blossoms and adorned with ancient graven stones and carved gilt statues. The air was sweet. Mr. Tutt was very tired . . .

"Let him sleep!" nodded Buddha, deftly conveying to his wrinkled lips a delicate morsel of guy yemg dun. "Let him sleep! He has earned his sleep. He has saved our face!"

It was after midnight when Mr. Tutt, heavily laden with princely gifts of ivory and jade and boxes of priceless teas, emerged from the side door of the Shanghai and Hongkong American-Chinese Restaurant. The sky was brilliant with stars and the sidewalks of Doyers and Pell Streets were crowded with pedestrians. Near by a lantern-bedecked rubber-neck wagon was in process of unloading its cargo of seekers after the curious and unwholesome. On either side of him walked Wong Get and Buddha. They had hardly reached the corner when five shots echoed in quick succession above the noise of the traffic and the crowd turned with one accord and rushed in the direction from which he had just come.

Mr. Tutt, startled, stopped and looked back. Courteously also stopped Wong Get and Buddha. A throng was fast gathering in front of the Shanghai and Hongkong Restaurant.

Then Murtha appeared, shouldering his way roughly through the mob. Catching sight of Mr. Tutt, he paused long enough to whisper hoarsely in the lawyer's ear: "Well, they got Mock Hen! Five bullets in him! But if they were going to, why in hell couldn't they have done it three months ago?"

SAMUEL AND DELILAH

"And it came to pass, when she pressed him daily with her words, and urged him, so that his soul was vexed unto death; that he told her all his heart, and said unto her, There hath not come a razor upon mine head; . . . if I be shaven, then my strength will go from me, and I shall become weak and be like any other man."—JUDGES XVI, 16, 17.

"Have you seen '76 Fed.' anywhere, Mr. Tutt?" inquired Tutt, appearing suddenly in the doorway of his partner's office.

Mr. Tutt looked up from Page 364 of the opinion he was perusing in "The United States vs. One Hundred and Thirty-two Packages of Spirituous Liquors and Wines."

"Got it here in front of me," he answered shortly. "What do you want it for?"

Tutt looked over his shoulder.

"That's a grand name for a case, isn't it? 'Packages of Wines!'" he chuckled. "I made a note once of a matter entitled 'United States vs. Forty-three Cases of Frozen Eggs'; and of another called 'United States vs. One Feather Mattress and One Hundred and Fifty Pounds of Butter'—along in 197 Federal Reports, if I remember correctly. And you recall that accident case we had—Bump against the Railroad?"

"You can't tell me anything about names," remarked Mr. Tutt. "I once tried a divorce action. Fuss against Fuss; and another, Love against Love. Do you really want this book?"

"Not if you are using it," replied Tutt. "I just wanted to show an authority to Mr. Sorg, the president of the Fat and Skinny Club. You know our application for a certificate of incorporation was denied yesterday by Justice McAlpin."

"No, I didn't know it," returned Mr. Tutt. "Why?"

"Here's his memorandum in the Law Journal," answered his partner. "Read it for yourself":

Matter of Fat and Skinny Club, Inc. This is an application for approval of a certificate of incorporation as a membership corporation. The stated purposes are to promote and encourage social intercourse and good fellowship and to advance the interests of the community. The name selected is the Fat and Skinny Club. If this be the most appropriate name descriptive of its membership it is better that it remain unincorporated. Application denied.

"Now who says the law isn't the perfection of common sense?" ruminated Mr. Tutt. "Its general principles are magnificent."

"And yet," mused Tutt, "only last week Judge McAlpin granted the petition of one Solomon Swackhamer to change his name to Phillips Brooks Vanderbilt. Is that right? Is that justice? Is it equity? I ask you!—when he turns down the Fat and Skinnies?"

"Oh, yes it is," retorted Mr. Tutt. "When you consider that Mr. Swackhamer could have assumed the appellation of P.B. Vanderbilt or any other name he chose without asking the court's permission at all."

"What!" protested Tutt incredulously.

"That's the law," returned the senior partner. "A man can call himself what he chooses and change his name as often as he likes—so long, of course, as he doesn't do it to defraud. The mere fact that a statute likewise gives him the right to apply to the courts to accomplish the same result makes no difference."

"Of course it might make him feel a little more comfortable about it to do it that way," suggested Tutt. "Do you know, as long as I've practised law in this town I've always assumed that one had to get permission to change one's name."

"You've learned something," said Mr. Tutt suavely. "I hope you will put it to good account. Here's '76 Fed.' Take it out and console the Fat and Skinny Club with it if you can."

Mr. Tutt surrendered the volume without apparent regret and Tutt retired to his own office and to the task of soothing the injured feelings of Mr. Sorg.

A simple-minded little man was Tutt, for all his professional shrewdness and ingenuity. Like many a hero of the battlefield and of the bar, once inside the palings of his own fence he became modest, gentle, even timorous. For Abigail, his wife, had no illusions about him and did not affect to have any. To her neither Tutt nor Mr. Tutt was any such great shakes. Had Tutt dared to let her know of many of the schemes which he devised for the profit or safety of his clients she would have thought less of him still; in fact, she might have parted with him forever. In a sense Mrs. Tutt was an exacting woman. Though she somewhat reluctantly consented to view the hours from nine a.m. to five p.m. in her husband's day as belonging to the law, she emphatically regarded the rest of the twenty-four hours as belonging to her.

The law may be, as Judge Holmes has called it, "a jealous mistress," but in the case of Tutt it was not nearly so jealous as his wife. So Tutt was compelled to walk the straight-and-narrow path whether he liked it or not. On the whole he liked it well enough, but there were times—usually in the spring—when without being conscious of what was the matter with him he mourned his lost youth. For Tutt was only forty-eight and he had had a grandfather who had lived strenuously to upward of twice that age. He was vigorous, sprightly, bright-eyed and as hard as nails, even if somewhat resembling in his contours the late Mr. Pickwick. Mrs. Tutt was tall, spare, capable and sardonic. She made Tutt comfortable, but she no longer appealed to his sense of romance. Still she held him. As the playwright hath said "It isn't good looks they want, but good nature; if a warm welcome won't hold them, cold cream won't."

However, Tutt got neither looks nor cold cream. His welcome, in fact, was warm only if he stayed out too late, and then the later the warmer. His relationship to his wife was prosaic, respectful. In his heart of hearts he occasionally thought of her as exceedingly unattractive. In a word Mrs. Tutt performed her wifely functions in a purely matter-of-fact way. Anything else would have seemed to her unseemly. She dressed in a manner that would have been regarded as conservative even on Beacon Hill. She had no intention of making an old fool of herself or of letting him be one either. When people had been married thirty years they could take some things for granted. Few persons therefore had ever observed Mr. Tutt in the act of caressing Mrs. Tutt; and there were those who said that he never had. Frankly, she was a trifle forbidding: superficially not the sort of person to excite a great deal of sentiment; and occasionally, as we have hinted, in the spring Tutt yearned for a little sentiment.

He did his yearning, however, entirely on the side and within those hours consecrated to the law. In his wife's society he yearned not at all. In her company he carefully kept his thoughts and his language inside the innermost circle of decorum. At home his talk was entirely "Yea, yea," and "Nay, nay," and dealt principally with politics and the feminist movement, in which Abigail was deeply interested.

And by this we do not mean to suggest that at other times or places Tutt was anything but conventionally proper. He was not. He only yearned to be, well knowing that he was deficient in courage if not in everything else.

But habit or no habit, likely or unlikely, Mrs. Tutt had no intention of taking any chances so far as Tutt was concerned. If he did not reach home precisely at six explanations were in order, and if he came in half an hour later he had to demonstrate his integrity beyond a reasonable doubt according to the established rules of evidence.

Perhaps Mrs. Tutt did wisely to hold Tutt thus in leash considering the character of many of the firm's clients. For it was quite impossible to conceal the nature of the practise of Tutt & Tutt; much of which figured flamboyantly in the newspapers. Some women would have taken it for granted under like circumstances that their husbands had acquired a touch at least of the wisdom of the serpent even if they remained quite harmless. Abigail countenanced no thought of any demoralization in her spouse. To her he was like the artist who smears himself and his smock with paint while in his studio, but appears at dinner in spotless linen without even a whiff of benzine about him to suggest his occupation. So Tutt, though hand and glove in his office with the most notorious of the elite of Longacre Square, came home to supper with the naiveté and innocence of a theological student for whom an evening at a picture show is the height of dissipation.

Yet Tutt was no more of a Doctor Jekyll and Mr. Hyde than most of us. Merely, his daily transition was a little more abrupt. And when all is said and done most of the devices invented by his fertile little brain to further the interests of his clients were no more worthy of condemnation than those put forward by far higher-priced and much more celebrated attorneys.

Not that Mrs. Tutt was blind to the dangers to which her husband by virtue of his occupation was exposed. Far from it. Indeed she made it her business to pay periodical visits to the office, ostensibly to see whether or not it was properly cleaned and the windows washed, but in reality—or at least so Tutt suspected—to find out whether the personnel was entirely suitable for a firm of their standing and particularly for a junior partner of his susceptibilities.

But she never discovered anything to give her the slightest cause for alarm. The dramatis personae of the offices of Tutt & Tutt were characteristic of the firm, none of their employees—except Miss Sondheim, the tumultous-haired lady stenographer—and Willie, the office boy, being under forty years of age.

When not engaged in running errands or fussing over his postage-stamp album, Willie spent most of his time teasing old Scraggs, the scrivener, an unsuccessful teetotaler. A faint odor of alcohol emanated from the cage in which he performed his labors and lent an atmosphere of cheerfulness to what might otherwise have seemed to Broadway clients an unsympathetic environment, though there were long annual periods during which he was as sober as a Kansas judge. The winds of March were apt, however, to take hold of him. Perhaps it was the spring in his case also.

The backbone of the establishment was Miss Minerva Wiggin. In every law office there is usually some one person who keeps the shop going. Sometimes it is a man. If so, he is probably a sublimated stenographer or law clerk who, having worked for years to get himself admitted to the bar, finds, after achieving that ambition, that he has neither the ability nor the inclination to brave the struggle for a livelihood by himself. Perchance as a youth he has had visions of himself arguing test cases before the Court of Appeals while the leaders of the bar hung upon his every word, of an office crowded with millionaire clients and servile employees, even as he is servile to the man for whom he labors for a miserly ten dollars a week.

His ambition takes him by the hand and leads him to high places, from which he gazes down into the land of his future prosperity and greatness. The law seems a mysterious, alluring, fascinating profession, combining the romance of the drama with the gratifications of the intellect. He springs to answer his master's bell; he sits up until all hours running down citations and making extracts from opinions; he rushes to court and answers the calendar and sometimes carries the lawyer's brief case and attends him throughout a trial. Three years go by—five—and he finds that he is still doing the same thing. He is now a member of the bar, he has become the managing clerk, he attends to fairly important matters, engages the office force, superintends transfer of title, occasionally argues a motion. Five years more go by and perhaps his salary is raised a trifle more. Then one day he awakes to the realization that his future is to be only that of a trusted servitor.

Perchance he is married and has a baby. The time has come for him to choose whether he will go forth and put his fortune to the test "to win or lose it all" or settle down into the position of faithful legal hired man. He is getting a bit bald, he has had one or two tussles with his bank about accidental overdrafts. The world looks pretty bleak outside and the big machine of the law goes grinding on heartless, inevitable. Who is he to challenge the future? The old job is fairly easy; they can't get on without him, they say; here is where he belongs; he knows his business—give him his thirty-five hundred a year and let him stay!

That is Binks, or Calkins, or Shivers, or any one of those worried gray-haired men who sit in the outer office behind a desk strewn with papers and make sure that no mistakes have been made. To them every doubtful question of practise is referred and they answer instantly—sometimes wrongly, but always instantly. They know the last day for serving the demurrer in Bilbank against Terwilliger and whether or not you can tax a referee's fee as a disbursement in a bill of costs; they are experts on the precise form for orders in matrimonial actions and the rule in regard to filing a summons and complaint in Oneida County; they stand between the members of the firm and disagreeable clients; they hire and discharge the office boys; they do everything from writing a brief for the Supreme Court of the United States down to making the contract with the window cleaners; they are the only lawyers who really know anything and they were once promising young men, who have found out at last that life and the Sunday-school books are very far apart; but they run the works and make the law a gentleman's profession for the rest of us. They are always there. Others come, grow older, go away, but they remain. Many of them drink. All of which would be irrelevant, incompetent and immaterial if this were not a legal story.

Scraggs had been one of these, but he had also been one of those who drank, and now he was merely a bookkeeper. Miss Wiggin reigned in his stead.

A woman and not a man kept Tutt & Tutt on the map. When this sort of thing occurs it is usually because the woman in question is the ablest and very likely also the best person in the outfit, and she assumes the control of affairs by a process of natural selection. Miss Wiggin was the conscience, if Mr. Tutt was the heart, of Tutt & Tutt. Nobody, unless it was Mr. Tutt, knew where she had come from or why she was working if at all in only a semi-respectable law office. Without her something dreadful would have happened to the general morale. Everybody recognized that fact.

Her very appearance gave the place tone—neutralized the faint odor of alcohol from the cage. For in truth she was a fine-looking woman. Had she been costumed by a Fifth Avenue dressmaker and done her coiffure differently she would have been pretty. Because she drew her gray hair straight back from her low forehead and tied it in a knob on the back of her head, wore paper cuffs and a black dress, she looked nearer fifty than forty-one, which she was. Two hundred dollars would have taken twenty years off her apparent age—a year for every ten dollars; but she would not have looked a particle less a lady.

Her duties were ambiguous. She was always the first to arrive at the office and was the only person permitted to open the firm mail outside of its members. She overlooked the books that Scraggs kept and sent out the bills. She kept the key to the cash box and had charge of the safe. She made the entries in the docket and performed most of the duties of a regular managing clerk. She had been admitted to the bar. She checked up the charge accounts and on Saturdays paid off the office force. In addition to all these things she occasionally took a hand at a brief, drew most of the pleadings, and kept track of everything that was done in the various cases.

But her chief function, one which made her invaluable was that of receiving clients who came to the office, and in the first instance ascertaining just what their troubles were; and she was so sympathetic and at the same time so sensible that many a stranger who casually drifted in and would otherwise just as casually have drifted out again remained a permanent fixture in the firm's clientele. Scraggs and William adored her in spite of her being an utter enigma to them. She was quiet but businesslike, of few words but with a latent sense of humor that not infrequently broke through the surface of her gravity, and she proceeded upon the excellent postulate that everyone with whom she came in contact was actuated by the highest sense of honor. She acted as a spiritual tonic to both Mr. Tutt and Tutt—especially to the latter, who was the more in need of it. If they were ever tempted to stray across the line of professional rectitude her simple assumption that the thing couldn't be done usually settled the matter once and for all. On delicate questions Mr. Tutt frankly consulted her. Without her, Tutt & Tutt would have been shysters; with her they were almost respectable. She received a salary of three thousand dollars a year and earned double that amount, for she served where she loved and her first thought was of Tutt & Tutt. If you can get a woman like that to run your law office do not waste any time or consideration upon a man. Her price is indeed above rubies.

Yet even Miss Wiggin could not keep the shadow of the vernal equinox off the simple heart of the junior Tutt. She had seen it coming for several weeks, had scented danger in the way Tutt's childish eye had lingered upon Miss Sondheim's tumultous black hair and in the rather rakish, familiar way he had guided the ladies who came to get divorces out to the elevator. And then there swam into his life the beautiful Mrs. Allison, and for a time Tutt became not only hysterically young again, but—well, you shall see.

Yet, curiously enough, though we are a long way from where this story opened, it all goes back to Phillips Brooks Vanderbilt and the Fat and Skinny Club and the right to call ourselves by what names we please.

Moreover, as must be apparent, all that happened occurred beyond Miss Wiggin's sphere of spiritual influence. Yet, had it not, even she could not have harnessed Leviathan or loosed the bands of Orion—to say nothing of counteracting the effect of spring.

When Tutt returned with "76 Fed." after the departure of Mr. Sorg he found his partner smoking the usual stogy and gazing pensively down upon the harbor. The immediate foreground was composed of rectangular roofs of divers colors, mostly reddish, ornamented with eccentrically shaped chimney pots, pent-houses, skylights and water tanks, in addition to various curious whistle-like protuberances from which white wraiths of steam whirled and danced in the gay breeze. Beyond, in the middle distance, a great highway of sparkling jewels led across the waves to the distant faintly green hills of Staten Island. Three tiny aeroplanes wove invisible threads against the blue woof of the sky above the New Jersey shore. It was not a day to practise law at all. It was a day to lie on one's back in the grass and watch the clouds or throw one's weight against the tugging helm of a racing sloop and bite the spindrift blown across her bows—not a day for lawyers but for lovers!

"Here's '76 Fed.'," said Tutt.

"What's become of Sorg?"

"Gone. Mad. Says the whole point of the Fat and Skinny Club is in the name."

"I fancy—from looking at Mr. Sorg—that that is quite true," remarked Mr. Tutt. He paused and reaching down into a lower compartment of his desk, lifted out a tumbler and his bottle of malt extract, which he placed carefully at his elbow and leaned back again contemplatively. "Look here, Tutt," he said. "I want to ask you something. Is there anything the matter with you?"

Tutt regarded him with the air of a small boy caught peeking through a knot hole.

"Why,—no!" he protested lamely. "That is—nothing in particular. I do feel a bit restless—sort of vaguely dissatisfied."

Mr. Tutt nodded sympathetically.

"How old are you, Tutt?"

"Forty-eight."

"And you feel just at present as if life were 'flat, stale and unprofitable?'"

"Why—yes; you might put it that way. The fact is every day seems just like every other day. I don't even get any pleasure out of eating. The very sight of a boiled egg beside my plate at breakfast gives me the willies. I can't eat boiled eggs any more. They sicken me!"

"Exactly!" Mr. Tutt poured out a glass of the malt extract.

"I feel the same way about a lot of things," Tutt hurried on. "Special demurrers, for instance. They bore me horribly. And supplementary proceedings get most frightfully upon my nerves."

"Exactly!" repeated Mr. Tutt.

"What do you mean by 'exactly?'" snapped Tutt.

"You're bored," explained his partner.

"Rather!" agreed Tutt. "Bored to death. Not with anything special, you understand; just everything. I feel as if I'd like to do something devilish."

"When a man feels like that he better go to a doctor," declared Mr. Tutt.

"A doctor!" exclaimed Tutt derisively. "What good would a doctor do me?"

"He might keep you from getting into trouble."

"Oh, you needn't be alarmed. I won't get into any trouble."

"It's the dangerous age," said Mr. Tutt. "I've known a lot of respectable married men to do the most surprising things round fifty."

Tutt looked interested.

"Have you now?" he inquired. "Well, I've no doubt it did some of 'em a world of good. Tell you frankly sometimes I feel as if I'd rather like to take a bit of a fling myself!"

"Your professional experience ought to be enough to warn you of the dangers of that sort of experiment," answered Mr. Tutt gravely. "It's bad enough when it occurs inadvertently, so to speak, but when a man in your condition of life deliberately goes out to invite trouble it's a sad, sad spectacle."

"Do you mean to imply that I'm not able to take care of myself?" demanded Tutt.

"I mean to imply that no man is too wise to be made a fool of by some woman."

"That every Samson has his Delilah?"

"If you want to put it that way—yes."

"And that in the end he'll get his hair cut?"

Mr. Tutt took a sip from the tumbler of malt and relit his stogy.

"What do you know about Samson and Delilah, Tutt?" he challenged.

"Oh, about as much as you do, I guess, Mr. Tutt," answered his partner modestly.

"Well, who cut Samson's hair?" demanded the senior member.

He emptied the dregs of the malt-extract bottle into his glass and holding it to the light examined it critically.

"Delilah, of course!" ejaculated Tutt.

Mr. Tutt shook his head.

"There you go off at half-cock again, Tutt!" he retorted whimsically. "You wrong her. She did no such thing."

"Why, I'll bet you a hundred dollars on it!" cried Tutt excitedly.

"Make it a simple dinner at the Claridge Grill and I'll go you."

"Done!"

There were four books on the desk near Mr. Tutt's right hand— the New York Code of Civil Procedure, an almanac, a Shakesperean concordance and a Bible.

"Look it up for yourself," said Mr. Tutt, waving his arm with a gesture of the utmost impartiality. "That is, if you happen to know in what part of Holy Writ said Delilah is to be found."

Tutt followed the gesture and sat down at the opposite side of the desk.

"There!" he exclaimed, after fumbling over the leaves for several minutes. "What did I tell you? Listen, Mr. Tutt! It's in the sixteenth chapter of Judges: 'And it came to pass, when she pressed him daily with her words, and urged him, so that his soul was vexed unto death; That he told her all his heart, and said unto her, There hath not come a razor upon mine head.' Um—um."

"Read on, Tutt!" ordered Mr. Tutt.

"Um. 'And when Delilah saw that he had told her all his heart, she sent and called for the lords of the Philistines, saying, Come up this once.' Um-um."

"Yes, go on!"

"'And she made him sleep upon her knees; and she called for a man, and she caused him to shave off the seven locks of his head.' Well, I'll be hanged!" exclaimed Tutt. "Now, I would have staked a thousand dollars on it. But look here, you don't win! Delilah did cut Samson's hair—through her agent. *'Qui facit per alium facit per se!'*"

"Your point is overruled," said Mr. Tutt. "A barber cut Samson's hair. Let it be a lesson to you never to take anything on hearsay. Always look up your authorities yourself. Moreover"—and he looked severely at Tutt—"the cerebral fluid—like malt extract—tends to become cloudy with age."

"Well, anyhow, I'm no Samson," protested Tutt. "And I haven't met anyone that looked like a Delilah. I guess after the procession of adventuresses that have trailed through this office in the last twenty years I'm reasonably safe."

"No man is safe," meditated Mr. Tutt. "For the reason that no man knows the power of expansion of his heart. He thinks it's reached its limit—and then he finds to his horror or his delight that it hasn't. To put it another way, a man's capacity to love may be likened to a thermometer. At twenty-five or thirty he meets some young person, falls in love with her, thinks his amatory thermometer has reached the boiling-point and accordingly marries her. In point of fact it hasn't—it's only marking summer heat—hasn't even registered the temperature of the blood. Well, he goes merrily on life's way and some fine day another lady breezes by, and this safe and sane citizen, who supposes his capacity for affection was reached in early youth, suddenly discovers to his amazement that his mercury is on the jump and presently that his old thermometer has blown its top off."

"Very interesting, Mr. Tutt," observed Tutt after a moment's silence. "You seem to have made something of a study of these things."

"Only in a business way—only in a business way!" Mr. Tutt assured him. "Now, if you're feeling stale—and we all are apt to get that way this time of year—why don't you take a run down to Atlantic City?"

Now Tutt would have liked to go to Atlantic City could he have gone by himself, but the idea of taking Abigail along robbed the idea of its attraction. She had got more than ever on his nerves of late. But his reply, whatever it might have been, was interrupted by the announcement of Miss Wiggin, who entered at that moment, that a lady wished to see him.

"She asked for Mr. Tutt," explained Minerva.

"But I think her case is more in your line," and she nodded to Tutt.

"Good looking?" inquired Tutt roguishly.

"Very," returned Miss Wiggin. "A blonde."

"Thanks," answered Tutt, smoothing his hair; "I'm on my way."

Now this free, almost vulgar manner of speech was in reality foreign to both Tutt and Miss Wiggin and it was born of the instant, due doubtless to some peculiar juxtaposition of astral bodies in Cupid's horoscope unknown to them, but which none the less had its influence. Strange things happen on the eve of St. Agnes and on Midsummer Night—even in law offices.

Mrs. Allison was sitting by the window in Tutt's office when he came in, and for a full minute he paused upon the threshold while she pretended she did not know that he was there. The deluge of sunlight that fell upon her face betrayed no crack or wrinkle—no flaw of any kind—in the white marble of its perfection. It was indeed a lovely face, classic in the chiseling of its transparent alabaster; and when she turned, her eyes were like misty lakes of blue. Bar none, she was the most beautiful creature—and there had been many—that had ever wandered into the offices of Tutt & Tutt. He sought for a word. "Wonderful"; that was, it, she was "wonderful." His stale spirit soared in ecstasy, and left him tongue-tied. In vulgar parlance he was rattled to death, this commonplace little lawyer who for a score of years had dealt cynically with the loves and lives of the flock of female butterflies who fluttered annually in and out of the office. Throughout that period he had sat unemotionally behind his desk and listened in an aloof, cold, professional manner to the stories of their wrongs as they sobbed or hissed them forth. Wise little lawyer that he was, he had regarded them all as just what they were and nothing else—specimens of the Cecropia. And he had not even patted them upon the shoulder or squeezed their hands when he had bade them good-by—maintaining always an impersonal and dignified demeanor.

Therefore he was surprised to hear himself say in soothing, almost cooing tones:

"Well, my dear, what can I do for you?"

Shades of Abigail! "Well, my dear!" Tutt—Tutt! Tutt!

"I am in great trouble," faltered Mrs. Allison, gazing in misty helplessness out of her blue grottoes at him while her beautiful red lips trembled.

"I hope I can help you!" he breathed. "Tell me all about it! Take your time. May I relieve you of your wrap?"

She wriggled out of it gratefully and he saw for the first time the round, slender pillar of her neck. What a head she had—in its nimbus of hazy gold. What a figure! His forty-eight-year-old lawyer's heart trembled under its heavy layer of half-calf dust. He found difficulty in articulating. He stammered, staring at her most shamelessly both of which symptoms she did not notice. She was used to them in the other sex. Tutt did not know what was the matter with him. He had in fact entered upon that phase at which the wise man, be he old or young, turns and runs.

But Tutt did not run. In legal phrase he stopped, looked and listened, experiencing a curious feeling of expansion. This enchanting creature transmuted the dingy office lined with its rows of calfskin bindings into a golden grot in which he stood spellbound by the low murmur of her voice. A sense of infinite leisure emanated from her—a subtle denial of the ordinary responsibilities—very relaxing and delightful to Tutt. But what twitched his very heartstrings was the dimple that came and went with that pathetic little twisted smile of hers.

"I came to you," said Mrs. Allison, "because I knew you were both kind and clever."

Tutt smiled sweetly.

"Kind, perhaps—not clever!" he beamed.

"Why, everyone says you are one of the cleverest lawyers in New York," she protested. Then, raising her innocent China-blue eyes to his she murmured, "And I so need kindness!"

Tutt's breast swelled with an emotion which he was forced to admit was not altogether avuncular—that curious sentimental mixture that middle-aged men feel of paternal pity, Platonic tenderness and protectiveness, together with all those other euphemistic synonyms, that make them eager to assist the weak and fragile, to try to educate and elevate, and particularly to find out just how weak, fragile, uneducated and unelevated a helpless lady may be. But in spite of his half century of experience Tutt's knowledge of these things was purely vicarious. He could have told another man when to run, but he didn't know when to run himself.

He could have saved another, himself he could not save—at any rate from Mrs. Allison.

He had never seen anyone like her. He pulled his chair a little nearer. She was so slender, so supple, so—what was it?—svelte! And she had an air of childish dignity that appealed to him tremendously. There was nothing, he assured himself, of the vamp about her at all.

"I only want to get my rights," she said, tremulously. "I'm nearly out of my mind. I don't know what to do or where to turn!"

"Is there"—he forced himself to utter the word with difficulty— "a—a man involved?"

She flushed and bowed her head sadly, and instantly a poignant rage possessed him.

"A man I trusted absolutely," she replied in a low voice.

"His name?"

"Winthrop Oaklander."

Tutt gasped audibly, for the name was that of one of Manhattan's most distinguished families, the founder of which had swapped glass beads and red-flannel shirts with the aborigines for what was now the most precious water frontage in the world—and moreover, Mrs. Allison informed Tutt, he was a clergyman.

"I don't wonder you're surprised!" agreed Mrs. Allison.

"Why—I—I'm—not surprised at all!" prevaricated Tutt, at the same time groping for his silk handkerchief. "You don't mean to say you've got a case against this man Oaklander!"

"I have indeed!" she retorted with firmly compressed lips. "That is, if it is what you call a case for a man to promise to marry a woman and then in the end refuse to do so."

"Of course it is!" answered Tutt. "But why on earth wouldn't he?"

"He found out I had been divorced," she explained. "Up to that time everything had been lovely. You see he thought I was a widow."

"Ah!"

Mr. Tutt experienced another pang of resentment against mankind in general.

"I had a leading part in one of the season's successes on Broadway," she continued miserably. "But when Mr. Oaklander promised to marry me I left the stage; and now—I have nothing!"

"Poor child!" sighed Tutt.

He would have liked to take her in his arms and comfort her, but he always kept the door into the outer office open on principle.

"You know, Mr. Oaklander is the pastor of St. Lukes-Over-the-Way," said Mrs. Allison. "I thought that maybe rather than have any publicity he might do a little something for me."

"I suppose you've got something in the way of evidence, haven't you? Letters or photographs or something?" inquired Tutt, reverting absent-mindedly to his more professional manner.

"No," she answered. "We never wrote to one another. And when we went out it was usually in the evening. I don't suppose half a dozen people have ever seen us together."

"That's awkward!" meditated Tutt, "if he denies it."

"Of course he will deny it!"

"You can't tell. He may not."

"Oh, yes, he will! Why, he even refuses to admit that he ever met me!" declared Mrs. Allison indignantly.

Now, to Tutt's credit be it said that neither at this point nor at any other did any suspicion of Mrs. Allison's sincerity enter his mind. For the first time in his professional existence he accepted what a lady client told him at its face value. Indeed he felt that no one, not even a clergyman, could help loving so miraculous a woman, or that loving her one could refrain from marrying her save for some religious or other permanent obstacle He was sublimely, ecstatically happy in the mere thought that he, Tutt, might be of help to such a celestial being, and he desired no reward other than the privilege of being her willing slave and of reading her gratitude in those melting, misty eyes.

Mrs. Allison went away just before lunch time, leaving her telephone number, her handkerchief, a pungent odor of violet talc, and a disconsolate but highly excited Tutt. Never, at any rate within twenty years, had he felt so young. Life seemed tinged with every color of the spectrum. The radiant fact was that he would—he simply had to—see her again. What he might do for her professionally—all that aspect of the affair was shoved far into the background of his mind. His only thought was how to get her back into his office at the earliest possible moment.

"Shall I enter the lady's name in the address book?" inquired Miss Wiggin coldly as he went out to get a bite of lunch.

Tutt hesitated.

"Mrs. Georgie Allison is her name," he said in a detached sort of way.

"Address?"

Tutt felt in his waistcoat pocket.

"By George!" he muttered, "I didn't take it. But her telephone number is Lincoln Square 9187."

To chronicle the details of Tutt's second blooming would be needlessly to derogate from the dignity of the history of Tutt & Tutt. There is a silly season in the life of everyone—even of every lawyer—who can call himself a man, and out of such silliness comes the gravity of knowledge. Tutt found it necessary for his new client to come to the office almost every day, and as she usually arrived about the noon hour what was more natural than that he should invite her out to lunch? Twice he walked home with her. The telephone was busy constantly. And the only thorn in the rose of Tutt's delirious happiness was the fear lest Abigail might discover something. The thought gave him many an anxious hour, cost him several sleepless nights. At times this nervousness about his wife almost exceeded the delight of having Mrs. Allison for a friend. Yet each day he became on more and more cordial terms with her, and the lunches became longer and more intimate.

The Reverend Winthrop Oaklander gave no sign of life, however. The customary barrage of legal letters had been laid down, but without eliciting any response. The Reverend Winthrop must be a wise one, opined Tutt, and he began to have a hearty contempt as well as hatred for his quarry. The first letter had been the usual vague hint that the clergyman might and probably would find it to his advantage to call at the offices of Tutt & Tutt, and so on. The Reverend Winthrop, however did not seem to care to secure said advantage whatever it might be. The second epistle gave the name of the client and proposed a friendly discussion of her affairs. No reply. The third hinted at legal proceedings. Total silence. The fourth demanded ten thousand dollars damages and threatened immediate suit.

In answer to this last appeared the Reverend Winthrop himself. He was a fine-looking young chap with a clear eye—almost as blue as Georgie's—and a skin even pinker than hers, and he stood six feet five in his Oxfords and his fist looked to Tutt as big as a coconut.

"Are you the blackmailer who's been writing me those letters?" he demanded, springing into Tutt's office. "If you are, let me tell you something. You've got hold of the wrong monkey. I've been dealing with fellows of your variety ever since I got out of the seminary. I don't know the lady you pretend to represent, and I never heard of her. If I get any more letters from you I'll go down and lay the case before the district attorney; and if he doesn't put you in jail I'll come up here and knock your head off. Understand? Good day!"

At any other period in his existence Tutt could not have failed to be impressed with the honesty of this husky exponent of the church militant, but he was drugged as by the drowsy mandragora. The blatant defiance of this muscular preacher outraged him. This canting hypocrite, this wolf in priest's clothing must be brought to book. But how? Mrs. Allison had admitted the literal truth when she had told him that there were no letters, no photographs. There was no use commencing an action for breach of promise if there was no evidence to support it. And once the papers were filed their bolt would have been shot. Some way must be devised whereby the Reverend Winthrop Oaklander could be made to perceive that Tutt & Tutt meant business, and—equally imperative—whereby Georgie would be impressed with the fact that not for nothing had she come to them—that is, to him—for help.

The fact of the matter was that the whole thing had become rather hysterical. Tutt, though having nothing seriously to reproach himself with, was constantly haunted by a sense of being rather ridiculous and doing something behind his wife's back. He told himself that his Platonic regard for Georgie was a noble thing and did him honor, but it was an honor which he preferred to wear as an entirely private decoration. He was conscious of being laughed at by Willie and Scraggs and disapproved of by Miss Wiggin, who was very snippy to him. And in addition there was the omnipresent horror of having Abigail unearth his philandering. He now not only thought of Mrs. Allison as Georgie but addressed her thus, and there was quite a tidy little bill at the florist's for flowers that he had sent her. In one respect only did he exhibit even the most elementary caution—he wrote and signed all his letters to her himself upon the typewriter, and filed copies in the safe.

"So there we are!" he sighed as he gave to Mrs. Allison a somewhat expurgated, or rather emasculated version of the Reverend Winthrop's visit. "We have got to hand him something hot or make up our minds to surrender. In a word we have got to scare him—Georgie."

And then it was that, like the apocryphal mosquito, the Fat and Skinny Club justified its attempted existence. For the indefatigable Sorg made an unheralded reappearance in the outer office and insisted upon seeing Tutt, loudly asserting that he had reason to believe that if a new application were now made to another judge—whom he knew—it would be more favorably received. Tutt went to the doorway and stood there barring the entrance and expostulating with him.

"All right!" shouted Sorg. "All right! I hear you! But don't tell me that a man named Solomon Swackhamer can change his name to Phillips

Brooks Vanderbilt and in the same breath a reputable body of citizens be denied the right to call themselves what they please!"

"He don't understand!" explained Tutt to Georgie, who had listened with wide, dreamy eyes. "He don't appreciate the difference between doing a thing as an individual and as a group."

"What thing?"

"Why, taking a name."

"I don't get you," said Georgie.

"Sorg wanted to call his crowd the Fat and Skinny Club, and the court wouldn't let him—thought it was silly."

"Well?"

"But he could have called himself Mr. Fat or Mr. Skinny or Mr. Anything Else without having to ask anybody—Oh, I say!"

Tutt had stiffened into sculpture.

"What is it?" demanded Georgie fascinated.

"I've got an idea," he cried. "You can call yourself anything you like. Why not call yourself Mrs. Winthrop Oaklander?"

"But what good would that do?" she asked vaguely.

"Look here!" directed Tutt. "This is the surest thing you know! Just go up to the Biltmore and register as Mrs. Winthrop Oaklander. You have a perfect legal right to do it. You could call yourself Mrs. Julius Caesar if you wanted to. Take a room and stay there until our young Christian soldier offers you a suitable inducement to move along. Even if you're violating the law somehow his first attempt to make trouble for you will bring about the very publicity he is anxious to avoid. Why, it's marvelous—and absolutely safe? They can't touch you. He'll come across inside of two hours. If he doesn't a word to the reporters will start things in the right direction."

For a moment Mrs. Allison looked puzzled. Then her beautiful face broke into an enthusiastic classic smile and she laid her little hand softly on his arm.

"What a clever boy you are—Sammy!"

A subdued snigger came from the direction of the desk usually occupied by William. Tutt flushed. It was one thing to call Mrs. Allison "Georgie" in private and another to have her "Sammy" him within hearing of the office force. And just then Miss Wiggin passed by with her nose slightly in the air.

"What a perfectly wonderful idea!" went on Mrs. Allison rapturously. "A perfectly wonderful idea!"

Then she smiled a strange, mysterious, significant smile that almost tore Tutt's heart out by the roots.

"Listen, Sammy," she whispered, with a new light in those beautiful eyes. "I want five thousand dollars."

"Five?" repeated Tutt simply. "I thought you wanted ten thousand!"

"Only five from you, Sammy!"

"Me!" he gagged.

"You—dearest!"

Tutt turned blazing hot; then cold, dizzy and sea-sick. His sight was slightly blurred. Slowly he groped for the door and closed it cautiously.

"What—are—you—talking about?" he choked, though he knew perfectly well.

Georgie had thrown herself back in the leather chair by his desk and had opened her gold mesh-bag.

"About five thousand dollars," she replied with the careful enunciation of a New England school-mistress.

"What five thousand dollars?"

"The five you're going to hand me before I leave this office, Sammy darling," she retorted dazzlingly.

Tutt's head swam and he sank weakly into his swivel chair. It was incredible that he, a veteran of the criminal bar, should have been so tricked. Instantly, as when a reagent is injected into a retort of chemicals and a precipitate is formed leaving the previously cloudy liquid like crystal, Tutt's addled brain cleared. He was caught! The victim of his own asininity. He dared not look at this woman who had wound him thus round her finger, innocent as he was of any wrongdoing; he was ashamed to think of his wife.

"My Lord!" he murmured, realizing for the first time the depth of his weakness.

"Oh, it isn't as bad as that!" she laughed. "Remember you were going to charge Oaklander ten thousand. This costs you only five. Special rates for physicians and lawyers!"

"And suppose I don't choose to give it to you?" he asked.

"Listen here, you funny little man!" she answered in caressing tones that made him writhe. "You'd stand for twenty if I insisted on it. Oh, don't jump! I'm not going to. You're getting off easy—too easy. But I want to stay on good terms with you. I may need you sometime in my business. Your certified check for five thousand dollars—and I leave you."

She struck a match and started to light a tiny gold-tipped cigarette.

"Don't!" he gasped. "Not in the office."

"Do I get the five thousand?"

He ground his teeth, not yet willing to concede defeat.

"You silly old bird!" she said. "Do you know how many times you've had me down here in your office in the last three weeks? Fifteen. How many times you've taken me out to lunch? Ten. How often you've called me on the telephone? Eighty-nine How many times you've sent me flowers? Twelve. How many letters you've written me? Eleven! Oh, I realize they're typewritten, but a photograph enlargement would show they were typed in your office. Every typewriter has its own individuality, you know. Your clerks and office boy have heard me call you Sammy. Why, every time you've moved with me beside you someone has seen you. That's enough, isn't it? But now, on top of all that, you go and hand me exactly what I need on a gold plate."

He gazed at her stupidly.

"Why, if now you don't give me that check I shall simply go up to the Biltmore and register as Mrs. Samuel Tutt. I shall take a room and stay there until you offer me a proper inducement to move on." She giggled delightedly. "It's marvelous—absolutely safe," she quoted. "They can't touch me. You'll come across inside of two hours. If you don't a word to the reporters will start things in the right direction."

"Don't!" he groaned. "I must have been crazy. That was simply blackmail!"

"That's exactly what it was!" she agreed. "There aren't any letters except these typewritten ones, or photographs, or any evidence at all, but you're going to give me five thousand dollars just the same. Just so that your wife won't know what a silly old fool you've been. Where's your check book, Sam?"

Tutt pulled out the bottom drawer of his desk and slowly removed his personal check book. With his fountain pen in his hand he paused and looked at her.

"Rather than give you another cent I'd stand the gaff," he remarked defiantly.

"I know it," she answered. "I looked you up before I came here the first time. You are good for exactly five thousand dollars."

Tutt filled out the check to cash and sent Willie across the street to the bank to have it certified. The sun was just sinking over the Jersey shore beyond the Statue of Liberty and the surface of the harbor undulated like iridescent watered silk. The clouds were torn into golden-purple rents, and the air was so clear that one could look down the Narrows far out to the open sea. Standing there by the window Mrs. Allison looked as innocently beautiful as the day Tutt had first beheld her. After all, he thought, perhaps the experience had been worth the money.

Something of the same thought may have occurred to the lady, for as she took the check and carefully examined the certification she remarked with a distinct access of cordiality: "Really, Sammy, you're quite a nice little man. I rather like you."

Tutt stood after she had gone watching the sunset until the west was only a mass of leaden shadows Then, strangely relieved, he took his hat and started out of the office. Somewhat to his surprise he found Miss Wiggin still at her desk.

"By the way," she remarked casually as he passed her, "what shall I charge that check to? The one you just drew to cash for five thousand dollars?"

"Charge it to life insurance," he said shortly.

He felt almost gay as he threaded his way through the crowds along Broadway. Somehow a tremendous load had been lifted from his shoulders He would no longer be obliged to lead a sneaking, surreptitious existence. He felt like shouting with joy now that he could look the world frankly in the face. The genuine agony he had endured during the past three weeks loomed like a sickness behind him. He had been a fool—and there was no fool like an old one. Just let him get back to his old Abigail and there'd be no more wandering-boy business for him! Abigail might not have the figure or the complexion that Georgie had, but she was a darn sight more reliable. Henceforth she could have him from five p.m. to nine a.m. without reserve. As for kicking over the traces, sowing wild oats and that sort of thing, there was nothing in it for him. Give him Friend Wife.

He stopped at the florist's and, having paid a bill of thirty-six dollars for Georgie's flowers, purchased a double bunch of violets and carried them home with him. Abigail was watching for him out of the window. Something warm rushed to his heart at the sight of her. Through the lace curtains she looked quite trim.

"Hello, old girl!" he cried, as she opened the door. "Waiting for me, eh? Here's a bunch of posies for you."

And he kissed her on the cheek.

"That's more than I ever did to Georgie," he said to himself.

"Why, Samuel!" laughed Abigail with a faded blush. "What's ever got into you?"

"Dunno!" he retorted gaily. "The spring, I guess. What do you say to a little dinner at a restaurant and then going to the play?"

She bridled—being one of the generation who did such things—with pleasure.

"Seems to me you're getting rather extravagant." she objected. "Still—"

"Oh, come along!" he bullied her. "One of my clients collected five thousand dollars this afternoon."

Tutt summoned a taxi and they drove to the brightest, most glittering of Broadway hostelries. Abigail had never been in such a chic place before. It half terrified and shocked her, all those women in dresses that hardly came up to their armpits. Some of them were handsome though. That slim one at the table by the pillar, for instance. She was really quite lovely with that mass of yellow-golden hair, that startlingly white skin, and those misty China-blue eyes. And the gentleman with her, the tall man with the pink cheeks, was very handsome, too.

"Look, Samuel," she said, touching his hand. "See that good-looking couple over there."

But Samuel was looking at them already—intently. And just then the beautiful woman turned and, catching sight of the Tutts, smiled cordially if somewhat roguishly and raised her glass, as did her companion. Mechanically Tutt elevated his. The three drank to one another.

"Do you know those people, Samuel?" inquired Mrs. Tutt somewhat stiffly. "Who are they?"

"Oh, those over there?" he repeated absently. "I don't really know what the lady's name is, she's been down to our office a few times. But the man is Winthrop Oaklander—and the funny part of it is, I always thought he was a clergyman."

Later in the evening he turned to her between the acts and remarked inconsequently: "Say, Abbie, do I look as if I'd just had my hair cut?"

THE DOG ANDREW

"Every dog is entitled to one bite."—UNREPORTED
OPINION OF THE APPELLATE DIVISION OF THE NEW
YORK SUPREME COURT.

"Now see here!" shouted Mr. Appleboy, coming out of the boathouse,
where he was cleaning his morning's catch of perch, as his neighbor Mr.
Tunnygate crashed through the hedge and cut across Appleboy's parched
lawn to the beach. "See here, Tunnygate, I won't have you trespassing on
my place! I've told you so at least a dozen times! Look at the hole you've
made in that hedge, now! Why can't you stay in the path?"

His ordinarily good-natured countenance was suffused with anger
and perspiration. His irritation with Mr. Tunnygate had reached the point
of explosion. Tunnygate was a thankless friend and he was a great cross
to Mr. Appleboy. Aforetime the two had been intimate in the fraternal,
taciturn intimacy characteristic of fat men, an attraction perhaps akin to
that exerted for one another by celestial bodies of great mass, for it is
a fact that stout people do gravitate toward one another—and hang or
float in placid juxtaposition, perhaps merely as a physical result of their
avoirdupois. So Appleboy and Tunnygate had swum into each other's
spheres of influence, either blown by the dallying winds of chance or
drawn by some mysterious animal magnetism, and, being both addicted
to the delights of the soporific sport sanctified by Izaak Walton, had
raised unto themselves portable temples upon the shores of Long Island
Sound in that part of the geographical limits of the Greater City known
as Throggs Neck.

Every morn during the heat of the summer months Appleboy would rouse Tunnygate or conversely Tunnygate would rouse Appleboy, and each in his own wobbly skiff would row out to the spot which seemed most propitious to the piscatorial art. There, under two green umbrellas, like two fat rajahs in their shaking howdahs upon the backs of two white elephants, the friends would sit in solemn equanimity awaiting the evasive cunner, the vagrant perch or cod or the occasional flirtatious eel. They rarely spoke and when they did the edifice of their conversation—their Tower of Babel, so to speak—was monosyllabic. Thus:

"Huh! Ain't had a bite!"

"Huh!"

"Huh!"

Silence for forty minutes. Then: "Huh! Had a bite?"

"Nope!"

"Huh!"

That was generally the sum total of their interchange Yet it satisfied them, for their souls were in harmony. To them it was pregnant of unutterable meanings, of philosophic mysteries more subtle than those of the esoterics, of flowers and poetry, of bird-song and twilight, of all the nuances of softly whispered avowals, of the elusive harmonies of love's half-fainting ecstasy.

"Huh!"

"Huh!"

And then into this Eden—only not by virtue of the excision of any vertebra such as was originally necessary in the case of Adam—burst woman. There was silence no longer. The air was rent with clamor; for both Appleboy and Tunnygate, within a month of one another, took unto themselves wives. Wives after their own image!

For a while things went well enough; it takes ladies a few weeks to find out each other's weak points. But then the new Mrs. Tunnygate unexpectedly yet undeniably began to exhibit the serpent's tooth, the adder's tongue or the cloven hoof—as the reader's literary traditions may lead him to prefer. For no obvious reason at all she conceived a violent hatred of Mrs. Appleboy, a hatred that waxed all the more virulent on account of its object's innocently obstinate refusal to comprehend or recognize it. Indeed Mrs. Tunnygate found it so difficult to rouse Mrs. Appleboy into a state of belligerency sufficiently interesting that she soon transferred her energies to the more worthy task of making Appleboy's life a burden to him.

To this end she devoted herself with a truly Machiavellian ingenuity, devising all sorts of insults irritations and annoyances, and adding to the venom of her tongue the inventive cunning of a Malayan witch doctor. The Appleboys' flower-pots mysteriously fell off the piazza, their thole-pins disappeared, their milk bottles vanished, Mr. Appleboy's fish lines acquired a habit of derangement equaled only by barbed-wire entanglements, and his clams went bad! But these things might have been borne had it not been for the crowning achievement of her malevolence, the invasion of the Appleboys' cherished lawn, upon which they lavished all that anxious tenderness which otherwise they might have devoted to a child.

It was only about twenty feet by twenty, and it was bordered by a hedge of moth-eaten privet, but anyone who has ever attempted to induce a blade of grass to grow upon a sand dune will fully appreciate the deviltry of Mrs. Tunnygate's malignant mind. Already there was a horrid rent where Tunnygate had floundered through at her suggestion in order to save going round the pathetic grass plot which the Appleboys had struggled to create where Nature had obviously intended a floral vacuum. Undoubtedly it had been the sight of Mrs. Appleboy with her small watering pot patiently encouraging the recalcitrant blades that had suggested the malicious thought to Mrs. Tunnygate that maybe the Appleboys didn't own that far up the beach. They didn't—that was the mockery of it. Like many others they had built their porch on their boundary line, and, as Mrs. Tunnygate pointed out, they were claiming to own something that wasn't theirs. So Tunnygate, in daily obedience to his spouse, forced his way through the hedge to the beach, and daily the wrath of the Appleboys grew until they were driven almost to desperation.

Now when the two former friends sat fishing in their skiffs they either contemptuously ignored one another or, if they "Huh-Huhed!" at all the "Huhs!" resembled the angry growls of infuriated beasts. The worst of it was that the Appleboys couldn't properly do anything about it. Tunnygate had, as Mrs. Tunnygate sneeringly pointed out, a perfect legal right to push his way through the hedge and tramp across the lawn, and she didn't propose to allow the Appleboys to gain any rights by proscription, either. Not much!

Therefore, when Mr. Appleboy addressed to Mr. Tunnygate the remarks with which this story opens, the latter insolently replied in words, form or substance that Mr. Appleboy could go to hell. Moreover, as he went by Mr. Appleboy he took pains to kick over a clod of transplanted sea grass, nurtured by Mrs. Appleboy as the darling of her bosom, and designed to give an air of verisimilitude to an otherwise bare and unconvincing surface of sand. Mr. Appleboy almost cried with vexation.

"Oh!" he ejaculated, struggling for words to express the full content of his feeling. "Gosh, but you're—mean!"

He hit it! Curiously enough, that was exactly the word! Tunnygate was mean—and his meanness was second only to that of the fat hippopotama his wife.

Then, without knowing why, for he had no formulated ideas as to the future, and probably only intended to try to scare Tunnygate with vague threats, Appleboy added: "I warn you not to go through that hedge again! Understand—I warn you! And if you do I won't be responsible for the consequences!"

He really didn't mean a thing by the words, and Tunnygate knew it.

"Huh!" retorted the latter contemptuously. "You!"

Mr. Appleboy went inside the shack and banged the door. Mrs. Appleboy was peeling potatoes in the kitchen-living room.

"I can't stand it!" he cried weakly. "He's driving me wild!"

"Poor lamb!" soothed Mrs. Appleboy, peeling an interminable rind. "Ain't that just a sweetie? Look! It's most as long as your arm!"

She held it up dangling between her thumb and fore-finger. Then, with a groan she dropped it at his feet. "I know it's a real burden to you, deary!" she sighed.

Suddenly they both bent forward with startled eyes, hypnotized by the peel upon the floor.

Unmistakably it spelt "dog"! They looked at one another significantly.

"It is a symbol!" breathed Mrs. Appleboy in an awed whisper.

"Whatever it is, it's some grand idea!" exclaimed her husband. "Do you know anybody who's got one? I mean a—a—"

"I know just what you mean," she agreed. "I wonder we never thought of it before! But there wouldn't be any use in getting any dog!"

"Oh, no!" he concurred. "We want a real—dog!"

"One you know about!" she commented.

"The fact is," said he, rubbing his forehead, "if they know about 'em they do something to 'em. It ain't so easy to get the right kind."

"Oh, we'll get one!" she encouraged him. "Now Aunt Eliza up to Livornia used to have one. It made a lot of trouble and they ordered her—the selectmen did—to do away with it. But she only pretended she had—she didn't really—and I think she's got him yet."

"Gee!" said Mr. Appleboy tensely. "What sort was it?"

"A bull!" she replied. "With a big white face."

"That's the kind!" he agreed excitedly. "What was its name?"

"Andrew," she answered.

"That's a queer name for a dog!" he commented "Still, I don't care what his name is, so long as he's the right kind of dog! Why don't you write to Aunt Eliza to-night?"

"Of course Andrew may be dead," she hazarded. "Dogs do die."

"Oh, I guess Andrew isn't dead!" he said hopefully "That tough kind of dog lasts a long time. What will you say to Aunt Eliza?"

104

Mrs. Appleboy went to the dresser and took a pad and pencil from one of the shelves.

"Oh, something like this," she answered, poising the pencil over the pad in her lap:

"Dear Aunt Eliza: I hope you are quite well. It is sort of lonely living down here on the beach and there are a good many rough characters, so we are looking for a dog for companionship and protection Almost any kind of healthy dog would do and you may be sure he would have a good home. Hoping to see you soon. Your affectionate niece, Bashemath."

"I hope she'll send us Andrew," said Appleboy fervently.
"I guess she will!" nodded Bashemath.

* * * * *

"What on earth is that sign?" wrathfully demanded Mrs. Tunnygate one morning about a week later as she looked across the Appleboys' lawn from her kitchen window. "Can you read it, Herman?"

Herman stopped trying to adjust his collar and went out on the piazza.

"Something about 'dog'," he declared finally.

"Dog!" she exclaimed. "They haven't got a dog!"

"Well," he remarked, "that's what the sign says: 'Beware of the dog'! And there's something above it. Oh! 'No crossing this property. Trespassing forbidden.'"

"What impudence!" avowed Mrs. Tunnygate. "Did you ever know such people! First they try and take land that don't belong to them, and then they go and lie about having a dog. Where are they, anyway?"

"I haven't seen 'em this morning," he answered. "Maybe they've gone away and put up the sign so we won't go over. Think that'll stop us!"

"In that case they've got another think comin'!" she retorted angrily. "I've a good mind to have you go over and tear up the whole place!"

"'N pull up the hedge?" he concurred eagerly. "Good chance!"

Indeed, to Mr. Tunnygate it seemed the supreme opportunity both to distinguish himself in the eyes of his blushing bride and to gratify that perverse instinct inherited from our cave-dwelling ancestors to destroy utterly—in order, perhaps, that they may never seek to avenge themselves upon us—those whom we have wronged. Accordingly Mr. Tunnygate girded himself with his suspenders, and with a gleam of fiendish exultation in his eye stealthily descended from his porch and crossed to the hole in the hedge. No one was in sight except two barefooted searchers after clams a few hundred yards farther up the beach and a man working in a field half a mile away. The bay shimmered in the broiling August sun and from a distant grove came the rattle and wheeze of locusts. Throggs Neck blazed in silence, and utterly silent was the house of Appleboy.

With an air of bravado, but with a slightly accelerated heartbeat, Tunnygate thrust himself through the hole in the hedge and looked scornfully about the Appleboy lawn. A fierce rage worked through his veins. A lawn! What effrontery! What business had these condescending second-raters to presume to improve a perfectly good beach which was satisfactory to other folks? He'd show 'em! He took a step in the direction of the transplanted sea grass. Unexpectedly the door of the Appleboy kitchen opened.

"I warned you!" enunciated Mr. Appleboy with unnatural calmness, which with another background might have struck almost anybody as suspicious.

"Huh!" returned the startled Tunnygate, forced under the circumstances to assume a nonchalance that he did not altogether feel. "You!"

"Well," repeated Mr. Appleboy. "Don't ever say I didn't!"

"Pshaw!" ejaculated Mr. Tunnygate disdainfully.

With premeditation and deliberation, and with undeniable malice aforethought, he kicked the nearest bunch of sea grass several feet in the air. His violence carried his leg high in the air and he partially lost his equilibrium. Simultaneously a white streak shot from beneath the porch and something like a red-hot poker thrust itself savagely into an extremely tender part of his anatomy.

"Ouch! O—o—oh!" he yelled in agony. "Oh!"

"Come here, Andrew!" said Mr. Appleboy mildly. "Good doggy! Come here!"

But Andrew paid no attention. He had firmly affixed himself to the base of Mr. Tunnygate's personality without any intention of being immediately detached. And he had selected that place, taken aim, and discharged himself with an air of confidence and skill begotten of lifelong experience.

"Oh! O—o—oh!" screamed Tunnygate, turning wildly and clawing through the hedge, dragging Andrew after him. "Oh! O—oh!"

Mrs. Tunnygate rushed to the door in time to see her spouse lumbering up the beach with a white object gyrating in the air behind him.

"What's the matter?" she called out languidly. Then perceiving the matter she hastily followed. The Appleboys were standing on their lawn viewing the whole proceeding with ostentatious indifference.

Up the beach fled Tunnygate, his cries becoming fainter and fainter. The two clam diggers watched him curiously, but made no attempt to go to his assistance. The man in the field leaned luxuriously upon his hoe and surrendered himself to unalloyed delight. Tunnygate was now but a white flicker against the distant sand. His wails had a dying fall: "O—o—oh!"

"Well, we warned him!" remarked Mr. Appleboy to Bashemath with a smile in which, however, lurked a slight trace of apprehension.

"We certainly did!" she replied. Then after a moment she added a trifle anxiously: "I wonder what will happen to Andrew!"

Tunnygate did not return. Neither did Andrew. Secluded in their kitchen living-room the Appleboys heard a motor arrive and through a crack in the door saw it carry Mrs. Tunnygate away bedecked as for some momentous ceremonial. At four o'clock, while Appleboy was digging bait, he observed another motor making its wriggly way along the dunes. It was fitted longitudinally with seats, had a wire grating and was marked "N.Y.P.D." Two policemen in uniform sat in front. Instinctively Appleboy realized that the gods had called him. His heart sank among the clams. Slowly he made his way back to the lawn where the wagon had stopped outside the hedge.

"Hey there!" called out the driver. "Is your name Appleboy?"

Appleboy nodded.

"Put your coat on, then, and come along," directed the other. "I've got a warrant for you."

"Warrant?" stammered Appleboy dizzily.

"What's that?" cried Bashemath, appearing at the door. "Warrant for what?"

The officer slowly descended and handed Appleboy a paper.

"For assault," he replied. "I guess you know what for, all right!"

"We haven't assaulted anybody," protested Mrs. Appleboy heatedly. "Andrew—"

"You can explain all that to the judge," retorted the cop. "Meantime put on your duds and climb in. If you don't expect to spend the night at the station you'd better bring along the deed of your house so you can give bail."

"But who's the warrant for?" persisted Mrs. Appleboy.

"For Enoch Appleboy," retorted the cop wearily. "Can't you read?"

"But Enoch didn't do a thing!" she declared. "It was Andrew!"

"Who's Andrew?" inquired the officer of the law mistrustfully.

"Andrew's a dog," she explained.

* * * * *

"Mr. Tutt," announced Tutt, leaning against his senior partner's door jamb with a formal-looking paper in his hand, "I have landed a case that will delight your legal soul."

"Indeed?" queried the elder lawyer. "I have never differentiated between my legal soul and any other I may possess. However, I assume from your remark that we have been retained in a matter presenting some peculiarly absurd, archaic or otherwise interesting doctrine of law?"

"Not directly," responded Tutt. "Though you will doubtless find it entertaining enough, but indirectly—atmospherically so to speak—it touches upon doctrines of jurisprudence, of religion and of philosophy, replete with historic fascination."

"Good!" exclaimed Mr. Tutt, laying down his stogy. "What kind of a case is it?"

"It's a dog case!" said the junior partner, waving the paper. "The dog bit somebody."

"Ah!" exclaimed Mr. Tutt, perceptibly brightening. "Doubtless we shall find a precedent in Oliver Goldsmith's famous elegy:

> "And in that town a dog was found,
>   As many dogs there be,
> Both mongrel, puppy, whelp, and hound,
>   And curs of low degree."

"Only," explained Tutt, "in this case, though the man recovered of the bite, the dog refused to die!"

"And so they want to prosecute the dog? It can't be done. An animal hasn't been brought to the bar of justice for several centuries."

"No, no!" interrupted Tutt. "They don't—"

"There was a case," went on Mr. Tutt reminiscently "Let me see—at Sauvigny, I think it was—about 1457, when they tried a sow and three pigs for killing a child. The court assigned a lawyer to defend her, but like many assigned counsel he couldn't think of anything to say in her behalf.

As regards the little pigs he did enter the plea that no animus was shown, that they had merely followed the example of their mother, and that at worst they were under age and irresponsible. However, the court found them all guilty, and the sow was publicly hanged in the market place."

"What did they do with the three little pigs?" inquired Tutt with some interest.

"They were pardoned on account of their extreme youth," said Mr. Tutt, "and turned loose again—with a warning."

"I'm glad of that!" sighed Tutt. "Is that a real case?"

"Absolutely," replied his partner. "I've read it in the Sauvigny records."

"I'll be hanged!" exclaimed Tutt. "I never knew that animals were ever held personally responsible."

"Why, of course they were!" said Mr. Tutt. "Why shouldn't they be? If animals have souls why shouldn't they be responsible for their acts?"

"But they haven't any souls!" protested Tutt.

"Haven't they now?" remarked the elder lawyer. "I've seen many an old horse that had a great deal more conscience than his master. And on general principles wouldn't it be far more just and humane to have the law deal with a vicious animal that had injured somebody than to leave its punishment to an irresponsible and arbitrary owner who might be guilty of extreme brutality?"

"If the punishment would do any good—yes!" agreed Tutt.

"Well, who knows?" meditated Mr. Tutt. "I wonder if it ever does any good? But anybody would have to agree that responsibility for one's acts should depend upon the degree of one's intelligence—and from that point of view many of our friends are really much less responsible than sheep."

"Which, as you so sagely point out, would, however be a poor reason for letting their families punish them in case they did wrong. Just think how such a privilege might be abused! If Uncle John didn't behave himself as his nephews thought proper they could simply set upon him and briskly beat him up."

"Yes, of course, the law even to-day recognizes the right to exercise physical discipline within the family. Even homicide is excusable, under

"That's a fine relic of barbarism!" remarked Tutt. "But the child soon passes through that dangerous zone and becomes entitled to be tried for his offenses by a jury of his peers; the animal never does."

"Well, an animal couldn't be tried by a jury of his peers, anyhow," said Mr. Tutt.

"I've seen juries that were more like nanny goats than men!" commentated Tutt. "I'd like to see some of our clients tried by juries of geese or woodchucks."

"The field of criminal responsibility is the No Man's Land of the law," mused Mr. Tutt. "Roughly, mental capacity to understand the nature of one's acts is the test, but it is applied arbitrarily in the case of human beings and a mere point of time is taken beyond which, irrespective of his actual intelligence, a man is held accountable for whatever he does. Of course that is theoretically unsound. The more intelligent a person is the more responsible he should be held to be and the higher the quality of conduct demanded of him by his fellows. Yet after twenty-one all are held equally responsible—unless they're actually insane. It isn't equity! In theory no man or animal should be subject to the power of discretionary punishment on the part of another—even his own father or master. I've often wondered what earthly right we have to make the animals work for us—to bind them to slavery when we denounce slavery as a crime. It would horrify us to see a human being put up and sold at auction. Yet we tear the families of animals apart, subject them to lives of toil, and kill them whenever we see fit. We say we do this because their intelligence is limited and they cannot exercise any discrimination in their conduct, that they are always in the zone of irresponsibility and so have no rights. But I've seen animals that were shrewder than men, and men who were vastly less intelligent than animals."

"Right-o!" assented Tutt. "Take Scraggs, for instance. He's no more responsible than a chipmunk."

"Nevertheless, the law has always been consistent," said Mr. Tutt, "and has never discriminated between animals any more than it has between men on the ground of varying degrees of intelligence. They used to try 'em all, big and little, wild and domesticated, mammals and invertebrates."

"Oh, come!" exclaimed Tutt. "I may not know much law, but—"

"Between 1120 and 1740 they prosecuted in France alone no less than ninety-two animals. The last one was a cow."

"A cow hasn't much intelligence," observed Tutt.

"And they tried fleas," added Mr. Tutt.

"They have a lot!" commented his junior partner. "I knew a flea once, who—"

"They had a regular form of procedure," continued Mr. Tutt, brushing the flea aside, "which was adhered to with the utmost technical accuracy. You could try an individual animal, either in person or by proxy, or you could try a whole family, swarm or herd. If a town was infested by rats, for example, they first assigned counsel—an advocate, he was called— and then the defendants were summoned three times publicly to appear. If they didn't show up on the third and last call they were tried *in absentia*, and if convicted were ordered out of the country before a certain date under penalty of being exorcised."

"What happened if they were exorcised?" asked Tutt curiously.

"It depended a good deal on the local power of Satan," answered the old lawyer dryly. "Sometimes they became even more prolific and destructive than they were before, and sometimes they promptly died. All the leeches were prosecuted at Lausanne in 1451. A few selected representatives were brought into court, tried, convicted and ordered to depart within a fixed period. Maybe they didn't fully grasp their obligations or perhaps were just acting contemptuously, but they didn't depart and so were promptly exorcised. Immediately they began to die off and before long there were none left in the country."

"I know some rats and mice I'd like to have exorcised," mused Tutt.

"At Autun in the fifteenth century the rats won their case," said Mr. Tutt.

"Who got 'em off?" asked Tutt.

"M. Chassensée, the advocate appointed to defend them. They had been a great nuisance and were ordered to appear in court. But none of them turned up. M. Chassensée therefore argued that a default should not be taken because *all* the rats had been summoned, and some were either so young or so old and decrepit that they needed more time. The court thereupon granted him an extension. However, they didn't arrive on the day set, and this time their lawyer claimed that they were under duress and restrained by bodily fear—of the townspeople's cats. That all these cats, therefore should first be bound over to keep the peace! The court admitted the reasonableness of this, but the townsfolk refused to be responsible for their cats and the judge dismissed the case!"

"What did Chassensée get out of it?" inquired Tutt.

"There is no record of who paid him or what was his fee."

"He was a pretty slick lawyer," observed Tutt. "Did they ever try birds?"

"Oh, yes!" answered Mr. Tutt. "They tried a cock at Basel in 1474—for the crime of laying an egg."

"Why was that a crime?" asked Tutt. "I should call it a *tour de force.*"

"Be that as it may," said his partner, "from a cock's egg is hatched the cockatrice, or basilisk, the glance of whose eye turns the beholder to stone. Therefore they tried the cock, found him guilty and burned him and his egg together at the stake. That is why cocks don't lay eggs now."

"I'm glad to know that," said Tutt. "When did they give up trying animals?"

"Nearly two hundred years ago," answered Mr. Tutt. "But for some time after that they continued to try inanimate objects for causing injury to people. I've heard they tried one of the first locomotives that ran over a man and declared it forfeit to the crown as a deodand."

"I wonder if you couldn't get 'em to try Andrew," hazarded Tutt, "and maybe declare him forfeited to somebody as a deodand."

"Deodand means 'given to God,'" explained Mr. Tutt.

"Well, I'd give Andrew to God—if God would take him," declared Tutt devoutly.

"But who is Andrew?" asked Mr. Tutt.

"Andrew is a dog," said Tutt, "who bit one Tunnygate, and now the Grand Jury have indicted not the dog, as it is clear from your historical disquisition they should have done, but the dog's owner, Mr. Enoch Appleboy."

"What for?"

"Assault in the second degree with a dangerous weapon."

"What was the weapon?" inquired Mr. Tutt simply.

"The dog."

"What are you talking about?" cried Mr. Tutt. "What nonsense!"

"Yes, it is nonsense!" agreed Tutt. "But they've done it all the same. Read it for yourself!" And he handed Mr. Tutt the indictment.

* * * * *

"The Grand Jury of the County of New York by this indictment accuse Enoch Appleboy of the crime of assault in the second degree, committed as follows:

"Said Enoch Appleboy, late of the Borough of Bronx, City and County aforesaid, on the 21st day of July, in the year of our Lord one thousand nine hundred and fifteen, at the Borough and County aforesaid, with force and arms in and upon one Herman Tunnygate, in the peace of the State and People then and there being, feloniously did willfully and wrongfully make an assault in and upon the legs and body of him the said Herman Tunnygate, by means of a certain dangerous weapon, to wit: one dog, of the form, style and breed known as 'bull,' being of the name of 'Andrew,' then and there being within control of the said Enoch Appleboy, which said dog, being of the name of 'Andrew,' the said Enoch Appleboy did then and there feloniously, willfully and wrongfully incite, provoke, and encourage, then and there being, to bite him, the said Herman Tunnygate, by means whereof said dog 'Andrew' did then and there grievously bite the said Herman Tunnygate in and upon the legs and body of him, the said Herman Tunnygate, and the said Enoch Appleboy thus then and there feloniously did willfully and wrongfully cut, tear, lacerate and bruise, and did then and there by the means of the dog 'Andrew' aforesaid feloniously, willfully and wrongfully inflict grievous bodily harm upon the said Herman Tunnygate, against the form of the statute in such case made and provided, and against the peace of the People of the State of New York and their dignity."

"That," asserted Mr. Tutt, wiping his spectacles, "is a document worthy of preservation in the Congressional Library. Who drew it?"

"Don't know," answered Tutt, "but whoever he was he was a humorist!"

"It's no good. There isn't any allegation of *scienter* in it," affirmed Mr. Tutt.

"What of it? It says he assaulted Tunnygate with a dangerous weapon. You don't have to set forth that he knew it was a dangerous weapon if you assert that he did it willfully. You don't have to allege in an indictment charging an assault with a pistol that the defendant knew it was loaded."

"But a dog is different!" reasoned Mr. Tutt. "A dog is not *per se* a dangerous weapon. Saying so doesn't make it so, and that part of the indictment is bad on its face—unless, to be sure, it means that he hit him with a dead dog, which it is clear from the context that he didn't. The other part—that he set the dog on him—lacks the allegation that the dog was vicious and that Appleboy knew it; in other words an allegation of *scienter*. It ought to read that said Enoch Appleboy 'well knowing that said dog Andrew was a dangerous and ferocious animal and would, if incited, provoked and encouraged, bite the legs and body of him the said Herman—did then and there feloniously, willfully and wrongfully incite, provoke and encourage the said Andrew, and so forth.'"

"I get you!" exclaimed Tutt enthusiastically. "Of course an allegation of *scienter* is necessary! In other words you could demur to the indictment for insufficiency?"

Mr. Tutt nodded.

"But in that case they'd merely go before the Grand Jury and find another—a good one. It's much better to try and knock the case out on the trial once and for all."

"Well, the Appleboys are waiting to see you," said Tutt. "They are in my office. Bonnie Doon got the case for us off his local district leader, who's a member of the same lodge of the Abyssinian Mysteries— Bonnie's been Supreme Exalted Ruler of the Purple Mountain for over a year—and he's pulled in quite a lot of good stuff, not all dog cases either! Appleboy's an Abyssinian too."

"I'll see them," consented Mr. Tutt, "but I'm going to have you try the case. I shall insist upon acting solely in an advisory capacity. Dog trials aren't in my line. There are some things which are *infra dig*—even for Ephraim Tutt."

* * * * *

Mr. Appleboy sat stolidly at the bar of justice, pale but resolute. Beside him sat Mrs. Appleboy, also pale but even more resolute. A jury had been selected without much manifest attention by Tutt, who had nevertheless managed to slip in an Abyssinian brother on the back row, and an ex-dog fancier for Number Six. Also among those present were a delicatessen man from East Houston Street, a dealer in rubber novelties, a plumber and the editor of Baby's World. The foreman was almost as fat as Mr. Appleboy, but Tutt regarded this as an even break on account of the size of Tunnygate. As Tutt confidently whispered to Mrs. Appleboy, it was as rotten a jury as he could get.

Mrs. Appleboy didn't understand why Tutt should want a rotten jury, but she nevertheless imbibed some vicarious confidence from this statement and squeezed Appleboy's hand encouragingly. For Appleboy, in spite of his apparent calm, was a very much frightened man, and under the creases of his floppy waistcoat his heart was beating like a tom-tom. The penalty for assault in the second degree was ten years in state's prison, and life with Bashemath, even in the vicinity of the Tunnygates, seemed sweet. The thought of breaking stones under the summer sun— it was a peculiarly hot summer—was awful. Ten years! He could never live through it! And yet as his glance fell upon the Tunnygates, arrayed in their best finery and sitting with an air of importance upon the front bench of the court room, he told himself that he would do the whole thing all over again—yes, he would! He had only stood up for his rights, and Tunnygate's blood was upon his own head—or wherever it was. So he squeezed Bashemath's hand tenderly in response.

Upon the bench Judge Witherspoon, assigned from somewhere upstate to help keep down the ever-lengthening criminal calendar of the Metropolitan District, finished the letter he was writing to his wife in Genesee County, sealed it and settled back in his chair. An old war horse of the country bar, he had in his time been mixed up in almost every kind of litigation, but as he looked over the indictment he with difficulty repressed a smile. Thirty years ago he'd had a dog case himself; also of the form, style and breed known as bull.

"You may proceed, Mister District Attorney!" he announced, and little Pepperill, the youngest of the D.A.'s staff, just out of the law school, begoggled and with his hair plastered evenly down on either side of his small round head, rose with serious mien, and with a high piping voice opened the prosecution.

It was, he told them, a most unusual and hence most important case. The defendant Appleboy had maliciously procured a savage dog of the most vicious sort and loosed it upon the innocent complainant as he was on his way to work, with the result that the latter had nearly been torn to shreds. It was a horrible, dastardly, incredible, fiendish crime, he would expect them to do their full duty in the premises, and they should hear Mr. Tunnygate's story from his own lips.

Mr. Tunnygate limped with difficulty to the stand, and having been sworn gingerly sat down—partially. Then turning his broadside to the gaping jury he recounted his woes with indignant gasps.

"Have you the trousers which you wore upon that occasion?" inquired Pepperill.

Mr. Tunnygate bowed solemnly and lifted from the floor a paper parcel which he untied and from which he drew what remained of that now historic garment.

"These are they," he announced dramatically.

"I offer them in evidence," exclaimed Pepperill, "and I ask the jury to examine them with great care."

They did so.

Tutt waited until the trousers had been passed from hand to hand and returned to their owner; then, rotund, chipper and birdlike as ever, began his cross-examination much like a woodpecker attacking a stout stump. The witness had been an old friend of Mr. Appleboy's, had he not? Tunnygate admitted it, and Tutt pecked him again. Never had done him any wrong, had he? Nothing in particular. Well, any wrong? Tunnygate hesitated. Why, yes, Appleboy had tried to fence in the public beach that belonged to everybody. Well, did that do the witness any harm? The witness declared that it did; compelled him to go round when he had a right to go across. Oh! Tutt put his head on one side and glanced at the jury. How many feet? About twenty feet. Then Tutt pecked a little harder.

"Didn't you tear a hole in the hedge and stamp down the grass when by taking a few extra steps you could have reached the beach without difficulty?"

"I—I simply tried to remove an illegal obstruction," declared Tunnygate indignantly.

"Didn't Mr. Appleboy ask you to keep off?"

"Sure—yes!"

"Didn't you obstinately refuse to do so?"

Mr. Pepperill objected to "obstinately" and it was stricken out.

"I wasn't going to stay off where I had a right to go," asserted the witness.

"And didn't you have warning that the dog was there?"

"Look here!" suddenly burst out Tunnygate. "You can't hector me into anything. Appleboy never had a dog before. He got a dog just to sic him on me! He put up a sign 'Beware of the dog,' but he knew that I'd think it was just a bluff. It was a plant, that's what it was! And just as soon as I got inside the hedge that dog went for me and nearly tore me to bits. It was a rotten thing to do and you know it!"

He subsided, panting.

Tutt bowed complacently.

"I move that the witness' remarks be stricken out on the grounds first, that they are unresponsive; second, that they are irrelevant, incompetent and immaterial; third, that they contain expressions of opinion and hearsay; and fourth, that they are abusive and generally improper."

"Strike them out!" directed Judge Witherspoon. Then he turned to Tunnygate. "The essence of your testimony is that the defendant set a dog on you, is it not? You had quarreled with the defendant, with whom you had formerly been on friendly terms. You entered on premises claimed to be owned by him, though a sign warned you to beware of a dog. The dog attacked and bit you? That's the case, isn't it?"

"Yes, Your Honor."

"Had you ever seen that dog before?"

"No, sir."

"Do you know where he got it?"

"My wife told me—"

"Never mind what your wife told you. Do you—"

"He don't know where the dog came from, judge!" suddenly called out Mrs. Tunnygate in strident tones from where she was sitting. "But I know!" she added venomously. "That woman of his got it from—"

Judge Witherspoon fixed her coldly with an impassive and judicial eye.

"Will you kindly be silent, madam? You will no doubt be given an opportunity to testify as fully as you wish. That is all, sir, unless Mr. Tutt has some more questions."

Tutt waved the witness from the stand contemptuously.

"Well, I'd like a chance to testify!" shrilled Mrs. Tunnygate, rising in full panoply.

"This way, madam," said the clerk, motioning her round the back of the jury box. And she swept ponderously into the offing like a full-rigged bark and came to anchor in the witness chair, her chin rising and falling upon her heaving bosom like the figurehead of a vessel upon a heavy harbor swell.

Now it has never been satisfactorily explained just why the character of an individual should be in any way deducible from such irrelevant attributes as facial anatomy, bodily structure or the shape of the cranium. Perhaps it is not, and in reality we discern disposition from something far more subtle—the tone of the voice, the expression of the eyes, the lines of the face or even from an aura unperceived by the senses. However that may be, the wisdom of the Constitutional safeguard guaranteeing that every person charged with crime shall be confronted by the witnesses against him was instantly made apparent when Mrs. Tunnygate took the stand, for without hearing a word from her firmly compressed lips the jury simultaneously swept her with one comprehensive glance and turned away. Students of women, experienced adventurers in matrimony, these plumbers, bird merchants "delicatessens" and the rest looked, perceived and comprehended that here was the very devil of a woman—a virago, a shrew, a termagant, a natural-born trouble-maker; and they shivered and thanked God that she was Tunnygate's and not theirs; their unformulated sentiment best expressed in Pope's immortal couplet:

> Oh woman, woman! when to ill thy mind
> Is bent, all hell contains no fouler fiend.

She had said no word. Between the judge and jury nothing had passed, and yet through the alpha rays of that mysterious medium of communication by which all men as men are united where woman is concerned, the thought was directly transmitted and unanimously acknowledged that here for sure was a hell cat!

It was as naught to them that she testified to the outrageous illegality of the Appleboys' territorial ambitions, the irascibility of the wife, the violent threats of the husband; or that Mrs. Appleboy had been observed to mail a suspicious letter shortly before the date of the canine assault. They disregarded her. Yet when Tutt upon cross-examination sought to attack her credibility by asking her various pertinent questions they unhesitatingly accepted his implied accusations as true, though under the rules of evidence he was bound by her denials.

Peck 1: "Did you not knock Mrs. Appleboy's flower pots off the piazza?" he demanded significantly.

"Never! I never did!" she declared passionately

But they knew in their hearts that she had.

Peck 2: "Didn't you steal her milk bottles?"

"What a lie! It's absolutely false!"

Yet they knew that she did.

Peck 3: "Didn't you tangle up their fish lines and take their thole-pins?"

"Well, I never! You ought to be ashamed to ask a lady such questions!"

They found her guilty.

"I move to dismiss, Your Honor," chirped Tutt blithely at the conclusion of her testimony.

Judge Witherspoon shook his head.

"I want to hear the other side," he remarked. "The mere fact that the defendant put up a sign warning the public against the dog may be taken as some evidence that he had knowledge of the animal's vicious propensities. I shall let the case go to the jury unless this evidence is contradicted or explained. Reserve your motion."

"Very well, Your Honor," agreed Tutt, patting himself upon the abdomen. "I will follow your suggestion and call the defendant. Mr. Appleboy, take the stand."

Mr. Appleboy heavily rose and the heart of every fat man upon the jury, and particularly that of the Abyssinian brother upon the back row, went out to him. For just as they had known without being told that the new Mrs. Tunnygate was a vixen, they realized that Appleboy was a kind, good-natured man—a little soft, perhaps, like his clams, but no more dangerous. Moreover, it was plain that he had suffered and was, indeed, still suffering, and they had pity for him. Appleboy's voice shook and so did the rest of his person as he recounted his ancient friendship for Tunnygate and their piscatorial association, their common matrimonial experiences, the sudden change in the temperature of the society of Throggs Neck, the malicious destruction of their property and the unexplained aggressions of Tunnygate upon the lawn. And the jury, believing, understood.

Then like the sword of Damocles the bessemer voice of Pepperill severed the general atmosphere of amiability: "Where did you get that dog?"

Mr. Appleboy looked round helplessly, distress pictured in every feature.

"My wife's aunt lent it to us."

"How did she come to lend it to you?"

"Bashemath wrote and asked for it."

"Oh! Did you know anything about the dog before you sent for it?"

"Of your own knowledge?" interjected Tutt sharply.

"Oh, no!" returned Appleboy.

"Didn't you know it was a vicious beast?" sharply challenged Pepperill.

"Of your own knowledge?" again warned Tutt.

"I'd never seen the dog."

"Didn't your wife tell you about it?"

Tutt sprang to his feet, wildly waving his arms: "I object; on the ground that what passed between husband and wife upon this subject must be regarded as confidential."

"I will so rule," said Judge Witherspoon, smiling. "Excluded."

Pepperill shrugged his shoulders.

"I would like to ask a question," interpolated the editor of Baby's World.

"Do!" exclaimed Tutt eagerly.

The editor, who was a fat editor, rose in an embarrassed manner.

"Mr. Appleboy!" he began.

"Yes, sir!" responded Appleboy.

"I want to get this straight. You and your wife had a row with the Tunnygates. He tried to tear up your front lawn. You warned him off. He kept on doing it. You got a dog and put up a sign and when he disregarded it you sicked the dog on him. Is that right?"

He was manifestly friendly, merely a bit cloudy in the cerebellum. The Abyssinian brother pulled him sharply by the coat tails.

"Sit down," he whispered hoarsely. "You're gumming it all up."

"I didn't sic Andrew on him!" protested Appleboy.

"But I say, why shouldn't he have?" demanded the baby's editor. "That's what anybody would do!"

Pepperill sprang frantically to his feet.

"Oh, I object! This juryman is showing bias. This is entirely improper."

"I am, am I?" sputtered the fat editor angrily. "I'll show you—"

"You want to be fair, don't you?" whined Pepperill. "I've proved that the Appleboys had no right to hedge in the beach!"

"Oh, pooh!" sneered the Abyssinian, now also getting to his feet. "Supposing they hadn't? Who cares a damn? This man Tunnygate deserved all he's got!"

"Gentlemen! Gentlemen!" expostulated the judge firmly. "Take your seats or I shall declare a mistrial. Go on, Mr. Tutt. Call your next witness."

"Mrs. Appleboy," called out Tutt, "will you kindly take the chair?" And that good lady, looking as if all her adipose existence had been devoted to the production of the sort of pies that mother used to make, placidly made her way to the witness stand.

"Did you know that Andrew was a vicious dog?" inquired Tutt.

"No!" answered Mrs. Appleboy firmly. "I didn't."

O woman!

"That is all," declared Tutt with a triumphant smile.

"Then," snapped Pepperill, "why did you send for him?"

"I was lonely," answered Bashemath unblushingly.

"Do you mean to tell this jury that you didn't know that that dog was one of the worst biters in Livornia?"

"I do!" she replied. "I only knew Aunt Eliza had a dog. I didn't know anything about the dog personally."

"What did you say to your aunt in your letter?"

"I said I was lonely and wanted protection."

"Didn't you hope the dog would bite Mr. Tunnygate?"

"Why, no!" she declared. "I didn't want him to bite anybody."

At that the delicatessen man poked the plumber in the ribs and they both grinned happily at one another.

Pepperill gave her a last disgusted look and sank back in his seat.

"That is all!" he ejaculated feebly.

"One question, if you please, madam," said Judge Witherspoon. "May I be permitted to"—he coughed as a suppressed snicker ran round the court—"that is—may I not—er—Oh, look here! How did you happen to have the idea of getting a dog?"

Mrs. Appleboy turned the full moon of her homely countenance upon the court.

"The potato peel came down that way!" she explained blandly.

"What!" exploded the dealer in rubber novelties.

"The potato peel—it spelled 'dog,'" she repeated artlessly.

"Lord!" deeply suspirated Pepperill. "What a case! Carry me out!"

"Well, Mr. Tutt," said the judge, "now I will hear what you may wish to say upon the question of whether this issue should be submitted to the jury. However, I shall rule that the indictment is sufficient."

Tutt elegantly rose.

"Having due respect to Your Honor's ruling as to the sufficiency of the indictment I shall address myself simply to the question of *scienter*. I might, of course, dwell upon the impropriety of charging the defendant with criminal responsibility for the act of another free agent even if that agent be an animal—but I will leave that, if necessary, for the Court of Appeals. If anybody were to be indicted in this case I hold it should have been the dog Andrew. Nay, I do not jest! But I can see by Your Honor's expression that any argument upon that score would be without avail."

"Entirely," remarked Witherspoon. "Kindly go on!"

"Well," continued Tutt, "the law of this matter needs no elucidation. It has been settled since the time of Moses."

"Of whom?" inquired Witherspoon. "You don't need to go back farther than Chief Justice Marshall so far as I am concerned."

Tutt bowed.

"It is an established doctrine of the common law both of England and America that it is wholly proper for one to keep a domestic animal for his use, pleasure or protection, until, as Dykeman, J., says in Muller vs. McKesson, 10 Hun., 45, 'some vicious propensity is developed and brought out to the knowledge of the owner.' Up to that time the man who keeps a dog or other animal cannot be charged with liability for his acts. This has always been the law.

"In the twenty-first chapter of Exodus at the twenty-eighth verse it is written: 'If an ox gore a man or a woman, that they die; then the ox shall be surely stoned, and his flesh shall not be eaten; but the owner of the ox shall be quit. But if the ox were wont to push with his horn in time past, and it hath been testified to his owner, and he hath not kept him in, but that he hath killed a man or a woman; the ox shall be stoned, and his owner also shall be put to death.'

"In the old English case of Smith vs. Pehal, 2 Strange, 1264, it was said by the court: 'If a dog has once bit a man, and the owner having notice thereof keeps the dog, and lets him go about or lie at his door, an action will lie against him at the suit of a person who is bit, though it happened by such person's treading on the dog's toes; for it was owing to his not hanging the dog on the first notice. And the safety of the king's subjects ought not afterwards to be endangered.' That is sound law; but it is equally good law that 'if a person with full knowledge of the evil propensities of an animal wantonly excites him or voluntarily and unnecessarily puts himself in the way of such an animal he would be adjudged to have brought the injury upon himself, and ought not to be entitled to recover. In such a case it cannot be said in a legal sense that the keeping of the animal, which is the gravamen of the offense, produced the injury.'

"Now in the case at bar, first there is clearly no evidence that this defendant knew or ever suspected that the dog Andrew was otherwise than of a mild and gentle disposition. That is, there is no evidence whatever of *scienter*. In fact, except in this single instance there is no evidence that Andrew ever bit anybody. Thus, in the word of Holy Writ the defendant

Appleboy should be quit, and in the language of our own courts he must be held harmless. Secondly, moreover, it appears that the complainant deliberately put himself in the way of the dog Andrew, after full warning. I move that the jury be directed to return a verdict of not guilty."

"Motion granted," nodded Judge Witherspoon, burying his nose in his handkerchief. "I hold that every dog is entitled to one bite."

"Gentlemen of the jury," chanted the clerk: "How say you? Do you find the defendant guilty or not guilty?"

"Not guilty," returned the foreman eagerly, amid audible evidences of satisfaction from the Abyssinian brother, the Baby's World editor and the others. Mr. Appleboy clung to Tutt's hand, overcome by emotion.

"Adjourn court!" ordered the judge. Then he beckoned to Mr. Appleboy. "Come up here!" he directed.

Timidly Mr. Appleboy approached the dais.

"Don't do it again!" remarked His Honor shortly.

"Eh? Beg pardon, Your Honor, I mean—"

"I said: 'Don't do it again!'" repeated the judge with a twinkle in his eye. Then lowering his voice he whispered: "You see I come from Livornia, and I've known Andrew for a long time."

As Tutt guided the Appleboys out into the corridor the party came face to face with Mr. and Mrs. Tunnygate.

"Huh!" sneered Tunnygate.

"Huh!" retorted Appleboy.

WILE *VERSUS* GUILE

For 'tis the sport to have the engineer
Hoist with his own petar.—HAMLET.

It was a mouse by virtue of which Ephraim Tutt had leaped into fame. It is true that other characters famous in song and story—particularly in "Mother Goose"—have similarly owed their celebrity in whole or part to rodents, but there is, it is submitted, no other case of a mouse, as mouse *per se*, reported in the annals of the law, except Tutt's mouse, from Doomsday Book down to the present time.

Yet it is doubtful whether without his mouse Ephraim Tutt would ever have been heard of at all, and same would equally have been true if when pursued by the chef's gray cat the mouse aforesaid had jumped in another direction. But as luck would have it, said mouse leaped foolishly into an open casserole upon a stove in the kitchen of the Comers Hotel, and Mr. Tutt became in his way a leader of the bar.

It is quite true that the tragic end of the mouse in question has nothing to do with our present narrative except as a side light upon the vagaries of the legal career, but it illustrates how an attorney if he expects to succeed in his profession, must be ready for anything that comes along—even if it be a mouse.

The two Tutts composing the firm of Tutt & Tutt were both, at the time of the mouse case, comparatively young men. Tutt was a native of Bangor, Maine, and numbered among his childhood friends one Newbegin, a commercial wayfarer in the shingle and clapboard line; and as he hoped at some future time to draw Newbegin's will or to incorporate for him some business venture Tutt made a practise of entertaining his prospective client at dinner upon his various visits to the metropolis, first at one New York hostelry and then at another.

Chance led them one night to the Comers, and there amid the imitation palms and imitation French waiters of the imitation French restaurant Tutt invited his friend Newbegin to select what dish he chose from those upon the bill of fare; and Newbegin chose kidney stew. It was at about that moment that the adventure which has been referred to occurred in the hotel kitchen. The gray cat was cheated of its prey, and in due course the casserole containing the stew was borne into the dining room and the dish was served.

Suddenly Mr. Newbegin contorted his mouth and exclaimed:

"Heck! A mouse!"

It was. The head waiter was summoned, the manager, the owner. Guests and garçons crowded about Tutt and Mr. Newbegin to inspect what had so unexpectedly been found. No one could deny that it was, mouse—cooked mouse; and Newbegin had ordered kidney stew. Then Tutt had had his inspiration.

"You shall pay well for this!" he cried, frowning at the distressed proprietor, while Newbegin leaned piteously against a pâpier-maché pillar. "This is an outrage! You shall be held liable in heavy damages for my client's indigestion!"

And thus Tutt & Tutt got their first case out of Newbegin, for under the influence of the eloquence of Mr. Tutt a jury was induced to give him a verdict of one thousand dollars against the Comers Hotel, which the Court of Appeals sustained in the following words, quoting verbatim from the learned brief furnished by Tutt & Tutt, Ephraim Tutt of counsel:

"The only legal question in the case, or so it appears to us, is whether there is such a sale of food to a guest on the part of the proprietor as will sustain a warranty. If we are not in error, however, the law is settled and has been since the reign of Henry the Sixth. In the Ninth Year Book of that Monarch's reign there is a case in which it was held that 'if I go to a tavern to eat, and the taverner gives and sells me meat and it corrupted, whereby I am made very sick, action lies against him without any express warranty, for there is a warranty in law'; and in the time of Henry the Seventh the learned Justice Keilway said, 'No man can justify selling corrupt victual, but an action on the case lies against the seller, whether the victual was warranted to be good or not.' Now, certainly, whether mouse meat be or be not deleterious to health a guest at a hotel who orders a portion of kidney stew has the right to expect, and the hotel keeper impliedly warrants, that such dish will contain no ingredients beyond those ordinarily placed therein."

* * * * *

"A thousand dollars!" exulted Tutt when the verdict was rendered. "Why, anyone would eat mouse for a thousand dollars!"

The Comers Hotel became in due course a client of Tutt & Tutt, and the mouse which made Mr. Tutt famous did not die in vain, for the case became celebrated throughout the length and breadth of the land, to the glory of the firm and a vast improvement in the culinary conditions existing in hotels.

"Come in, Mr. Barrows! Come right in! I haven't seen you for—well, how long is it?" exclaimed Mr. Tutt, extending a long welcoming arm toward a human scarecrow upon the threshold.

"Five years," answered the visitor. "I only got out day before yesterday. Fourteen months off for good behavior."

He coughed and put down carefully beside him a large dress-suit case marked E.V.B., Pottsville, N.Y.

"Well, well!" sighed Mr. Tutt. "So it is. How time flies!"

"Not in Sing Sing!" replied Mr. Barrows ruefully.

"I suppose not. Still, it must feel good to be out!"

Mr. Barrows made no reply but dusted off his felt hat. He was but the shadow of a man, an old man at that, as was attested by his long gray beard, his faded blue eyes, and the thin white hair about his fine domelike forehead.

"I forget what your trouble was about," said Mr. Tutt gently. "Won't you have a stogy?"

Mr. Barrows shook his head.

"I ain't used to it," he answered. "Makes me cough." He gazed about him vaguely.

"Something about bonds, wasn't it?" asked Mr. Tutt.

"Yes," replied Mr. Barrows; "Great Lakes and Canadian Southern."

"Of course! Of course!"

"A wonderful property," murmured Mr. Barrows regretfully. "The bonds were perfectly good. There was a defect in the foreclosure proceedings which made them a permanent underlying security of the reorganized company—under The Northern Pacific R.R. Co. vs. Boyd; you know—but the court refused to hold that way. They never will hold the way you want, will they?" He looked innocently at Mr. Tutt.

"No," agreed the latter with conviction, "they never will!"

"Now those bonds were as good as gold," went on the old man; "and yet they said I had to go to prison. You know all about it. You were my lawyer."

"Yes," assented Mr. Tutt, "I remember all about it now."

Indeed it had all come back to him with the vividness of a landscape seen during a lightning flash—the crowded court, old Doc Barrows upon the witness stand, charged with getting money on the strength of defaulted and outlawed bonds—picked up heaven knows where—pathetically trying to persuade an unsympathetic court that for some reason they were still worth their face value, though the mortgage securing the debt which they represented had long since been foreclosed and the money distributed.

"I'd paid for 'em—actual cash," he rambled on. "Not much, to be sure—but real money. If I got 'em cheap that was my good luck, wasn't it? It was because my brain was sharper than other folks'! I said they had value and I say so now—only nobody will believe it or take the trouble to find out. I learned a lot up there in Sing Sing too," he continued, warming to his subject. "Do you know, sir, there are fortunes lying all about us? Take gold, for instance! There's a fraction of a grain in every ton of sea water. But the big people don't want it taken out because it would depress the standard of exchange. I say it's a conspiracy—and yet they jailed a man for it! There's great mineral deposits all about just waiting for the right man to come along and develop 'em."

His lifted eye rested upon the engraving of Abraham Lincoln over Mr. Tutt's desk. "There was a man!" he exclaimed inconsequently; then stopped and ran his transparent, heavily veined old hand over his forehead. "Where was I? Let me see. Oh, yes—gold. All those great properties could be bought at one time or another for a song. It needed a pioneer! That's what I was—a pioneer to find the gold where other people couldn't find it. That's not any crime; it's a service to humanity! If only they'd have a little faith—instead of locking you up. The judge never looked up the law about those Great Lakes bonds! If he had he'd have found out I was right! I'd looked it up. I studied law once myself."

"I know," said Mr. Tutt, almost moved to tears by the sight of the wreck before him. "You practised up state, didn't you?"

"Yes," responded Doc Barrows eagerly. "And in Chicago too. I'm a member of the Cook County bar. I'll tell you something! If the Supreme Court of Illinois hadn't been wrong in its law I'd be the richest man in the world—in the whole world!" He grabbed Mr. Tutt by the arm and stared hard into his eyes. "Didn't I show you my papers? I own seven feet of water front clean round Lake Michigan all through the city of Chicago I got it for a song from the man who found out the flaw in the original title deed of 1817; he was dying. 'I'll sell my secret to you,' he says, 'because I'm passing on. May it bring you luck!' I looked it all up and it was just as he said. So I got up a corporation—The Chicago Water Front and Terminal Company—and sold bonds to fight my claim in the courts. But all the people who had deeds to my land conspired against me and had me arrested! They sent me to the penitentiary. There's justice for you!"

"That was too bad!" said Mr. Tutt in a soothing voice. "But after all what good would all that money have done you?"

"I don't want money!" affirmed Doc plaintively. "I've never needed money. I know enough secrets to make me rich a dozen times over. Not money but justice is what I want—my legal rights. But I'm tired of fighting against 'em. They've beaten me! Yes, they've beaten me! I'm going to retire. That's why I came in to see you, Mr. Tutt. I never paid you for your services as my attorney. I'm going away. You see my married daughter lost her husband the other day and she wants me to come up and live with her on the farm to keep her from being lonely. Of course it won't be much like life in Wall Street—but I owe her some duty and I'm getting on—I am, Mr. Tutt, I really am!"

He smiled.

"And I haven't seen Louisa for three years—my only daughter. I shall enjoy being with her. She was such a dear little girl! I'll tell you another secret"—his voice dropped to a whisper—"I've found out there's a gold mine on her farm, only she doesn't know it. A rich vein runs right through her cow pasture. We'll be rich! Wouldn't it be fine, Mr. Tutt, to be rich? Then I'm going to pay you in real money for all you've done for me—thousands! But until then I'm going to let you have these—all my securities; my own, you know, every one of them."

He placed the suitcase in front of Mr. Tutt and opened the clasps with his shaking old fingers. It bulged with bonds, and he dumped them forth until they covered the top of the desk.

"These are my jewels!" he said. "There's millions represented here!" He lifted one tenderly and held it to the light, fresh as it came from the engraver's press—a thousand dollar first-mortgage bond of The Chicago

Water Front and Terminal Company. "Look at that! Good as gold—if the courts only knew the law."

He took up a yellow package of valueless obligations upon the top of which an old-fashioned locomotive from whose bell-shaped funnel the smoke poured in picturesque black clouds, dragging behind it a chain of funny little passenger coaches, drove furiously along beside a rushing river through fields rich with corn and wheat amid a border of dollar signs.

"The Great Lakes and Canadian Southern," he crooned lovingly. "The child of my heart! The district attorney kept all the rest—as evidence, he claimed, but some day you'll see he'll bring an action against the Lake Shore or the New York Central based on these bonds. Yes, sir! They're all right!"

He pawed them over, picking out favorites here and there and excitedly extolling the merits of the imaginary properties they represented. There were the repudiated bonds of Southern states and municipalities of railroads upon whose tracks no wheel had ever turned; of factories never built except in Doc Barrows' addled brain; of companies which had defaulted and given stock for their worthless obligations; certificates of oil, mining and land companies; deeds to tracts now covered with sky scrapers in Pittsburgh, St. Louis and New York—each and every one of them not worth the paper they were printed on except to some crook who dealt in high finance. But they were exquisitely engraved, quite lovely to look at, and Doc Barrows gloated upon them with scintillating eyes.

"Ain't they beauties?" he sighed. "Some day—yes sir!—some day they'll be worth real money. I paid it for some of 'em. But they're yours—all yours."

He gathered them up with care and returned them to the suitcase, then fastened the clasps and patted the leather cover with his hand.

"They are yours, sir!" he exclaimed dramatically.

"As you say," agreed Mr. Tutt, "there's gold lying round everywhere if we only had sense enough to look for it. But I think you're wise to retire. After all, you have the satisfaction of knowing that your enterprises were sound even if other people disagreed with you."

"If this was 1819 instead of 1919 I'd own Chicago," began Doc, a gleam appearing in his eye. "But they don't want to upset the status quo—that's why I haven't got a fair chance. But they needn't worry! I'd be generous with 'em—give 'em easy terms—long leases and nominal rents."

"But you'll like living with your daughter, I'm sure," said Mr. Tutt. "It will make a new man of you in no time."

"Healthiest spot in northern New York," exclaimed Doc. "Within two miles of a lake—fishing, shooting, outdoor recreation of all kinds, an ideal site for a mammoth summer hotel."

Mr. Tutt rose and laid his arms round old Doc Barrows' shoulders.

"Thank you a thousand times," he said gratefully, "for the securities. I'll be glad to keep them for you in my vault." His lips puckered in a stealthy smile which he tried hard to conceal.

"Louisa may want to repaper the farmhouse some time," he added to himself.

"Oh, they're all yours to keep!" insisted Doc. "I want you to have them!" His voice trembled.

"Well, well!" answered Mr. Tutt. "Leave it that way; but if you ever should want them they'll be here waiting for you."

"I'm no Indian giver!" replied Doc with dignity. "Give, give, give a thing—never take it back again."

He laughed rather childishly. He was evidently embarrassed.

"Could—could you let me have the loan of seventy-five cents?" he asked shyly.

* * * * *

Down below, inside a doorway upon the other side of the street, Sergeant Murtha of the Detective Bureau waited for Doc Barrows to come out and be arrested again. Murtha had known Doc for fifteen years as a harmless old nut who had rarely succeeded in cheating anybody, but who was regarded as generally undesirable by the authorities and sent away every few years in order to keep him out of mischief. There was no danger that the public would accept Doc's version of the nature or value of his securities, but there was always the chance that some of his worthless bonds—those bastard offsprings of his cracked old brain—would find their way into less honest but saner hands. So Doc rattled about from penitentiary to prison and from prison to madhouse and out again, constantly taking appeals and securing writs of habeas corpus, and feeling mildly resentful, but not particularly so, that people should be so interfering with his business. Now as from force of long habit he peered out of the doorway before making his exit; he looked like one of the John Sargent's prophets gone a little madder than usual—a Jeremiah or a Habakkuk.

"Hello, Doc!" called Murtha in hearty, friendly tones. "Hie spy! Come on out!"

"Oh, how d'ye do, captain!" responded Doc. "How are you? I was just interviewing my solicitor."

"Sorry," said Murtha. "The inspector wants to see you."

Doc flinched.

"But they've just let me go!" he protested faintly.

"It's one of those old indictments—Chicago Water Front or something. Anyhow—Here! Hold on to yourself!"

He threw his arms around the old man, who seemed on the point of falling.

"Oh, captain! That's all over! I served time for that out in Illinois!" For some strange reason all the insanity had gone out of his bearing.

"Not in this state," answered Murtha. New pity for this poor old wastrel took hold upon him. "What were you going to do?"

"I was going to retire, captain," said Doc faintly. "My daughter's husband—he owned a farm up in Cayuga County—well, he died and I was planning to go up there and live with her."

"And sting all the boobs?" grinned Murtha not unsympathetically. "How much money have you got?"

"Seventy-five cents."

"How much is the ticket?"

"About nine dollars," quavered Doc. "But I know a man down on Chatham Square who might buy a block of stock in the Last Chance Gold Mining Company; I could get the money that way."

"What's the Last Chance Gold Mining Company?" asked Murtha sharply.

"It's a company I'm going to organize. I'll tell you a secret, Murtha. There's a vein of gold runs right through my daughter Louisa's cow pasture—she doesn't know anything about it—"

"Oh, hell!" exclaimed Murtha. "Come along to the station. I'll let you have the nine bones. And you can put me down for half a million of the underwriting."

* * * * *

That same evening Mr. Tutt was toasting his carpet slippers before the sea-coal fire in his library, sipping a hot toddy and rereading for the eleventh time the "Lives of the Chancellors" when Miranda, who had not yet finished washing the few dishes incident to her master's meager supper, pushed open the door and announced that a lady was calling.

"She said you'd know her sho' enough, Mis' Tutt," grinned Miranda, swinging her dishrag, "'case you and she used to live tergidder when you was a young man."

This scandalous announcement did not have the startling effect upon the respectable Mr. Tutt which might naturally have been anticipated, since he was quite used to Miranda's forms of expression.

"It must be Mrs. Effingham," he remarked, closing the career of Lord Eldon and removing his feet from the fender.

"Dat's who it is!" answered Miranda. "She's downstairs waitin' to come up."

"Well, let her come," directed Mr. Tutt, wondering what his old boarding-house keeper could want of him, for he had not seen Mrs. Effingham for more than fifteen years, at which time she was well provided with husband, three children and a going business. Indeed, it required some mental adjustment on his part to recognize the withered little old lady in widow's weeds and rusty black with a gold star on her sleeve who so timidly, a moment later, followed Miranda into the room.

"I'm afraid you don't recognize me," she said with a pitiful attempt at faded coquetry. "I don't blame you, Mr. Tutt. You don't look a day older yourself. But a great deal has happened to me!"

"I should have recognized you anywhere," he protested gallantly. "Do sit down, Mrs. Effingham won't you? I am delighted to see you. How would you like a glass of toddy? Just to show there's no ill-feeling!"

He forced a glass into her hand and filled it from the teakettle standing on the hearth, while Miranda brought a sofa cushion and tucked it behind the old lady's back.

Mrs. Effingham sighed, tasted the toddy and leaned back deliciously. She was very wrinkled and her hair under the bonnet was startlingly white in contrast with the crepe of her veil, but there were still traces of beauty in her face.

"I've come to you, Mr. Tutt," she explained apologetically, "because I always said that if I ever was in trouble you'd be the one to whom I should go to help me out."

"What greater compliment could I receive?"

"Well, in those days I never thought that time would come," she went on. "You remember my husband—Jim? Jim died two years ago. And little Jimmy—our eldest—he was only fourteen when you boarded with us—he was killed at the Front last July." She paused and felt for her

138

handkerchief, but could not find it. "I still keep the house; but do you know how old I am, Mr. Tutt? I'm seventy-one! And the two older girls got married long ago and I'm all alone except for Jessie, the youngest— and I haven't told her anything about it."

"Yes?" said Mr. Tutt sympathetically. "What haven't you told her about?"

"My trouble. You see, Jessie's not a well girl—she really ought to live out West somewhere, the doctor says—and Jim and I had saved up all these years so that after we were gone she would have something to live on. We saved twelve thousand dollars—and put it into Government bonds."

"You couldn't have anything safer, at any rate," remarked the lawyer. "I think you did exceedingly well."

"Now comes the awful part of it all!" exclaimed Mrs. Effingham, clasping her hands. "I'm afraid it's gone—gone forever. I should have consulted you first before I did it, but it all seemed so fair and above-board that I never thought."

"Have you got rid of your bonds?"

"Yes—no—that is, the bank has them. You see I borrowed ten thousand dollars on them and gave it to Mr. Badger to invest in his oil company for me."

Mr. Tutt groaned inwardly. Badger was the most celebrated of Wall Street's near-financiers.

"Where on earth did you meet Badger?" he demanded.

"Why, he boarded with me—for a long time," she answered. "I've no complaint to make of Mr. Badger. He's a very handsome polite gentleman. And I don't feel altogether right about coming to you and saying anything that might be taken against him—but lately I've heard so many things—"

"Don't worry about Badger!" growled Mr. Tutt. "How did you come to invest in his oil stock?"

"I was there when he got the telegram telling how they had found oil on the property; it came one night at dinner. He was tickled to death. The stock had been selling at three cents a share, and, of course, after the oil was discovered he said it would go right up to ten dollars. But he was real nice about it—he said anybody who had been living there in the house could share his good fortune with him, come in on the ground floor, and have it just the same for three cents. A week later there came a photograph of the gusher and almost all of us decided to buy stock."

At this point in the narrative Mr. Tutt kicked the coal hod violently and uttered a smothered ejaculation.

"Of course I didn't have any ready money," explained Mrs. Effingham, "but I had the bonds—they only paid two per cent and the oil stock was going to pay twenty—and so I took them down to the bank and borrowed ten thousand dollars on them. I had to sign a note and pay five per cent interest. I was making the difference—fifteen hundred dollars every year."

"What has it paid?" demanded Mr. Tutt ironically.

"Twenty per cent," replied Mrs. Effingham. "I get Mr. Badger's check regularly every six months."

"How many times have you got it?"

"Twice."

"Well, why don't you like your investment?" inquired Mr. Tutt blandly. "I'd like something that would pay me twenty per cent a year!"

"Because I'm afraid Mr. Badger isn't quite truthful, and one of the ladies—that old Mrs. Channing; you remember her, don't you—the one with the curls?—she tried to sell her stock and nobody would make a bid on it at all—and when she spoke to Mr. Badger about it he became very angry and swore right in front of her. Then somebody told me that Mr. Badger had been arrested once for something—and—and—Oh, I wish I hadn't given him the money, because if it's lost Jessie won't have anything to live on after I'm dead—and she's too sick to work. What do you think, Mr. Tutt? Do you suppose Mr. Badger would buy the stock back?"

Mr. Tutt smiled grimly.

"Not if I know him! Have you got your stock with you?"

She nodded. Fumbling in her black bag she pulled forth a flaring certificate—of the regulation kind, not even engraved—which evidenced that Sarah Maria Ann Effingham was the legal owner of three hundred and thirty thousand shares of the capital stock of the Great Geyser Texan Petroleum and Llano Estacado Land Company.

Mr. Tutt took it gingerly between his thumb and forefinger. It was signed ALFRED HAYNES BADGER, Pres., and he had an almost irresistible temptation to twist it into a spill and light a stogy with it. But he used a match instead, while Mrs. Effingham watched him apprehensively. Then he handed the stock back to her and poured out another glass of toddy.

"Ever been in Mr. Badger's office?"

"Oh, yes!" she answered. "It's a lovely office. You can see 'way down the harbor—and over to New Jersey. It's real elegant."

"Would you mind going there again? That is, are you on friendly terms with him?"

Already a strange, rather desperate plan was half formulated in his mind.

"Oh, we're perfectly friendly," she smiled. "I generally go down there to get my check."

"Whose check is it—his or the company's?"

"I really don't know," she answered simply. "What difference would it make?"

"Oh, nothing—except that he might claim that he'd loaned you the money."

"Loaned it? To me?"

"Why, yes. One hears of such things."

"But it is my money!" she cried, stiffening.

"You paid that for the stock."

She shook her head helplessly.

"I don't understand these things," she murmured. "If Jim had been alive it wouldn't have happened. He was so careful."

"Husbands have some uses occasionally."

Suddenly she put her hands to her face.

"Oh, Mr. Tutt! Please get the money back from him. If you don't something terrible will happen to Jessie!"

"I'll do my best," he said gently, laying his hand on her fragile shoulder. "But I may not be able to do it—and anyhow I'll need your help."

"What can I do?"

"I want you to go down to Mr. Badger's office to-morrow morning and tell him that you are so much pleased with your investment that you would like to turn all your securities over to him to sell and put the money into the Great Geyser Texan Petroleum and Llano Estacado Land Company."

He rolled out the words with unction.

"But I don't!"

"Oh, yes, you do!" he assured her. "You want to do just what I tell you, don't you?"

"Of course," she answered. "But I thought you didn't like Mr. Badger's oil company."

"Whether I like it or not makes no difference. I want you to say just what I tell you."

"Oh, very well, Mr. Tutt."

"Then you must tell him about the note, and that first it will have to be paid off."

"Yes."

"And then you must hand him a letter which I will dictate to you now."

She flushed slightly, her eyes bright with excitement.

"You're sure it's perfectly honest, Mr. Tutt? I wouldn't want to do anything unfair!"

"Would you be honest with a burglar?"

"But Mr. Badger isn't a burglar!"

"No—he's only about a thousand times worse. He's a robber of widows and orphans. He isn't man enough to take a chance at housebreaking."

"I don't know what you mean," she sighed. "Where shall I write?"

Mr. Tutt cleared a space upon his desk, handed her a pad and dipped a pen in the ink while she took off her gloves.

"Address the note to the bank," he directed.

She did so.

"Now say: 'Kindly deliver to Mr. Badger all the securities I have on deposit with you, whenever he pays my note. Very truly yours, Sarah Maria Ann Effingham.'"

"But I don't want him to have my securities!" she retorted.

"Oh, you won't mind! You'll be lucky to get Mr. Badger to take back your oil stock on any terms. Leave the certificate with me," laughed Mr. Tutt, rubbing his long thin hands together almost gleefully. "And now as it is getting rather late perhaps you will do me the honor of letting me escort you home."

It was midnight before Mr. Tutt went to bed. In the first place he had felt himself so neglectful of Mrs. Effingham that after he had taken her home he had sat there a long time talking over the old lady's affairs and making the acquaintance of the phthisical Jessie, who turned out to be a wistful little creature with great liquid eyes and a delicate transparent skin that foretold only too clearly what was to be her future. There was only one place for her, Mr. Tutt told himself—Arizona; and by the grace of God she should go there, Badger or no Badger!

As the old lawyer walked slowly home with his hands clasped behind his back he pondered upon the seeming mockery and injustice of the law that forced a lonely, half-demented old fellow with the fixed delusion that he was a financier behind prison bars and left free the sharp slick crook who had no bowels or mercies and would snatch away the widow's mite and leave her and her consumptive daughter to die in the poorhouse. Yet such was the case, and there they all were! Could you blame people for being Bolsheviks? And yet old Doc Barrows was as far from a Bolshevik as anyone could well be.

Mr. Tutt passed a restless night, dreaming, when he slept at all, of mines from which poured myriads of pieces of yellow gold, of gushers spouting columns of blood-red oil hundreds of feet into the air, and of old-fashioned locomotives dragging picturesque trains of cars across bright green prairies studded with cacti in the shape of dollar signs. Old Doc Barrows was with him, and from time to time he would lean toward him and whisper "Listen, Mr. Tutt, I'll tell you a secret! There's a vein of gold runs right through my daughter's cow pasture!"

When Willie next morning at half past eight reached the office he found the door already unlocked and Mr. Tutt busy at his desk, up to his elbows in a great mass of bonds and stock certificates.

"Gee!" he exclaimed to Miss Sondheim, the stenographer, when she made her appearance at a quarter past nine. "Just peek in the old man's door if you want to feel rich! Say, he must ha' struck pay dirt! I wonder if we'll all get a raise?"

But all the securities on Mr. Tutt's desk would not have justified even the modest advance of five dollars in Miss Sondheim's salary, and their employer was merely sorting out and making an inventory of Doc Barrows' imaginary wealth. By the time Mrs. Effingham arrived by appointment at ten o'clock he had them all arranged and labeled; and in a special bundle neatly tied with a piece of red tape were what on their face were securities worth upward of seventy thousand dollars. There were ten of the beautiful bonds of the Great Lakes and Canadian Southern Railroad Company with their miniature locomotives and fields of wheat, and ten equally lovely bits of engraving belonging to the long-since defunct Bluff Creek and Iowa Central, ten more superb lithographs issued by the Mohawk and Housatonic in 1867 and paid off in 1882, and a variety of gorgeous chromos of Indians and buffaloes, and of factories and steamships spouting clouds of soft-coal smoke; and on the top of all was a pile of the First Mortgage Gold Six Per Cent obligations of the Chicago Water Front and Terminal Company—all of them fresh and crisp, with that faintly acrid smell which though not agreeable to the nostrils nevertheless delights the banker's soul.

"Ah! Good morning to you, Mrs. Effingham!" Mr. Tutt cried, waving her in when that lady was announced. "You are not the only millionaire, you see! In fact, I've stumbled into a few barrels of securities myself— only I didn't pay anything for them."

"Gracious!" cried Mrs. Effingham, her eyes lighting with astonishment. "Wherever did you get them? And such exquisite pictures! Look at that lamb!"

"It ought to have been a wolf!" muttered Mr. Tutt. "Well, Mrs. Effingham, I've decided to make you a present—just a few pounds of Chicago Water Front and Canadian Southern—those over there in that pile; and now if you say so we'll just go along to your bank."

"Give them to me!" she protested. "What on earth for? You're joking, Mr. Tutt."

"Not a bit of it!" he retorted. "I don't make any pretensions as to the value of my gift, but they're yours for whatever they're worth."

He wrapped them carefully in a piece of paper and returned the balance to Doc Barrows' dress-suit case.

"Aren't you afraid to leave them that way?" she asked, surprised.

"Not at all! Not at all!" he laughed. "You see there are fortunes lying all about us everywhere if we only know where to look. Now the first thing to do is to get your bonds back from the bank."

Mr. Thomas McKeever, the popular loan clerk of the Mustardseed National, was just getting ready for the annual visit of the state bank examiner when Mr. Tutt, followed by Mrs. Effingham, entered the exquisitely furnished boudoir where lady clients were induced by all modern conveniences except manicures and shower baths to become depositors. Mr. Tutt and Mr. McKeever belonged to the same Saturday evening poker game at the Colophon Club, familiarly known as The Bible Class.

"Morning, Tom," said Mr. Tutt. "This is my client, Mrs. Effingham. You hold her note, I believe, for ten thousand dollars secured by some government bonds. She has a use for those bonds and I thought that you might be willing to take my indorsement instead. You know I'm good for the money."

"Why, I guess we can accommodate her, Mr. Tutt!" answered the Chesterfieldian Mr. McKeever. "Certainly we can. Sit down, Mrs. Effingham, while I send for your bonds. See the morning paper?"

Mrs. Effingham blushingly acknowledged that she had not seen the paper. In fact, she was much too excited to see anything.

"Sign here!" said the loan clerk, placing the note before the lawyer.

Mr. Tutt indorsed it in his strange, humpbacked chirography.

"Here are your bonds," said Mr. McKeever, handing Mrs. Effingham a small package in a manila envelope. She took them in a half-frightened way, as if she thought she was doing something wrong.

"And now," said Mr. Tutt, "the lady would like a box in your safe-deposit vaults; a small one—about five dollars a year—will do. She has quite a bundle of securities with her, which I am looking into. Most if not all of them are of little or no value, but I have told her she might just as well leave them as security for what they are worth, in addition to my indorsement. Really it's just a slick game of ours to get the bank to look after them for nothing. Isn't it, Mrs. Effingham?"

"Ye-es!" stammered Mrs. Effingham, not understanding what he was talking about.

"Well," answered Mr. McKeever, "we never refuse collateral. I'll put the bonds with the note—" His eye caught the edges of the bundle. "Great Scott, Tutt! What are you leaving all these bonds here for against that note? There must be nearly a hundred thousand dol—"

"I thought you never refused collateral, Mr. McKeever!" challenged Mr. Tutt sternly.

146

Twenty minutes later the exquisite blonde that acted as Mr. Badger's financial accomplice learned from Mrs. Effingham's faltering lips that the widow would like to see the great man in regard to further investments.

"How does it look, Mabel?" inquired the financier from behind his massive mahogany desk covered with a six by five sheet of plate glass. "Is it a squeal or a fall?"

"Easy money," answered Mabel with confidence. "She wants to put a mortgage on the farm."

"Keep her about fourteen minutes, tell her the story of my philanthropies, and then shoot her in," directed Badger.

So Mrs. Effingham listened politely while Mabel showed her the photographs of Mr. Badger's home for consumptives out in Tyrone, New Mexico, and of his wife and children, taken on the porch of his summer home at Seabright, New Jersey; and then, exactly fourteen minutes having elapsed, she was shot in.

"Ah! Mrs. Effingham! Delighted! Do be seated!" Mr. Badger's smile was like that of the boa constrictor about to swallow the rabbit.

"About my oil stock," hesitated Mrs. Effingham.

"Well, what about it?" demanded Badger sharply. "Are you dissatisfied with your twenty per cent?"

"Oh, no!" stammered the old lady. "Not at all! I just thought if I could only get the note paid off at the Mustardseed Bank I might ask you to sell the collateral and invest the proceeds in your gusher."

"Oh!" Mr. Badger beamed with pleasure. "Do you really wish to have me dispose of your securities for you?"

He did not regard it as necessary to inquire into the nature of the collateral. If it was satisfactory to the Mustardseed National it must of course exceed considerably the amount of the note.

"Yes," answered Mrs. Effingham timidly; and she handed him the letter dictated by Mr. Tutt.

"Well," replied Mr. Badger thoughtfully, after reading it, "what you ask is rather unusual—quite unusual, I may say, but I think I may be able to attend to the matter for you. Leave it in my hands and think no more about it. How have you been, my dear Mrs. Effingham? You're looking extraordinarily well!"

Mr. McKeever had about concluded his arrangements for welcoming the state bank examiner when the telephone on his desk buzzed, and on taking up the receiver he heard the ingratiating voice of Alfred Haynes Badger.

"Is this the Loan Department of the Mustardseed National?"

"It is," he answered shortly.

"I understand you hold a note of a certain Mrs. Effingham for ten thousand dollars. May I ask if it is secured?"

"Who is this?" snapped McKeever.

"One of her friends," replied Mr. Badger amicably.

"Well, we don't discuss our clients' affairs over the telephone. You had better come in here if you have any inquiries to make."

"But I want to pay the note," expostulated Mr. Badger.

"Oh! Well, anybody can pay the note who wants to."

"And of course in that case you would turn over whatever collateral is on deposit to secure the note?"

"If we were so directed."

"May I ask what collateral there is?"

"I don't know."

"There is some collateral, I suppose?"

"Yes."

"Well, I have an order from Mrs. Effingham directing the bank to turn over whatever securities she has on deposit as collateral, on my payment of the note."

"In that case you'll get 'em," said Mr. McKeever gruffly. "I'll get them out and have 'em ready for you."

* * * * *

148

"Here is my certified check for ten thousand; dollars," announced Alfred Haynes Badger a few minutes later. "And here is the order from Mrs. Effingham. Now will you kindly turn over to me all the securities?"

Mr. McKeever, knowing something of the reputation of Mr. Badger, first called up the bank which had certified the latter's check, and having ascertained that the certification was genuine he marked Mrs. Effingham's note as paid and then took down from the top of his roll-top desk the bundle of beautifully engraved securities given him by Mr. Tutt. Badger watched him greedily.

"Thank you," he gurgled, stuffing them into his pocket. "Much obliged for your courtesy. Perhaps you would like me to open an account here?"

"Oh, anybody can open an account who wants to," remarked Mr. McKeever dryly, turning away from him to something else.

Mr. Badger fairly flew back to his office. The exquisite blonde had hardly ever before seen him exhibit so much agitation.

"What have you pulled this time?" she inquired dreamily. "Father's daguerreotype and the bracelet of mother's hair?"

"I've grabbed off the whole bag of tricks!" he cried. "Look at 'em! We've not seen so much of the real stuff in six months.

"Ten—twenty—thirty—forty—fifty—By gad!—sixty—seventy!"

"What are they?" asked Mabel curiously. "Some bonds—what?"

"I should say so!" he retorted gaily. "Say, girlie, I'll give you the swellest meal of your young life to-night! Chicago Water Front and Terminal, Great Lakes and Canadian Southern, Mohawk and Housatonic, Bluff Creek and Iowa Central. '*Oh, Mabel!*'"

It was at just about this period of the celebration that Mr. Tutt entered the outer office and sent in his name; and as Mr. Badger was at the height of his good humor he condescended to see him.

"I have called," said Mr. Tutt, "in regard to the bonds belonging to my client, Mrs. Effingham. I see you have them on the desk there in front of you. Unfortunately she has changed her mind. She has decided not to have you dispose of her securities."

Mr. Badger's expression instantly became hostile and defiant.

"It's too late!" he replied. "I have paid off her note and I am going to carry out the rest of the arrangement."

"Oh," said Mr. Tutt, "so you are going to sell all her securities and put the proceeds into your bogus oil company—whether she wishes it or not? If you do the district attorney will get after you."

"I stand on my rights," snarled Badger. "Anyhow I can sell enough of the securities to pay myself back my ten thousand dollars."

"And then you'll steal the rest?" inquired Mr. Tutt. "Be careful, my dear sir! Remember there is such a thing as equity, and such a place as Sing Sing."

Badger gave a cynical laugh.

"You're too late, my friend! I've got a written order—*a written order*—from your client, as you call her. She can't go back on it now. I've got the bonds and I'm going to dispose of them."

"Very well," said Mr. Tutt tolerantly. "You can do as you see fit. But"—and he produced ten genuine one-thousand-dollar bills and exhibited them to Mr. Badger at a safe distance—"I now on behalf of Mrs. Effingham make you a legal tender of the ten thousand dollars you have just paid out to cancel her note, and I demand the return of the securities. Incidentally I beg to inform you that they are not worth the paper they are printed on."

"Indeed!" sneered Badger. "Well, my dear! old friend, you might have saved yourself the trouble of coming round here. You and your client can go straight to hell. *You* can keep the money; *I'll* keep the bonds. See?"

Mr. Tutt sighed and shook his head hopelessly.

Then he put the bills back into his pocket and started slowly for the door.

"You absolutely and finally decline to give up the securities?" he asked plaintively.

"Absolutely and finally?" mocked Mr. Badger with a sweeping bow.

"Dear! Dear!" almost moaned Mr. Tutt. "I'd heard of you a great many times but I never realized before what an unscrupulous man you were! Anyhow, I'm glad to have had a look at you. By the way, if you take the trouble to dig through all that junk you'll find the certificate of stock in the Great Jehoshaphat Oil Company you used to flim flam Mrs. Effingham with out of her ten thousand dollars. Maybe you can use it on someone else! Anyhow, she's about two thousand dollars to the good. It isn't every widow who can get twenty per cent and then get her money back in full."

THE HEPPLEWHITE TRAMP

"No freeman shall be taken, or imprisoned, or disseized or outlawed, or exiled, or in any way harmed—nor will we go upon or send upon him—save by the lawful judgment of his peers or by the law of the land."—MAGNA CHARTA, Sec. 39.

"'Somebody has been lying in my bed—and here she is,' cried the Little, Small, Wee Bear, in his little, small, wee voice."—THE THREE BEARS.

One of the nicest men in New York was Mr. John De Puyster Hepplewhite. The chief reason for his niceness was his entire satisfaction with himself and the padded world in which he dwelt, where he was as protected from all shocking, rough or otherwise unpleasant things as a shrinking débutante from the coarse universe of fact. Being thus shielded from every annoyance and irritation by a host of sycophants he lived serenely in an atmosphere of unruffled calm, gazing down benignly and with a certain condescension from the rarefied altitude of his Fifth Avenue windows, pleased with the prospect of life as it appeared to him to be and only slightly conscious of the vileness of his fellow man.

Certainly he was not conscious at all of the existence of the celebrated law firm of Tutt & Tutt. Such vulgar persons were not of his sphere. His own lawyers were gray-headed, dignified, rather smart attorneys who moved only in the best social circles and practised their profession with an air of elegance. When Mr. Hepplewhite needed advice he sent for them and they came, chatted a while in subdued easy accents, and went away—like cheerful undertakers. Nobody ever spoke in loud tones near Mr. Hepplewhite because Mr. Hepplewhite did not like anything loud—not even clothes. He was, as we have said, quite one of the nicest men in New York.

At the moment when Mrs. Witherspoon made her appearance he was sitting in his library reading a copy of "Sainte-Beuve" and waiting for Bibby, the butler, to announce tea. It was eight minutes to five and there was still eight minutes to wait; so Mr. Hepplewhite went on reading "Sainte-Beuve."

Then "Mrs. Witherspoon!" intoned Bibby, and Mr. Hepplewhite rose quickly, adjusted his eye-glass and came punctiliously forward.

"My dear Mrs. Witherspoon!" he exclaimed crisply. "I am really delighted to see you. It was quite charming of you to give me this week-end."

"Adorable of you to ask me Mr. Hepplewhite!" returned the lady. "I've been looking forward to this visit for weeks. What a sweet room? Is that a Corot?"

"Yes—yes!" murmured her host modestly. "Rather nice, I think, eh? I'll show you my few belongings after tea. Now will you go upstairs first or have tea first?"

"Just as you say," beamed Mrs. Witherspoon. "Perhaps I had better run up and take off my veil."

"Whichever you prefer," he replied chivalrously. "Do exactly as you like. Tea will be ready in a couple of minutes."

"Then I think I'll run up."

"Very well. Bibby, show Mrs. Witherspoon—"

"Very good, sir. This way, please, madam. Stockin', fetch Mrs. Witherspoon's bag from the hall."

Mr. Hepplewhite stood rubbing his delicate hands in front of the fire, telling himself what a really great pleasure it was to have Mrs. Witherspoon staying with him over the week-end. He was having a dinner party for her that evening—of forty-eight. All that it had been necessary for him to do to have the party was to tell Mr. Sadducee, his secretary, that he wished to have it and direct him to send the invitations from List Number One and then to tell Bibby the same thing and to order the chef to serve Dinner Number Four—only to have Johannisberger Cabinet instead of Niersteiner.

All these things were highly important to Mr. Hepplewhite, for upon the absolute smoothness with which tea and dinner were served and the accuracy with which his valet selected socks to match his tie his entire happiness, to say nothing of his peace of mind, depended. His daily life consisted of a series of subdued and nicely adjusted social events. They were forecast for months ahead. Nothing was ever done on the spur of the moment at Mr. Hepplewhite's. He could tell to within a couple of seconds just exactly what was going to occur during the balance of the day, the remainder of Mrs. Witherspoon's stay and the rest of the month. It would have upset him very much not to know exactly what was going to happen, for he was a meticulously careful host and being a creature of habit the unexpected was apt to agitate him extremely.

So now as he stood rubbing his hands it was in the absolute certainty that in just a few more seconds one of the footmen would appear between the tapestry portières bearing aloft a silver tray with the tea things, and then Bibby would come in with the paper, and presently Mrs. Witherspoon would come down and she would make tea for him and they would talk about tea, and Aiken, and whether the Abner Fullertons were going to get a domestic or foreign divorce, and how his bridge was these days. It would be very nice, and he rubbed his hands very gently and waited for the Dresden clock to strike five in the subdued and decorous way that it had. But he did not hear it strike.

Instead a shriek rang out from the hall above, followed by yells and feet pounding down the stairs. Mr. Hepplewhite turned cold and something hard rose up in his throat. His sight dimmed. And then Bibby burst in, pale and with protruding eyes.

"There was a man in the guest room!" he gasped. "Stockin's got him. What shall we do?"

At that moment Mrs. Witherspoon followed.

"Oh, Mr. Hepplewhite! Oh, Mr. Hepplewhite!" she gasped, staggering toward him.

Mr. Hepplewhite would have taken her in his arms and attempted to comfort her only it was not done in Mr. Hepplewhite's set unless under extreme provocation. So he pressed an armchair upon her; or, rather, pressed her into an armchair; and leaned against the bookcase feeling very faint. He was extremely agitated.

"S-send for the police! S-s-send for B-burk!" he stuttered. Burk was a husky watchman who also acted as a personal guard for Mr. Hepplewhite.

An alarm began to beat a deafening staccato in the hall outside the library. Bibby rushed gurgling from the room. Several tall men in knee breeches and silk stockings dashed excitedly up and down stairs using expressions such as had never before been heard by Mr. Hepplewhite, and the clanging gong of a police wagon was audible as it clattered up the Avenue.

"Oh, Mr. Hepplewhite," whispered Mrs. Witherspoon, unconsciously seeking his hand. "I never was so frightened in my life!"

Then the gong stopped and the police poured into the house and up the stairs. There were muffled noises and suppressed ejaculations of "Aw, come on there, now! I've got him, Mike! No funny business now, you! Come along quiet!"

The whole house seemed blue with policemen, and Mr. Hepplewhite became aware of a very fat man in a blue cap marked Captain, who removed the cap deferentially and otherwise indicated that he was making obeisance. Behind the fat man stood three other equally fat men, who held between them with grim firmness, by arm, neck and shoulder, a much smaller—in fact, quite a small—man shabby, unkempt, and with a desperate look upon his unshaven face.

"We've got him, all right, Mr. Hepplewhite!" exulted the captain, obviously grateful that God had vouchsafed to deliver the criminal into his and not into other hands. "Shall I take him to the house—or do you want to examine him?"

"I?" ejaculated Mr. Hepplewhite. "Mercy, no! Take him away as quickly as possible!"

"As you say, sir," wheezed the captain. "Come along, boys! Take him over to court and arraign him!"

"Yes, do!" urged Mrs. Witherspoon. "And arraign him as hard as you can; for he really frightened me nearly to death, the terrible man!"

"Leave him to me, ma'am!" adjured the captain "Will you have your butler act as complainant sir?" he asked.

"Why—yes—Bibby will do whatever is proper," agreed Mr. Hepplewhite. "It will not be necessary for me to go to court, will it?"

"Oh, no!" answered the captain. "Mr. Bibby will do all right. I suppose we had better make the charge burglary, sir?"

"I suppose so," replied Mr. Hepplewhite vaguely.

"Get on, boys," ordered the captain. "Good evening, sir. Good evening, ma'am. Step lively, you!"

The blue cloud faded away, bearing with it both Bibby and the burglar. Then the third footman brought the belated tea.

"What a frightful thing to have happen!" grieved Mrs. Witherspoon as she poured out the tea for Mr. Hepplewhite. "You don't take cream, do you?"

"No, thanks," he answered. "I find too much cream hard to digest. I have to be rather careful, you know. By the way, you haven't told me where the burglar was or what he was doing when you went into the room."

"He was in the bed," said Mrs. Witherspoon.

"In the 'Decay of Lying,' Mr. Tutt," said Tutt thoughtfully, as he dropped in for a moment's chat after lunch, "Oscar Wilde says, 'There is no essential incongruity between crime and culture.'"

The senior partner removed his horn-rimmed spectacles and carefully polished the lenses with a bit of chamois, which he produced from his watch pocket, meanwhile resting the muscles of his forehead by elevating his eyebrows until he somewhat resembled an inquiring but good-natured owl.

"That's plain enough," he replied. "The most highly cultivated people are often the most unscrupulous. I go Oscar one better and declare that there is a distinct relationship between crime and progress!"

"You don't say, now!" ejaculated Tutt. "How do you make that out?"

Mr. Tutt readjusted his spectacles and slowly selected a stogy from the bundle in the dusty old cigar box.

"Crime," he announced, "is the violation of the will of the majority as expressed in the statutes. The law is wholly arbitrary and depends upon public opinion. Acts which are crimes in one century or country become virtues in another, and vice versa. Moreover, there is no difference, except one of degree, between infractions of etiquette and of law, each of which expresses the feelings and ideas of society at a given moment. Violations of good taste, manners, morals, illegalities, wrongs, crimes—they are all fundamentally the same thing, the insistence on one's own will in defiance of society as a whole. The man who keeps his hat on in a drawing-room is essentially a criminal because he prefers his own way of doing things to that adopted by his fellows."

"That's all right," answered Tutt. "But how about progress?"

"Why, that is simple," replied his partner. "The man who refuses to bow to habit, tradition, law—who thinks for himself and acts for himself, who evolves new theories, who has the courage of his convictions and stakes his life and liberty upon them—that man is either a statesman, a prophet or a criminal. And in the end he is either hailed as a hero and a liberator or is burned, cast into prison or crucified."

Tutt looked interested.

"Well, now," he returned, helping himself from the box, "I never thought of it, but, of course, it's true. Your proposition is that progress depends on development and development depends on new ideas. If the new idea is contrary to those of society it is probably criminal. If its inventor puts it across, gets away with it, and persuades society that he is right he is a leader in the march of progress. If he fails he goes to jail. Hence the relationship between crime and progress. Why not say that crime is progress?"

"If successful it is," answered Mr. Tutt. "But the moment it is successful it ceases to be crime."

"I get you," nodded Tutt. "Here to-day it is a crime to kill one's grandmother; but I recall reading that among certain savage tribes to do so is regarded as a highly virtuous act. Now if I convince society that to kill one's grandmother is a good thing it ceases to be a crime. Society has progressed. I am a public benefactor."

"And if you don't persuade society you go to the chair," remarked Mr. Tutt laconically.

"To use another illustration," exclaimed Tutt, warming to the subject, "the private ownership of property at the present time is recognized and protected by the law, but if we had a Bolshevik government it might be a crime to refuse to share one's property with others."

"In that case if you took your share of another's property by force, instead of being a thief you would be a Progressive," smiled his partner.

Tutt robbed his forehead.

"Looking at it that way, you know," said he, "makes it seem as if criminals were rather to be admired."

"Well, some of them are, and a great multitude of them certainly were," answered Mr. Tutt. "All the early Christian martyrs were criminals in the sense that they were law-breakers."

"And Martin Luther," suggested Tutt.

"And Garibaldi," added Mr. Tutt.

"And George Washington—maybe?" hazarded the junior partner.

Mr. Tutt shrugged his high shoulders.

"You press the analogy a long way, but—in a sense every successful revolutionist was in the beginning a criminal—as every rebel is and perforce must be," he replied.

"So," said Tutt, "if you're a big enough criminal you cease to be a criminal at all. If you're going to be a crook, don't be a piker—it's too risky. Grab everything in sight. Exterminate a whole nation, if possible. Don't be a common garden highwayman or pirate; be a Napoleon or a Willy Hohenzollern."

"You have the idea," replied Mr. Tutt. "Crime is unsuccessful defiance of the existing order of things. Once rebellion rises to the dignity of revolution murder becomes execution and the murderers become belligerents. Therefore, as all real progress involves a change in or defiance of existing law, those who advocate progress are essentially criminally minded, and if they attempt to secure progress by openly refusing to obey the law they are actual criminals. Then if they prevail, and from being in the minority come into power, they are taken out of jail, banquets are given in their honor, and they are called patriots and heroes. Hence the close connection between crime and progress."

Tutt scratched his chin doubtfully.

"That sounds pretty good," he admitted, "but"—and he shook his head—"there's something the matter with it. It doesn't work except in the case of crimes involving personal rights and liberties. I see your point that all progressives are criminals in the sense that they are 'agin the law' as it is, but—I also see the hole in your argument, which is that the fact that all progressives are criminals doesn't make all criminals progressive. Your proposition is only a half truth."

"You're quite wrong about my theory being a half truth," retorted Mr. Tutt. "It is fundamentally sound. The fellow who steals a razor or a few dollars is regarded as a mean thief, but if he loots a trust company or takes a million he's a financier. The criminal law, I maintain, is administered for the purpose of protecting the strong from the weak, the successful from the unsuccessful the rich from the poor. And, sir"—Mr. Tutt here

159

shook his fist at an imaginary jury—"the man who wears a red necktie in violation of the taste of his community or eats peas with his knife is just as much a criminal as a man who spits on the floor when there's a law against it. Don't you agree with me?"

"I do not!" replied Tutt. "But that makes no difference. Nevertheless what you say about the criminal law being devised to protect the rich from the poor interests me very much—very much indeed But I think there's a flaw in that argument too, isn't there? Your proposition is true only to the extent that the criminal law is invoked to protect property rights—and not life and liberty. Naturally the laws that protect property are chiefly of benefit to those who have it—the rich."

"However that may be," declared Mr. Tutt fiercely, "I claim that the criminal laws are administered, interpreted and construed in favor of the rich as against the liberties of the poor, for the simple reason that the administrators of the criminal law desire to curry favor with the powers that be."

"The moral of which all is," retorted the other, "that the law ought to be very careful about locking up people."

"At any rate those who have violated laws upon which there can be a legitimate difference of opinion," agreed Mr. Tutt.

"That's where we come in," said Tutt. "We make the difference—even if there never was any before."

Mr. Tutt chuckled.

"We perform a dual service to society," he declared. "We prevent the law from making mistakes and so keep it from falling into disrepute, and we show up its weak points and thus enable it to be improved."

"And incidentally we keep many a future statesman and prophet from going to prison," said Tutt. "The name of the last one was Solomon Rabinovitch—and he was charged with stealing a second-hand razor from a colored person described in the papers as one Morris Cohen."

How long this specious philosophic discussion would have continued is problematical had it not been interrupted by the entry of a young gentleman dressed with a somewhat ostentatious elegance, whose wizened face bore an expression at once of vast good nature and of a deep and subtle wisdom.

It was clear that he held an intimate relationship to Tutt & Tutt from the familiar way in which he returned their cordial, if casual, salutations.

"Well, here we are again," remarked Mr. Doon pleasantly, seating himself upon the corner of Mr. Tutt's desk and spinning his bowler hat upon the forefinger of his left hand. "The hospitals are empty. The Tombs is as dry as a bone. Everybody's good and every day'll be Sunday by and by."

"How about that man who stole a razor?" asked Tutt.

"Discharged on the ground that the fact that he had a full beard created a reasonable doubt," replied Doon. "Honestly there's nothing doing in my line—unless you want a tramp case."

"A tramp case!" exclaimed Tutt & Tutt.

"I suppose you'd call it that," he answered blandly. "I don't think he was a burglar. Anyhow he's in the Tombs now, shouting for a lawyer. I listened to him and made a note of the case."

Mr. Tutt pushed over the box of stogies and leaned back attentively.

"You know the Hepplewhite house up on Fifth Avenue—that great stone one with the driveway?"

The Tutts nodded.

"Well, it appears that the prisoner—our prospective client—was snooping round looking for something to eat and found that the butler had left the front door slightly ajar. Filled with a natural curiosity to observe how the other half lived, he thrust his way cautiously in and found himself in the main hall—hung with tapestry and lined with stands of armor. No one was to be seen. Can't you imagine him standing there in his rags—the Weary Willy of the comic supplements—gazing about him at the *objets d'art*, the old masters, the onyx tables, the statuary— wondering where the pantry was and whether the housekeeper would be more likely to feed him or kick him out?"

"Weren't any of the domestics about?" inquired Tutt.

"Not one. They were all taking an afternoon off, except the third assistant second man who was reading 'The Pilgrim's Progress' in the servants' hall. To resume, our friend was not only very hungry, but very tired. He had walked all the way from Yonkers, and he needed everything from a Turkish bath to a manicuring. He had not been shaved for weeks. His feet sank almost out of sight in the thick nap of the carpets. It was quiet, warm, peaceful in there. A sense of relaxation stole over him. He hated to go away, he says, and he meditated no wrong. But he wanted to see what it was like upstairs.

"So up he went. It was like the palace of 'The Sleeping Beauty.' Everywhere his eyes were soothed by the sight of hothouse plants, marble floors, priceless rugs, luxurious divans—"

"Stop!" cried Tutt. "You are making me sleepy!"

"Well, that's what it did to him. He wandered along the upper hall, peeking into the different rooms, until finally he came to a beautiful chamber finished entirely in pink silk. It had a pink rug—of silk; the furniture was upholstered in pink silk, the walls were lined with pink silk and in the middle of the room was a great big bed with a pink silk coverlid and a canopy of the same. It seemed to him that that bed must have been predestined for him. Without a thought for the morrow he jumped into it, pulled the coverlid over his head and went fast asleep.

"Meanwhile, at tea time Mrs. De Lancy Witherspoon arrived for the week-end. Bibby, the butler, followed by Stocking, the second man, bearing the hand luggage, escorted the guest to the Bouguereau Room, as the pink-silk chamber is called."

Mr. Bonnie Doon, carried away by his own powers of description, waved his hand dramatically at the old leather couch against the side wall, in which Weary Willy was supposed to be reclining.

"Can't you see 'em?" he declaimed. "The haughty Bibby with nose in air, preceding the great dame of fashion, enters the pink room and comes to attention, 'This way, madam!' he declaims, and Mrs. Witherspoon sweeps across the threshold." Bonnie Doon, picking up an imaginary skirt, waddled round Mr. Tutt and approached the couch. Suddenly he started back.

"Oh, la, la!" he half shrieked, dancing about. "There is a man in the bed!"

Both Tutts stared hard at the couch as if fully expecting to see the form of Weary Willy thereon. Bonnie Doon had a way of making things appear very vivid.

"And sure enough," he concluded, "there underneath the coverlid in the middle of the bed was a huddled heap with a stubby beard projecting like Excalibur from a pink silk lake!"

"Excuse me," interrupted Tutt. "But may I ask what this is all about?"

"Why, your new case, to be sure," grinned Bonnie, who, had he been employed by any other firm, might have run the risk of being regarded as an ambulance chaser. "To make a long and tragic story short, they sent for the watchman, whistled for a policeman, telephoned for the hurry-up wagon, and haled the sleeper away to prison—where he is now, waiting to be tried."

"Tried!" ejaculated Mr. Tutt. "What for?"

"For crime, to be sure," answered Mr. Doon.

"What crime?"

"I don't know. They'll find one, of course."

Mr. Tutt swiftly lowered his legs from the desk and brought his fist down upon it with a bang.

"Outrageous! What was I just telling you, Tutt!" he cried, a flush coming into his wrinkled face. "This poor man is a victim of the overzealousness which the officers of the law exhibit in protecting the privileges and property of the rich. If John De Puyster Hepplewhite fell asleep in somebody's vestibule the policeman on post would send him home in a cab; but if a hungry tramp does the same thing he runs him in. If John De Puyster Hepplewhite should be arrested for some crime they would let him out on bail; while the tramp is imprisoned for weeks awaiting trial, though under the law he is presumed to be innocent. Is he presumed to be innocent? Not much! He is presumed to be guilty, otherwise he would not be there. But what is he presumed to be guilty of? That's what I want to know! Just because this poor man—hungry, thirsty and weary—happened to select a bed belonging to John De Puyster Hepplewhite to lie on he is thrown into prison, indicted by a grand jury, and tried for felony! Ye gods! 'Sweet land of liberty!'"

"Well, he hasn't been tried yet," replied Bonnie Doon. "If you feel that way about it why don't you defend him?"

"I will!" shouted Mr. Tutt, springing to his feet. "I'll defend him and acquit him!"

He seized his tall hat, placed it upon his head and strode rapidly through the door.

"He will too!" remarked Bonnie, winking at Tutt.

"He thinks that tramp is either a statesman or a prophet!" mused Tutt, his mind reverting to his partner's earlier remarks.

"He won't think so after he's seen him," replied Mr. Doon.

It sometimes happens that those who seek to establish great principles and redress social evils involve others in an involuntary martyrdom far from their desires. Mr. Tutt would have gone to the electric chair rather than see the Hepplewhite Tramp, as he was popularly called by the newspapers convicted of a crime, but the very fact that he had become his legal champion interjected a new element into the situation, particularly as O'Brien, Mr. Tutt's arch enemy in the district attorney's office, had been placed in charge of the case.

It would have been one thing to let Hans Schmidt—that was the tramp's name—go, if after remaining in the Tombs until he had been forgotten by the press he could have been unobtrusively hustled over the Bridge of Sighs to freedom. Then there would have been no comeback. But with Ephraim Tutt breathing fire and slaughter, accusing the police and district attorney of being trucklers to the rich and great, and oppressors of the poor—law breakers, in fact—O'Brien found himself in the position of one having an elephant by the tail and unable to let go.

In fact, it looked as if the case of the Hepplewhite Tramp might become a political issue. That there was something of a comic side to it made it all the worse.

"Holy cats, boys!" snorted District Attorney Peckham to the circle of disgruntled police officers and assistants gathered about him on the occasion described by the reporters as his making a personal investigation of the case, "Why in the name of common sense didn't you simply boot the fellow into the street?"

"I wish we had, counselor!" assented the captain of the Hepplewhite precinct mournfully. "But we thought he was a burglar. I guess he was, at that—and it was Mr. Hepplewhite's house."

"I've heard that until I'm sick of it!" retorted Peckham.

"One thing is sure—if we turn him out now Tutt will sue us all for false arrest and put the whole administration on the bum," snarled O'Brien.

"But I didn't know the tramp would get Mr. Tutt to defend him," expostulated the captain. "Anyhow, ain't it a crime to go to sleep in another man's bed?"

"If it ain't it ought to be!" declared his plain-clothes man sententiously. "Can't you indict him for burglary?"

"You can indict all day; the thing is to convict!" snapped Peckham. "It's up to you, O'Brien, to square this business so that the law is vindicated— somehow It must be a crime to go into a house on Fifth Avenue and use it as a hotel. Why, you can't cross the street faster than a walk these days without committing a crime. Everything's a crime."

"Sure thing," agreed the captain. "I never yet had any trouble finding a crime to charge a man with, once I got the nippers on him."

"That's so," interjected the plain-clothes man. "Did you ever know it was a crime to mismanage a steam boiler? Well, it is."

"Quite right," agreed Mr. Magnus, the indictment clerk. "The great difficulty for the perfectly honest man nowadays is to avoid some act or omission which the legislature has seen fit to make a crime without his knowledge. Refilling a Sarsaparilla bottle, for instance, or getting up a masquerade ball or going fishing or playing on Sunday or loitering about a building to overhear what people are talking about inside—"

"That's no crime," protested the captain scornfully.

"Yes, it is too!" retorted Mr. Magnus, otherwise known to his fellows as Caput, because of his supposed cerebral inflation. "Just like it is a crime to have any kind of a show or procession on Sunday except a funeral, in which case it's a crime to make a disbursing noise at it."

"What's a disbursing noise?" demanded O'Brien.

"I don't know," admitted Magnus. "But that's the law anyway. You can't make a disbursing noise at a funeral on Sunday."

"Oh, hell!" ejaculated the captain. "Come to think of it, it's a crime to spit. What man is safe?"

"It occurs to me," continued Mr. Magnus thoughtfully, "that it is a crime under the law to build a house on another man's land; now I should say that there was a close analogy between doing that and sleeping in his bed."

"Hear! Hear!" commented O'Brien. "Caput Magnus, otherwise known as Big Head, there is no doubt but that your fertile brain can easily devise a way out of our present difficulty."

"Well, I've no time to waste on tramp cases," remarked District Attorney Peckham. "I've something more important to attend to. Indict this fellow and send him up quick. Charge him with everything in sight and trust in the Lord. That's the only thing to be done. Don't bother me about it, that's all!"

Meantime Mr. Hepplewhite became more and more agitated. Entirely against his will and, so far as he could see, without any fault of his own, he suddenly found himself the center of a violent and acrimonious controversy respecting the fundamental and sacred rights of freemen which threatened to disrupt society and extinguish the supremacy of the dominant local political organization.

On the one hand he was acclaimed by the conservative pulpit and press as a public-spirited citizen who had done exactly the right thing—disinterestedly enforced the law regardless of his own convenience and safety as a matter of principle and for the sake of the community—a moral hero; on the other, though he was president of several charitable organizations and at least one orphan asylum he was execrated as a heartless brute, an oppressor of the poor, an octopus, a soulless capitalist who fattened on the innocent and helpless and who—Mr. Hepplewhite was a bachelor—probably if the truth could be known lived a life of horrid depravity and crime.

Indeed there was a man named Tutt, of whom Mr. Hepplewhite had never before heard, who publicly declared that he, Tutt, would show him, Hepplewhite, up for what he was and make him pay with his body and his blood, to say nothing of his money, for what he had done and caused to be done. And so Mr. Hepplewhite became even more agitated, until he dreamed of this Tutt as an enormous bird like the fabled roc, with a malignant face and a huge hooked beak that some day would nip him in the abdomen and fly, croaking, away with him. Mrs. Witherspoon had returned to Aiken, and after the first flood of commiserations from his friends on Lists Numbers One, Two, Three and Four he felt neglected, lonely and rather fearful.

And then one morning something happened that upset his equanimity entirely. He had just started out for a walk in the park when a flashy person who looked like an actor walked impudently up to him and handed him a piece of paper in which was wrapped a silver half dollar. In a word Mr. Hepplewhite was subpoenaed and the nervous excitement attendant upon that operation nearly caused his collapse. For he was thereby commanded to appear before the Court of General Sessions of the Peace upon the following Monday at ten a. m. as a witness in a criminal action prosecuted by the People of the State of New York against Hans Schmidt. Moreover, the paper was a dirty-brown color and bore the awful name of Tutt. He returned immediately to the house and telephoned for Mr. Edgerton, his lawyer, who at once jumped into a taxi on the corner of Wall and Broad Streets and hurried uptown.

"Edgerton," said Hepplewhite faintly as the lawyer entered his library, "this whole unfortunate affair has almost made me sick. I had nothing to do with the arrest of this man Schmidt. The police did everything. And now I'm ordered to appear as a witness! Why, I hardly looked at the man. I shouldn't know him if I saw him. Do I have to go to court?"

Mr. Edgerton smiled genially in a manner which he thought would encourage Mr. Hepplewhite.

"I suppose you'll have to go to court. You can't help that, you know, if you've been subpoenaed. But you can't testify to anything that I can see. It's just a formality."

"Formality!" groaned his client. "Well, I supposed the arrest was just a formality."

Mr. Edgerton smiled again rather unconvincingly.

"Well, you see, you can't always tell what will happen when you once start something," he began.

"But I didn't start anything," answered Mr. Hepplewhite. "I had nothing to say about it."

At that moment Bibby appeared in the doorway.

"Excuse me, sir," he said. "There is a young man outside who asked me to tell you that he has a paper he wishes to serve on you—and would you mind saving him the trouble of waiting for you to go out?"

"Another!" gagged Mr. Hepplewhite.

"Yes, sir! Thank you, sir," stammered Bibby.

Mr. Hepplewhite looked inquiringly at Mr. Edgerton and rose feebly.

"He'll get you sooner or later," declared the lawyer. "A man as well known as you can't avoid process."

Mr. Hepplewhite bit his lips and went out into the hall.

Presently he returned carrying a legal-looking bunch of papers.

"Well, what is it this time?" asked Edgerton jocosely.

"It's a suit for false imprisonment for one hundred thousand dollars!" choked Mr. Hepplewhite.

Mr. Edgerton looked shocked.

"Well, now you've got to convict him!" he declared.

"Convict him?" retorted Mr. Hepplewhite. "I don't want to convict him. I'd gladly give a hundred thousand dollars to get out of the—the—darn thing!"

Which was as near profanity as he had ever permitted himself to go.

* * * * *

Upon the following Monday Mr. Hepplewhite proceeded to court—flanked by his distinguished counsel in frock coats and tall hats—simply because he had been served with a dirty-brown subpoena by Tutt & Tutt; and his distress was not lessened by the crowd of reporters who joined him at the entrance of the Criminal Courts Building; or by the flashlight bomb that was exploded in the corridor in order that the evening papers might reproduce his picture on the front page. He had never been so much in the public eye before, and he felt slightly defiled. For some curious reason he had the feeling that he and not Schmidt was the actual defendant charged with being guilty of something; nor was this impression dispelled even by listening to the indictment by which the Grand Jury charged Schmidt in eleven counts with burglary in the first, second and third degrees and with the crime of entering his, Hepplewhite's, house under circumstances not amounting to a burglary but with intent to commit a felony, as follows:

"Therefore, to wit, on the eleventh day of January in the year of our Lord one thousand nine hundred and nineteen in the night-time of the said day at the ward, city and county aforesaid the dwelling house of one John De Puyster Hepplewhite there situate, feloniously and burglariously did break into and enter there being then and there a human being in said dwelling house, with intent to commit some crime therein, to wit, the goods, chattels, and personal property of the said John De Puyster Hepplewhite, then and there being found, then and there feloniously and burglariously to steal, take and carry away one silver tea service of the value of five hundred dollars and one pair of opera glasses of the value of five dollars each with force and arms—"

"But that silver tea service cost fifteen thousand dollars and weighs eight hundred pounds!" whispered Mr. Hepplewhite.

"Order in the court!" shouted Captain Phelan, pounding upon the oak rail of the bar, and Mr. Hepplewhite subsided.

Yet as he sat there between his lawyers listening to all the extraordinary things that the Grand Jury evidently had believed Schmidt intended to do, the suspicion began gradually to steal over him that something was not entirely right somewhere. Why, it was ridiculous to charge the man with trying to carry off a silver service weighing nearly half a ton when he simply had gone to bed and fallen asleep. Still, perhaps that was the law.

However, when the assistant district attorney opened the People's case to the jury Mr. Hepplewhite began to feel much more at ease. Indeed O'Brien made it very plain that the defendant had been guilty of a very grievous—he pronounced it "gree-vious"—offense in forcing his way into another man's private house. It might or might not be burglary—that would depend upon the testimony—but in any event it was a criminal, illegal entry and he should ask for a conviction. A man's house was his castle and—to quote from that most famous of orators and statesmen— Edmund Burke—"the wind might enter, the rain might enter, but the King of England might not enter!" Thus Schmidt could not enter the house of Hepplewhite without making himself amenable to the law.

Hepplewhite was filled with admiration for Mr. O'Brien, and his drooping spirits reared their wilted heads as the prosecutor called Bibby

170

to the stand and elicited from him the salient features of the case. The jury was vastly interested in the butler personally, as well as his account rendered in the choicest cockney of how he had discovered Schmidt in his master's bed. O'Brien bowed to Mr. Tutt and told him that he might cross-examine.

And then it was that Mr. Hepplewhite discovered why he had been haunted by that mysterious feeling of guilt; for by some occult and subtle method of suggestion on the part of Mr. Tutt, the case, instead of being a trial of Schmidt, resolved itself into an attack upon Mr. Hepplewhite and his retainers and upon the corrupt minions of the law who had violated every principle of justice, decency and morality in order to accomplish the unscrupulous purposes of a merciless aristocrat—meaning him. With biting sarcasm, Mr. Tutt forced from the writhing Bibby the admission that the prisoner was sound asleep in the pink silk fastnesses of the Bouguereau Room when he was discovered that he made no attempt to escape, that he did not assault anybody and that he had appeared comatose from exhaustion; that there was no sign of a break anywhere, and that the pair of opera glasses "worth five dollars *apiece*"—Tutt invited the court's attention to this ingenuous phraseology of Mr. Caput Magnus, as a literary curiosity—were a figment of the imagination.

In a word Mr. Tutt rolled Bibby up and threw him away, while his master shuddered at the open disclosure of his trusted major-domo's vulgarity, mendacity and general lack of sportsmanship. Somehow all at once the case began to break up and go all to pot. The jury got laughing at Bibby, the footmen and the cops as Mr. Tutt painted for their edification the scene following the arrival of Mrs. Witherspoon, when Schmidt was discovered asleep, as Mr. Tutt put it, like Goldilocks in the Little, Small, Wee Bear's bed.

Stocking was the next witness, and he fared no better than had Bibby. O'Brien, catching the judge's eye, made a wry face and imperceptibly lowered his left lid—on the side away from the jury, thus officially indicating that, of course, the case was a lemon but that there was nothing that could be done except to try it out to the bitter end.

Then he rose and called out unexpectedly: "Mr. John De Puyster Hepplewhite—take the stand!"

It was entirely unexpected. No one had suggested that he would be called for the prosecution. Possibly O'Brien was actuated by a slight touch of malice; possibly he wanted to be able, if the case was lost, to accuse Hepplewhite of losing it on his own testimony. But at any rate he certainly had no anticipation of what the ultimate consequence of his act would be.

Mr. Hepplewhite suddenly felt as though his entire intestinal mechanism had been removed. But he had no time to take counsel of his fears. Everybody in the courtroom turned with one accord and looked at him. He rose, feeling as one who dreams; that he is naked in the midst of a multitude. He shrank back hesitating, but hostile hands reached out and pushed him forward. Cringing, he slunk to the witness chair, and for the first time faced the sardonic eyes of the terrible Tutt, his adversary who looked scornfully from Hepplewhite to the jury and then from the jury back to Hepplewhite as if to say: "Look at him! Call you this a man?"

"You are the Mr. Hepplewhite who has been referred to in the testimony as the owner of the house in which the defendant was found?" inquired O'Brien.

"Yes—yes," answered Mr. Hepplewhite deprecatingly.

"The first witness—Bibby—is in your employ?"

"Yes—yes."

"Did you have a silver tea set of the value of—er—at least five hundred dollars in the house?"

"It was worth fifteen thousand," corrected Mr. Hepplewhite.

"Oh! Now, have you been served by the defendant's attorneys with a summons and complaint in an action for false arrest in which damages are claimed in the sum of one hundred thousand dollars?"

"I object!" shouted Mr. Tutt. "It is wholly irrelevant."

"I think it shows the importance of the result of this trial to the witness," argued O'Brien perfunctorily. "It shows this case isn't any joke—even if some people seem to think it is."

"Objection sustained," ruled the court. "The question is irrelevant. The jury is supposed to know that every case is important to those concerned—to the defendant as well as to those who charge him with crime."

O'Brien bowed.

"That's all. You may examine, Mr. Tutt."

The old lawyer slowly unfolded his tall frame and gazed quizzically down upon the shivering Hepplewhite.

"You have been sued by my client for one hundred thousand dollars, haven't you?" he demanded.

"Object!" shot out O'Brien.

"Overruled," snapped the court. "It is a proper question for cross-examination. It may show motive."

Mr. Hepplewhite sat helplessly until the shooting was over.

"Answer the question!" suddenly shouted Mr. Tutt.

"But I thought—" he began.

"Don't think!" retorted the court sarcastically. "The time to think has gone by. Answer!"

"I don't know what the question is," stammered Mr. Hepplewhite, thoroughly frightened.

"Lord! Lord!" groaned O'Brien in plain hearing of the jury.

Mr. Tutt sighed sympathetically in mock resignation.

"My dear sir," he began in icy tones, "when you had my client arrested and charged with being a burglar, had you made any personal inquiry as to the facts?"

"I didn't have him arrested!" protested the witness.

"You deny that you ordered Bibby to charge the defendant with burglary?" roared Mr. Tutt. "Take care! You know there is such a crime as perjury, do you not?"

"No—I mean yes," stuttered Mr. Hepplewhite abjectly. "That is, I've heard about perjury—but the police attended to everything for me."

"Aha!" cried Mr. Tutt, snorting angrily like the war horse depicted in the Book of Job. "The police 'attended' to my client for you, did they? What do you mean—for you? Did you pay them for their little attention?"

"I always send them something on Christmas," said Mr. Hepplewhite. "Just like the postmen."

Mr. Tutt looked significantly at the jury, while a titter ran round the court room.

"Well," he continued with patient irony, "what we wish to know is whether these friends of yours whom you so kindly remember at Christmas dragged the helpless man away from your house, threw him into jail and charged him with burglary by your authority?"

"I didn't think anything about it," asserted Hepplewhite "Really I didn't. I assumed that they knew what to do under such circumstances. I didn't suppose they needed any authority from me."

Mr. Tutt eyed sideways the twelve jurymen.

"Trying to get out of it, are you? Attempting to avoid responsibility? Are you thinking of what your position will be if the defendant is acquitted—with an action against you for one hundred thousand dollars?"

Ashamed, terrified, humiliated, Mr. Hepplewhite almost burst into tears. He had suffered a complete moral disintegration—did not know where to turn for help or sympathy. The whole world seemed to have risen against him. He opened his mouth to reply, but the words would not come. He looked appealingly at the judge, but the judge coldly ignored him. The whole room seemed crowded with a multitude of leering eyes. Why had God made him a rich man? Why was he compelled to suffer those terrible indignities? He was not responsible for what had been done—why then, was he being treated so abominably?

"I don't want this man punished!" he suddenly broke out in fervent expostulation. "I have nothing against him. I don't believe he intended to do any wrong. And I hope the jury will acquit him!"

"Oho!" whistled Mr. Tutt exultantly, while O'Brien gazed at Hepplewhite in stupefaction. *Was* this a man?

"So you admit that the charge against my client is without foundation?" insisted Mr. Tutt.

Hepplewhite nodded weakly.

"I don't know rightly what the charge is—but I don't think he meant any harm," he faltered.

"Then why did you have the police put him under arrest and hale him away?" challenged Mr. Tutt ferociously.

"I supposed they had to—if he came into my house," said Mr. Hepplewhite. Then he added shamefacedly: "I know it sounds silly—but frankly I did not know that I had anything to say in the matter. If your client has been injured by my fault or mistake I will gladly reimburse him as handsomely as you wish."

O'Brien gasped. Then he made a funnel of his hands and whispered toward the bench: "Take it away, for heaven's sake!"

"That is all!" remarked Mr. Tutt with deep sarcasm, making an elaborate bow in the direction of Mr. Hepplewhite. "Thank you for your excellent intentions!"

A snicker followed Mr. Hepplewhite as he dragged himself back to his seat among the spectators.

He felt as though he had passed through a clothes wringer. Dimly he heard Mr. Tutt addressing the court.

"And I move, Your Honor," the lawyer was paying, "that you take the counts for burglary in the first, second and third degrees away from the jury on the ground that there has been a complete failure of proof that my client broke into the house of this man Hepplewhite either by night or by day, or that he assaulted anybody or stole anything there, or ever intended to."

"Motion granted," agreed the judge. "I quite agree with you, Mr. Tutt. There is no evidence here of any breaking. In fact, the inferences are all the other way."

"I further move that you take from the consideration of the jury the remaining count of illegally entering the house with intent to commit a crime and direct the jury to acquit the defendant for lack of evidence," continued Mr. Tutt.

"But what was your client doing in the house?" inquired the judge. "He had no particular business in it, had he?"

"That does not make his presence a crime, Your Honor," retorted the lawyer. "A man is not guilty of a felony who falls asleep on my haycock. Why should he be if he falls asleep in my bed?"

The judge smiled.

"We have no illegal entry statute with respect to fields or meadows, Mr. Tutt," he remarked good-naturedly. "No, I shall be obliged to let the jury decide whether this defendant went into that house for an honest or dishonest purpose. It is clearly a proper question for them to pass upon. Proceed with your case."

Now when, as in the case of the Hepplewhite Tramp, the chief witness for the prosecution throws up his hands and offers to repay the defendant for the wrong he has done him, naturally it is all over but the shouting.

"There is no need for me to call the defendant," Mr. Tutt told the court, "in view of the admissions made by the last witness. I am ready to proceed with the summing up."

"As you deem wise," answered the judge. "Proceed then."

Through a blur of sight and sound Mr. Hepplewhite dimly heard Mr. Tutt addressing the jury and saw them lean forward to catch his every word.

Beside him Mr. Edgerton was saying protestingly: "May I ask why you made those fool statements on the witness stand?"

"Because I didn't want an innocent man convicted," returned Mr. Hepplewhite tartly.

"Well, you'll get your wish!" sniffed his lawyer. "And you'll get soaked for about twenty thousand dollars for false arrest!"

"I don't care," retorted the client. "And what's more I hope Mr. Tutt gets a substantial fee out of it. He strikes me as a lawyer who knows his business!"

The oldest and fattest court officers, men so old and fat that they remembered the trial of Boss Tweed and the days when Delancey Nicoll was the White Hope of the Brownstone Court House—declared Mr. Tutt's summation was the greatest that ever they heard. For the shrewd old lawyer had an artist's hand with which he played upon the keyboard of the jury and knew just when to pull out the stops of the *vox humana* of pathos and the grand diapason of indignation and defiance. So he began by tickling their sense of humor with an ironic description of afternoon tea at Mr. Hepplewhite's, with Bibby and Stocking as chief actors, until all twelve shook with suppressed laughter and the judge was forced to hide his face behind the *Law Journal*; ridiculed the idea of a criminal who wanted to commit a crime calmly going to sleep in a pink silk bed in broad daylight; and then brought tears to their eyes as he pictured the wretched homeless tramp, sick, footsore and starving, who, drawn by the need of food and warmth to this silk nest of luxury, was clubbed, arrested and jailed simply because he had violated the supposed sanctity of a rich man's home.

The jury watched him as intently as a dog watches a piece of meat held over its nose. They smiled with him, they wept with him, they glared at Mr. Hepplewhite and they gazed in a friendly way at Schmidt, whom Mr. Tutt had bailed out just before the trial. The very stars in their courses seemed warring for Tutt & Tutt. In the words of Phelan: "There was nothing to it!"

"Thank God," concluded Mr. Tutt eloquently, "that in this land of liberty in which we are privileged to dwell no man can be convicted of a crime except by a jury of his peers—a right sacred under our Constitution and inherited from Magna Charta, that foundation stone of English liberty, in which the barons forced King John to declare that 'No freeman shall be taken, or imprisoned, or disseized, or outlawed, or exiled, or in any way harmed . . . save by the lawful judgment of his peers or by the law of the land.'

"Had I the time I would demonstrate to you the arbitrary character of our laws and the inequality with which they are administered.

"But in this case the chief witness has already admitted the innocence of the defendant. There is nothing more to be said. The prosecution has cried '*Peccavi!*' I leave my client in your hands."

He resumed his seat contentedly and wiped his forehead with his silk handkerchief. The judge looked down at O'Brien with raised eyebrows.

"I will leave the case to the jury on Your Honor's charge," remarked the latter carelessly.

"Gentlemen of the jury," began the judge, "the defendant is accused of entering the house of Mr. Hepplewhite with the intent to commit a crime therein—"

Mr. Hepplewhite sat, his head upon his breast, for what seemed to him several hours. He had but one thought—to escape. His ordeal had been far worse than he had anticipated. But he had made a discovery. He had suddenly realized that one cannot avoid one's duties to one's fellows by leaving one's affairs to others—not even to the police. He perceived that he had lived with his head stuck in the sand. He had tried to escape from his responsibilities as a citizen by hiding behind the thick walls of his stone mansion on Fifth Avenue. He made up his mind that he would do differently if he ever had the chance. Meanwhile, was not the jury ever going to set the poor man free?

They had indeed remained out a surprisingly long time in order merely to reach a verdict which was a mere formality. Ah! There they were! Mr. Hepplewhite watched with palpitating heart while they straggled slowly in. The clerk made the ordinary perfunctory inquiry as to what their verdict was. Mr. Hepplewhite did not hear what the foreman said in reply, but he saw both the Tutts and O'Brien start from their seats and heard a loud murmur rise throughout the court room.

"What's that!" cried the clerk in astonished tones. "What did you say, Mister Foreman?"

"I said that we find the defendant guilty," replied the foreman calmly.

Mr. Tutt stared incredulously at the twelve traitors who had betrayed him.

"Never mind, Mr. Tutt," whispered Number Six confidentially. "You did the best you could. Your argument was fine—grand—but nobody could ever make us believe that your client went into that house for any purpose except to steal whatever he could lay his hands on. Besides, it wasn't Mr. Hepplewhite's fault. He means well. And anyhow a nut like that has got to be protected against himself."

He might have enlightened Mr. Tutt further upon the psychology of the situation had not the judge at that moment ordered the prisoner arraigned at the bar.

"Have you ever been convicted before?" asked His Honor sharply.

"Sure," replied the Hepplewhite Tramp carelessly. "I've done three or four bits, I'm a burglar. But you can't give me more than a year for illegal entry."

"That is quite true," admitted His Honor stiffly. "And it isn't half enough!" He hesitated. "Perhaps under the circumstances you'll tell us what you were doing in Mr. Hepplewhite's bed?"

"Oh, I don't mind," returned the defendant with the superior air of one who has put something over. "When I heard the guy in the knee breeches coming up the stairs I just dove for the slats and played I was asleep."

Leaving the courthouse Mr. Tutt encountered Bonnie Doon.

"Young man," he remarked severely, "you assured me that fellow was only a harmless tramp!"

"Well," answered Bonnie, "that's what he said."

"He says now he's a burglar," retorted Mr. Tutt wrathfully. "I don't believe he knows what he is. Did you ever hear of such an outrageous verdict? With not a scrap of evidence to support it?"

Bonnie lit a cigarette doubtfully.

"Oh, I don't know," he muttered. "The jury seems to have sized him up rather better than we did."

"Jury!" growled Mr. Tutt, rolling his eyes heavenward. "'Sweet land of liberty!'"

LALLAPALOOSA LIMITED

"Ethics: The doctrine of man's duty in respect to himself and the rights of others."—CENTURY DICTIONARY.

"I don't say that all these people couldn't be squared; but it is right to tell you that I shouldn't be sufficiently degraded in my own estimation unless I was insulted with a very considerable bribe."—POOH-BAH.

"I've been all over those securities," Miss Wiggin informed Mr. Tutt as he entered the office one morning, "and not a single one of them is listed on the Stock Exchange."

"What securities are those?" asked her employer, hanging his tall hat on the antiquated mahogany coat tree in the corner opposite the screen that ambushed the washing apparatus. "I don't remember any securities," he remarked as he applied a match to the off end of a particularly green and vicious-looking stogy.

"Why, of course you do, Mr. Tutt!" insisted Miss Wiggin. "Don't you remember those great piles of bonds and stocks that Doctor Barrows left here with you to keep for him?"

"Oh, those!" Mr. Tutt smiled inscrutably. "Mr. Barrows is not a physician," he corrected her, running his eye over the General Sessions calendar. "He's only a 'doc'—that is to say, one who doctors. You know you can doctor a lot of things besides the human anatomy. No, I guess they're not listed on the Stock Exchange or anywhere else."

"Well, here's a schedule I made of them—Miss Sondheim typed it—and their total face value is seventeen million eight hundred thousand dollars. I tried to find out all I could, but none of the firms on Wall Street had ever heard of any of them—excepting of one that was traded in on the curb up to within a few weeks. There's Great Lakes and Canadian Southern Railway Company," she went on, "Chicago Water Front and Terminal Company, Great Geyser Texan Petroleum and Llano Estacado Land Company—dozens and dozens of them, and not one has an office or, so far as I can find out, any tangible existence—but the one I spoke of."

"Which is this great exception?" queried Mr. Tutt absently as he searched through the *Law Journal* for the case he was going to try that afternoon. "You said one of them had been dealt in on the curb? You astonish me!"

"It's got a funny name," she answered. "It almost sounds as if they meant it for a joke—Horse's Neck Extension."

"I guess they meant it for a joke all right—on the public," chuckled her employer. "How many shares are there?"

"A hundred thousand," she answered.

"Jumping Jehoshaphat!" ejaculated Mr. Tutt. "How on earth did old Doc manage to get hold of them?"

"It sold for only ten cents a share!" replied Miss Wiggin. "That would mean ten thousand dollars—"

"If Doc paid for it," supplemented Mr. Tutt. "Which he probably didn't. What's it selling for now?"

"It isn't selling at all."

Mr. Tutt pressed the button that summoned Willie.

"When you haven't anything better to do," he said to her, "why don't you go round and see what has become of—of—Horse's Neck Extension?"

"I will," assented Miss Wiggin. "It makes me feel rich just to talk about such things. I just love it."

"Many a slick crook has taken advantage of just that kind of feeling," mused Mr. Tutt. "There are two things that women—particularly trained nurses—seem to like better than anything else in the world—babies and stock certificates."

Then upon the arrival of the recalcitrant William he gathered up his papers and took down his hat from the tree.

"I wish you'd let me get your hat ironed, Mr. Tutt," remarked Miss Wiggin. "It would cost you only fifty cents."

"That's all you know about it, my dear," he answered. "More likely it would cost me a hundred thousand dollars."

* * * * *

Mr. Tobias Greenbaum, of Scherer, Hunn, Greenbaum & Beck, carefully placed his cigar where it would not char his Italian Renaissance desk and smoothed out the list which Mr. Elderberry, the secretary of The Horse's Neck Extension Copper Mining Company, handed to him. The list was typed on thin sheets; of foolscap and contained the names of stockholders, but as it had lain rolled up in the bottom of Mr. Elderberry's desk for five years without being disturbed it was inclined to resist the gentle pressure of Mr. Greenbaum's fingers.

Mr. Greenbaum glanced sharply round the plate-glass lake that separated him from the other directors of Horse's Neck, rather as if he had detected his associates in a crime.

"Isaacs says," he announced in an arrogant, almost insulting tone, though below the surface he was an entirely genial person, "that the new vein in the Amphalula runs into the west drift of Horse's Neck almost to where we quit work in Number Nine five years ago."

"If it does it will make it a bonanza property," emphatically declared his partner, Mr. Scherer, a dolichocephalous person with very black hair and thin bluish cheeks. "It's a pity we didn't buy it all in at ten cents a share."

"We did!" retorted Greenbaum. "All that could be shaken out. We've got all the stock that hasn't gravitated to the cemeteries."

"Even if the Amphalula vein doesn't run into it it will come near enough to make Horse's Neck worth dollars per share. It's a heads-I-win-tails-you-lose proposition," commented Mr. Hunn dryly. "Who controls Amphalula?"

"We do," snapped Greenbaum.

"Then it's a cinch," returned Hunn mildly. "Shake out the sleepers, reorganize, and sell or hold as seems most advisable later on."

Mr. Elderberry cleared his throat tentatively.

"If you gentlemen will pardon me—I have been considering this matter for some little time," he hazarded. Mr. Elderberry was not only the professional salaried secretary of Horse's Neck but was also treasurer of the Amphalula, and general factotum, representative and interlocking director for Scherer, Hunn, Greenbaum & Beck in their various mining enterprises, combining in his person almost as many offices as, Pooh-Bah in "The Mikado." Though he could not have claimed to serve as "First Lord of the Treasury, Lord Chief Justice, Commander-in-Chief, Lord High Admiral, Master of the Buck Hounds, Groom of the Back Stairs, Archbishop of Titipu and Lord Mayor, both acting and elect, all rolled into one," he could with entire modesty have admitted the soft impeachment of being simultaneously treasurer of Amphalula, vice-president of Hooligan Gulch and Red Water, secretary of Horse's Neck, Holy Jo, Gargoyle Extension, Cowhide Number Five, Consolidated Bimetallic, Nevada Mastodon, Leaping Frog, Orelady Mine, Why Marry and Sol's Cliff Buttress, and president of Blimp Consolidated.

All these various properties were either owned or controlled by Scherer, Hunn, Greenbaum & Beck and had been acquired with the use of the same original capital in various entirely legal ways, which at the present moment are irrelevant. The firm was a strictly honorable business house, from both their own point of view and that of the Street. Everything they did was with and by the advice of counsel. Yet not one of these active-minded gentlemen, including Mr. Greenbaum, the dolichocephalous Scherer and the acephalous Hunn, had ever done a stroke of productive work or contributed anything toward the common weal. In fact, distress to somebody in some form, and usually to a large number of persons, inevitably followed whatever deal they undertook, since their business was speculating in mining properties and unloading the bad ones upon an unsuspecting public which Scherer, Hunn, Greenbaum & Beck had permitted to deceive itself.

Thus, when Greenbaum called upon Mr. Elderberry for advice, it savored strongly of Koko's consulting Pooh-Bah and was sometimes almost as confusing, for just as Pooh-Bah on these occasions was won't to reply, "Certainly. In which of my capacities? As First Lord of the Treasury, Lord Chamberlain, Attorney-General, Chancellor of the Exchequer, Privy Purse or Private Secretary?" so the financial and corporate Elderberry might equally well ask: "Exactly. But are you seeking my advice as secretary of Horse's Neck, of Holy Jo, of Cowhide Number Five, or as vice-president of Hooligan Gulch and Red Water, treasurer of Amphalula or president of Blimp Consolidated?"

Just now it was, of course, obvious that he was addressing the company in his capacity of secretary of Horse's Neck.

"It goes without saying, gentlemen, that this property is pretty nearly down and out. You will recall that most of the insiders sold out on the tail of the Goldfield Boom and waited for the market to sag until we could buy in again. The mines are full of water, work was abandoned over four years ago, and the property is practically defunct. The original capitalization was ten million shares at one dollar a share. We own or control at least four million shares, for which we paid ten to fifteen cents, while we had sold our original holdings for one dollar sixty to one dollar ninety-five a share. While Horse's Neck represents a handsome profit—in my opinion"—he cleared his throat again as if deprecating the vulgarity of his phrase—"it is good for another whirl."

"You say it's full of water?" inquired Hunn.

"It will cost about fifty thousand dollars to pump out the mines and a hundred thousand to repair the machinery. Then there's quite an indebtedness—about seventy-five thousand; and tax liens—another fifty. Half a million dollars would put Horse's Neck on the map, and if the Amphalula vein crosses the property it will be worth ten millions. If it doesn't, the chance that it is going to will make a market for the stock."

Mr. Elderberry swept with a bland inquiring eye the shore of the glassy sea about which his associates were gathered.

"I've been over the ground," announced Greenbaum "and it's a good gamble. We want Horse's Neck for ourselves—at any rate until we are confident that it's a real lemon. Half a million will do it. I'll personally put up a hundred thousand."

"How are you going to get rid of the fifty thousand other stockholders?" asked Mr. Beck dubiously "We don't want them trailing along with us."

"I propose," answered Mr. Elderberry brightly, in his capacity as chief conspirator for Scherer, Hunn, *et al.*, "that we organize a new corporation to be called 'Lallapaloosa Limited' and capitalize it at a million dollars—one million shares at a dollar a share. Then we will execute a contract between Horse's Neck and Lallapaloosa by the terms of which the old bankrupt corporation will sell to the new corporation all its assets for one hundred and twenty-five thousand dollars. We underwrite the stock of Lallapaloosa at fifty cents a share, thus supplying the new corporation with the funds with which to purchase the properties of the old. In a word we shall get Horse's Neck for a hundred and twenty-five thousand and have three hundred and seventy-five thousand left out of what we subscribe to underwrite the stock to put it on its feet."

"That's all right," debated Hunn. "But how about the other stockholders in Horse's Neck that Beck referred to? Where do they come in?"

"I've thought of that," returned Elderberry. "Of course you can't just squeeze 'em out entirely. That wouldn't be legal. They must be given the chance to subscribe at par to the stock of the new corporation on the basis of one share in the new for every ten they hold in the old; or, as

Horse's Neck is a Delaware corporation, to have their old stock appraised under the laws of Delaware. In point of fact, they've all written off their holdings in Horse's Neck as a total loss years ago and you couldn't drag 'em into putting in any new money. They'll simply let it go—forfeit their stock in Horse's Neck and be wiped out because they were not willing to go in and reorganize the property with us."

"They would if they knew about Amphalula," remarked Beck.

"Well, they don't!" snapped Greenbaum, "and we're under no obligations to tell 'em. They can infer what they like from the fact that Horse's Neck has been selling for ten cents a share for the last three years."

"Is that right, Chippingham?" inquired Beck of the attorney who was in attendance. "I mean—is it legal?"

"Perfectly legal," replied Mr. Chippingham conclusively. "A corporation has a perfect right to dispose of its entire assets for a proper consideration and if any minority stockholder feels aggrieved he can take the matter to the Delaware courts and get his equity assessed. Besides, everybody is treated alike—all the stockholders in Horse's Neck can subscribe pro rata for Lallapaloosa."

"Only they won't," grinned Scherer.

"And so, as they are wiped out—the new corporation—that is us—in fact gets their equity, just as much as if they had deeded it to us."

"That is, we get for nothing about one-half the value of the property," agreed Elderberry. "Now, I've been over the list and I don't think you'll hear a peep from any of them."

"He's got 'em on the list—he's got 'em on the list;
And they'll none of 'em be missed—they'll none of 'em be missed!"

hummed Mr. Beck. "It looks good to me! I'll take a hundred thousand."

"Mr. Chippingham has the papers drawn already," continued Elderberry. "Of course you've got to give the old stockholders notice, but we can rush the thing through and before anybody wakes up the thing will be done. Then they can holler all they want."

"Well, I'll come in," announced Hunn complacently.

"So will I," echoed Scherer. "And the firm can underwrite the last hundred thousand, and that will clean it up."

"Is it all right for us to underwrite the stock ourselves at half price?" inquired Mr. Beck. "I mean—is it legal?"

"Sure!" reiterated Mr. Chippingham. "Somebody's got to underwrite it; why not us?"

"Move we adjourn," said Mr. Greenbaum. "Elderberry—the usual."

Mr. Elderberry removed from his change pocket five glittering gold pieces and slid one across the glass sheet to each director.

"Second motion. Carried! All up—seventh inning!" smiled Mr. Scherer; and the directors, pocketing their gold pieces, arose.

If, as it has been defined, ethics consists of a "system of principles and rules concerning moral obligations and regard for the rights of others," it may be interesting to speculate as to whether or not these gentlemen had any or not, and, if so, what it may have been. But in considering this somewhat nice question it should be borne in mind that Messrs. Scherer, Hunn, Greenbaum & Beck were bankers of standing, and were advised by a firm of attorneys of the highest reputation. On its face, and as it was about to be represented to the stockholders of Horse's Neck, the proposition appeared fair enough.

The circular, shortly after sent out to all the names upon the list, stated succinctly that financial and labor conditions had been such that it had been found impossible to operate the mine profitably for several years, that it had depreciated greatly in value owing to the water which had accumulated in its lower levels, that it had exhausted its surplus, that a heavy indebtedness had accumulated, that the corporation's outstanding notes had been protested and that the property would be sold under foreclosure unless money was immediately raised to pay them, the interest due and taxes; that half a million dollars was needed to put the property in operation and that there was no way to secure it, as nobody was willing to loan money to a bankrupt mining concern. That under these circumstances no practical method had been proposed except to organize a new corporation capitalized at one million instead of ten, to the stock of which each shareholder in Horse's Neck might subscribe in proportion to his holdings, at par, and to which the assets of the old corporation should be transferred practically for its debts. That this, in a word, was the only way to save the situation and possibly make a go of a bad business, and that it was a gamble in which the old stockholders had a right, up to a certain date, to participate if they saw fit. Those that did not would find their stock in Horse's Neck entirely valueless as it would have no assets left which had not been transferred to Lallapaloosa. Stockholders who were dissatisfied could protest against the enabling resolution to be offered at the annual meeting of the stockholders of Horse's Neck to be held the following week at Wilmington, Delaware, and could avail themselves of the right to have their equity assessed under the laws of Delaware, but as the liabilities practically equaled the present value of the property that equity would naturally be highly problematical.

Now, as a matter of morals or of law the only thing that made the proposed reorganization unethical or inequitable was the single trifling fact that those responsible for it were the only ones who knew of the existence and proximity of the Amphalula vein. When a mining company, a railroad, an oil well or any other enterprise is down and out it is only fair that the majority stockholders, who are obliged to protect their investment, should have the right to call upon the rest to come forward and do their share or else drop out. A minority stockholder cannot appeal to any canon of fair play whereby he should be entitled to sit back and let the majority take all the risks and then claim his share of the profits.

The imponderable element of injustice in the situation consisted in the suppression of a fact which the directors concealed but concerning which, however, they made no representation, false or otherwise. They were going to risk half a million dollars of their own money and they wanted the whole gamble for themselves. They sincerely felt that nobody else was entitled to take that risk with them. Once they had floated Horse's Neck they had come to look upon it as their own private affair. The minority had no rights which they, the majority, were bound to respect. The minority were nothing but a lot of piking gamblers, anyway, who bought or sold for a rise or fall of a few cents. They knew nothing of the property and cared less for its real value. They were merely traders and if they lost they forgot it or tried to. On the other hand Scherer, Hunn, Greenbaum & Beck were promoters, who contributed something to the economic advancement of the nation.

* * * * *

"Regarding my hat, which you suggested this morning should be pressed at a cost of fifty cents," remarked Mr. Tutt to Miss Wiggin when he returned to the office upon the adjournment of court in the afternoon and replaced that ancient object in its accustomed resting-place— "regarding that precious hat of mine"—he eyed it affectionately—"I can only say that I would as soon send myself to a dry-cleaning establishment as to permit its profanation by the iron of a haberdasher."

Miss Wiggin laughed lightly.

"That doesn't explain your cryptic statement that it would probably cost you a hundred thousand dollars," she replied. "Still—"

Mr. Tutt turned suddenly upon his heel and held her with an upraised hand, the bony wrist of which was encircled, after an intervening space of some five inches, by a frayed cuff confined with a black onyx button the size of a quarter.

"Behold," he cried in the deep resonant voice that he used in addressing juries at the climax of a peroration, "the integuments of my personality—the ancient habiliments of an honorable profession—the panoply of the legal warrior. Here, my corslet"—he touched his dingy waistcoat with his left hand; "my greaves"—he brushed the baggy legs of his pantaloons; "my halberd"—he raised his old mahogany cane with its knot of yellow ivory; "my casque"—he indicated his ruffled stove-pipe "Arrayed in these I am Mr. Ephraim Tutt, attorney and counselor at law—the senior partner in Tutt & Tutt—a respected member of the bar duly accredited and authorized to practise before the Supreme Court of the State of New York, the Court of Appeals, the District Court of the United States, the Circuit Court of Appeals, the Supreme Court of the United States, the Court of Claims—"

"—the Police Court and the Coroner's Court," concluded Miss Wiggin, making him a mock curtsy.

"Without these indicia of my profession and my individuality I should be like David without his sling or Samson without his hair. I should be merely Tutt, a criminal lawyer—one of a multitude—regarded perhaps as a shyster. But in these robes of my high office I am a high priest of the law; just as you, my dear girl, are one of its many devoted and worthy priestesses. Can you imagine me going to court in a bowler hat or arguing to the jury in a cutaway coat or bobtail business suit? Can you picture Ephraim Tutt with his hair cut short or in an Ascot tie, any more than you can envisage him in riding breeches or wearing lilacs? No! There is but one Mr. Tutt, and these are his only garments. He who steals my hat may steal trash, but without it I should be like a disembodied spirit unable to return to my earthly dwelling-place.

"A paltry hundred thousand?

"Nay, without my hat—my helmet!—I should be valueless to myself and everybody else; so estimate my worth and you can assay the value of my hat. What am I worth in your opinion?"

And then Miss Wiggin, having glanced cautiously if quickly round, made a most astonishing declaration.

"Just about a million times more than anybody else in the whole world, you old dear!" she whispered and rising upon her toes she kissed his wrinkled cheek.

"Dear me! You really mustn't do that!" gasped Mr. Tutt.

"Well," she retorted, "you can discharge me if you like. But first sit down, light a cigar and let me tell you something."

Mr. Tutt did as he was bid, chuckling.

"Well," said Miss Wiggin, "there is such a thing as Horse's Neck Extension after all!"

"Um—you don't say?" he answered, struggling to make his stogy draw.

"And it has an office with about a hundred other corporations of various kinds—most of them with names that sound like the zoo—Yellow Wildcat, Jumping Leapfrog, and that sort of thing. It seems Horse's Neck is played out and they are going to reorganize it—"

"Who are?" demanded her employer, suddenly sitting erect.

"Scherer, Hunn, Greenbaum & Beck."

"The dickens they are!" he ejaculated. "That bunch of pirates? Not if I know it!"

"Why not?"

"Reorganize! Reorganize? Reorganization is my middle name!" cried Mr. Tutt. "So Scherer, Hunn, Greenbaum & Beck are going to reorganize something, are they? Let 'em try! Not so long as I've got my hat!"

"This is all very enigmatical to me," replied Miss Wiggin. "But then, I'm only a woman. Aren't they all right? Why shouldn't they reorganize a mine if it's exhausted?"

"If it's exhausted why do they want to reorganize it?" he demanded, climbing to his feet. "Let me tell you something, Minerva! All my life I've been fighting against tyranny—the tyranny of the law, the tyranny of power, the tyranny of money."

He drew fiercely on his stogy, which being desiccated flared like a Roman candle.

192

"You don't need to tell me what this plan of reorganization is; because they wouldn't propose one unless it was going to benefit them in some way, and the only way it can be made to benefit them is at the expense of the other stockholders. *Quod erat demonstrandum.*"

Mr. Tutt seemed to have become distended somehow and to have spread over the entire wall surface of his office like the genie which the fisherman innocently permitted to escape from the bottle.

"There isn't one reorganization scheme in a hundred that isn't crooked somewhere."

"According to that, if a business is unsuccessful it ought to be allowed to go to pot for fear that somebody might make a profit in putting it on its feet," she countered. "I think you're a violent, irascible, prejudiced old man!"

"All the same," he retorted, "show me a reorganization scheme and I'll show you a flimflam! What's this one? Bet you anything you like it's as crooked as a ram's horn. I don't have to hear about it. Don't want to read the plan. But I'll bust it—higher than Hades. See if I don't!"

He spat the remaining filaments of his stogy from the window and fished out another.

"How do we come into it, anyhow?" he demanded.

"Doctor—I mean Mister Barrows," replied Miss Wiggin.

"Oh, yes. Of course. Well, you send for him to come down here and sign the papers."

"What papers?"

"The complaint and order to show cause."

"But there isn't any."

"There will be, all right, by the time he gets here."

Miss Wiggin looked first puzzled and then pained.

"I don't understand," she said rather stiffly. "Do you mean that the firm of Tutt & Tutt is going to engage in the enterprise of trying to break up a plan of reorganization without knowing what it is? Won't you lay us all open to the accusation of being strikers?"

Mr. Tutt's ordinarily brown complexion became slightly tinged with purple.

"Let the court decide!" he cried hotly. "You say Scherer, Hunn, Greenbaum & Beck are proposing to reorganize a mining company? You admit we hold some of the stock? Well—as the natural-born and perennial champion of the outraged minority—I'm going to attack it, and bust it, and raise heck with it—on general principles. I'm going to throw that damned old hat of mine into the ring, my child, and play hell with everything."

And with a cluck Mr. Tutt leaned over, produced a dingy bottle wrapped in a coat of many colors and poured himself out a glass of malt extract.

* * * * *

When Mr. Greenbaum was summoned to the telephone and informed by Mr. Elderberry in disgruntled tones that somebody had just served upon him an order to show cause why the proposed reorganization of Horse's Neck should not be set aside and enjoined, he not only became instantly annoyed but highly excited.

"What!" he almost screamed.

"I'll read it to you, if you don't believe it!" said Mr. Elderberry.

"'United States District Court, Southern District of New York, Edward V. Barrows, Complainant against Horse's Neck Extension Mining Company, Defendant.

"'Upon the subpoena herein and the complaint duly verified the nineteenth day of February, 1919, and the affidavit of Ephraim Tutt and—'"

"Who in hell is Tutt?" shouted Greenbaum, interrupting.

"I don't know," retorted Elderberry; "or Barrows either."

"Well, skip all the legal rot and get to the point," directed Greenbaum.

"'Ordered—ordered, that the defendant, Horse's Neck Extension Mining Company, show cause at a stated term to be held in and for—'"

"I said to cut the legal rot!"

"Um—um—'why an injunction order should not be issued herein pending the trial of this action and enjoining the defendant from disposing of its assets and for the appointment of a receiver of the assets of the defendant corporation; and why the complainant should not have such other, further and different relief as may be equitable.'"

There was a long pause during which Mr. Elderberry was under a convincing delusion that he could actually hear the thoughts that were rattling round in Mr. Greenbaum's brain.

"You there?" he inquired presently.

"Oh, yes, I'm here!" retorted Greenbaum. "This is the devil of a note! Have you spoken to Chippingham?"

"Yes."

"What does he say?"

"He says it's awkward. They have got hold somewhere of one of our old circulars of 1914 in which the property is described as worth about ten million dollars—that was during the boom, you remember—and they claim we are selling it to ourselves for less than one million and that on its face it's a fraud on the minority stockholders who can't afford to buy stock in the new corporation—as of course it would be if the mine was really worth ten million or anything like it."

"Did we really ever get out any circular like that?" demanded Greenbaum in a protesting voice. "I don't recall any."

"That was when we were making a market for the stock," Elderberry reminded him. "We couldn't say enough. Honestly, to look at the thing now is enough to make you sick!"

"Well, it's just a hold-up—that's what it is. Some crook like this Tutt or this Barrows has found out about Amphalula and is bringing a strike suit. You'll have to call a meeting right away. I'd like to strangle all these shyster lawyers!"

And it never occurred to Mr. Greenbaum that the possible existence of the Amphalula vein was what in fact made the order to show cause justifiable—his actual ground of complaint being that anybody should, as he assumed, have found out about it in defiance of his plans.

* * * * *

"Yeronner," said Attendant Mike Horan as he helped Judge Pollak into his black bombazine gown in his chambers in the old Post-Office Building on the morning of the return day, "there's a great bunch out there in the court room waitin' for ye, an' no mistake!"

"Indeed!" remarked His Honor. "And who are they? What is the case?"

"Hanged if I know," answered Mike, snipping a piece of fluff off his judgeship's shoulder. "There's a white-bearded old guy, two or three swell gents with tall hats, Counselor Tutt and an attorney named Chippingham, besides that pretty Miss Wiggin; and they ain't speakin' none to one another, neither."

"It must be that mining-reorganization case," answered the judge. "Well, it's time to go in."

They walked down the dirty marble corridor and entered the court room, while the clerk rapped on the railing.

"Hear ye! Hear ye! Hear ye! All persons having any business to do with the District Court of the United States draw near, give your attention and you will be heard," he intoned with unctuous authority.

The "bunch" rose and made obeisance.

"Good morning," said the judge pleasantly, sitting down with a side switch of the bombazine. "Barrows against the—er—er—Horse's Neck Mining Company. Do you represent the complainant, Mr. Tutt?"

"I do," answered Mr. Tutt with great dignity. "Your Honor, this is a motion for an order to show cause why an injunction *pendente lite* should not issue restraining the sale of the assets, of this corporation to another

196

in fraud of its minority stockholders—and for a receiver. My client, an aged man living upon his farm in the northern part of the state, is the owner of one hundred thousand shares in the Horse's Neck Mining Company of the par value of one hundred thousand dollars. He has owned these securities for many years. They represent his entire capital. He is a bona fide stockholder—"

"May I be pardoned for interrupting?" sneered Chippingham, springing to his feet. "I think the court should be informed at the outset that this man, Barrows, is a notorious ex-convict."

Judge Pollak raised his eyebrows.

"This is an outrage!" thundered Mr. Tutt, his form rising ceilingward. "My client—like all of us—has had his misfortunes, but they are happily a thing of the past; he has the same rights as if he were an archbishop, the president of a university or—a judge of this honorable court."

"We are sitting in equity," remarked His Honor. "The question of *bona fides* is a vital one. *Is* the complainant an ex-convict?"

"This is the complainant, sir," cried Mr. Tutt, indicating old Doc, now for the first time in his life smartly arrayed in a new checked suit, red tie, patent-leather shoes and suède gloves, and with his beard neatly trimmed. "This is the unfortunate man whose honest savings of a lifetime are being wrested from him by an unscrupulous group of manipulators who—in my opinion—are more deserving of confinement behind prison walls than he ever was."

The gentlemen with the tall hats bit their lips and showed signs of poorly suppressed agitation.

"But *is* your client an ex-convict, Mr. Tutt?" repeated the judge quietly.

"Yes, Your Honor, he is."

"When and how did he become possessed of his stock?"

Mr. Tutt turned to Doc with an air of ineffectually striving to master his righteous indignation.

"Tell the court, Mr. Barrows," he cried, "in your own words."

197

Doc Barrows wonderingly rose.

"If you please, sir," he began, "it's quite a long story. You see, I was the owner of all the stock of The Chicago Water Front and Terminal Company—there was a flaw in the title deed which I can explain to you privately if you wish—and when I was—er—visiting—up on the Hudson—I met a man there who was the owner of a hundred thousand shares of Horse's Neck, and we agreed to exchange."

The judge tried to hide a slight smile.

"I see," he replied pleasantly. "And what was the man's name?"

"Oscar Bloom, sir."

The gentlemen with the tall hats exchanged agitated glances.

"Do you know how he got his stock?"

"No, sir."

"That is all. Go on, Mr. Tutt."

Doc sat down while Mr. Tutt again unhooked his lank form.

"To resume where I was interrupted, Your Honor, the directors controlling a majority of the stock of this corporation, the capital of which is ten millions of dollars, have made a contract to sell all of its properties to another corporation, organized by themselves and capitalized for one million, for the sum of one hundred and twenty-five thousand dollars!

"It is true that in their plan of reorganization they offer to permit any stockholder in the old corporation to subscribe for stock in the new at par—thus at first glance placing all upon what seems to be an equality; but any stockholder who does not see fit to subscribe or cannot afford to do so is wiped out, for there will be nothing left in the way of assets in Horse's Neck after the transfer is completed.

"Now these gentlemen have underwritten the stock in the new Lallapaloosa Company at fifty cents upon the dollar, and if this nefarious deal is permitted to go through they will thus acquire a property worth ten millions for five hundred thousand dollars, of which they will use only one hundred and twenty-five thousand in payment of old indebtedness. In effect, they confiscate the equity of all the minority stockholders in

Horse's Neck who cannot afford to subscribe for stock in Lallapaloosa."
He turned upon the uncomfortable tall hats with an arraigning eye.

"In the criminal courts, Your Honor, such a conspiracy would be properly described as grand larceny; in Wall Street perchance it may be viewed as high finance. But so long as there are courts of equity such a wrong upon a helpless stockholder will not go unrebuked. Have I made myself clear to Your Honor?"

Judge Pollak looked interested. He was a man famous for his protection of helpless minorities and his court had been selected by Mr. Tutt on this account.

"If the facts are as you state them, Mr. Tutt," he answered seriously, "the plan on its face would seem to be inequitable. If the property is worth ten million the consideration is palpably inadequate. Your client's equity, worth on that basis at least one hundred thousand dollars, would be entirely destroyed without any redress."

"Your Honor," burst out Mr. Chippingham, whose bald head had been bobbing about in excited contiguity with the tall hats, "this is a most misleading statement. The assets of Horse's Neck aren't worth a hundred thousand dollars. And if any of the minority don't want to come into the reorganization—and I assure Your Honor that we would welcome their participation—they can have their equity appraised under the laws of Delaware and the finding becomes a lien on the assets even after they have been transferred."

"What relief does that give a man like Mr. Barrows?" shouted Mr. Tutt. "He can't afford to go down to Wilmington with a carload of books and a corps of experts to prove the value of Horse's Neck. It would cost him more than his stock is worth!"

"That remedy is not exclusive, in any event," declared the judge. "If this complainant is going to be defrauded I will enjoin this contract *pendente lite* and appoint a receiver."

"Your Honor!" protested Chippingham in great agony. "It is not the fact that this mine is worth ten million. It isn't worth at the most more than one hundred thousand. It is, full of water, the machinery is rusted and falling to pieces and the workings are practically exhausted. The only way to rehabilitate this property is for everybody to come in and put up enough money by subscribing to the stock of the new corporation to pump it out, buy new engines and start producing again. Is it fair to the majority, who are willing to go on, put up more money, and make an attempt to save the property, to have this complainant—an ex-convict who never paid a cent for his stock, dug up from heaven knows where—enjoin their contract and throw the corporation into the hands of a receiver? This is nothing but a strike suit. I repeat—a strike suit!"

He glowered breathless at his adversary.

"Oh! Oh!" groaned Mr. Tutt in horrified tones.

"Gentlemen! Gentlemen!" expostulated the court. "This will not do!"

"I beg pardon—of the court," stammered Mr. Chippingham.

"Your Honor," mourned Mr. Tutt, "I have practised here for thirty years and this is the first time I have ever been insulted in open court. A strike suit? I hold in my hand"—he waved it threateningly at the tall hats—"a circular issued by these directors less than five years ago, in which they give the itemized value of this property as ten million dollars. Shortly after that circular was issued the stock sold in the open market at one dollar and ninety cents a share. In two years it sank to ten cents a share. Will a little water, a little rust, a little trouble with labor reduce the value of a great property like this from ten millions of dollars to one hundred thousand—one per cent of its appraised value? Either"—he fixed Chippingham with an exultant and terrifying glance—"they were lying then or they are lying now!"

"Let me look at that circular," directed Judge Pollak. He took it from Mr. Tutt's eager hand, glanced through it and turned sharply upon the quaking Chippingham.

"How long have you been attorney for Scherer, Hunn, Greenbaum & Beck?"

200

"Twelve years, Your Honor."

"Who is Wilson W. Elderberry?"

"He is the secretary of the Horse's Neck Extension, Your Honor."

"Is he in court?"

From a distant corner Mr. Elderberry bashfully rose.

"Come here!" ordered the court. And the Pooh-Bah of the Scherer-Hunn-Greenbaum-Beck enterprises came cringing to the bar.

"Did you sign this circular in 1914?" demanded Judge Pollak.

"Yes, Your Honor."

"Were the statements contained in it true?"

Elderberry squirmed.

"Ye-es, Your Honor. That is—they were to the best of my knowledge and belief. I was, of course, obliged to take what information was at hand—and—er—and—"

"Did you sign the other circular, issued last month, to the effect that the mine was practically valueless?"

"Yes, sir." Elderberry studiously examined the moldings on the cornice of the judge's canopy.

"Um!" remarked the court significantly.

There was a flurry among the tall hats. Then Mr. Greenbaum sprang to his feet.

"If you please, Your Honor," he announced, staccato, "we entirely disavow Mr. Elderberry's circular of 1914. It was issued without our knowledge or authority. It is no evidence that the mine was worth ten millions or any other amount at that time."

"Oh! Oh!" choked Mr. Tutt, while Miss Wiggin giggled delightedly into her brief case.

Judge Pollak bent upon Mr. Greenbaum a withering glance.

"Did your firm sell any of its holdings in Horse's Neck after the issuance of that circular?"

Greenbaum hesitated. He would have liked to wring that judge's neck.

"Why—how do I know? We may have."

"*Did* you?"

"Say 'yes,' for God's sake," hissed Chippingham "or you'll land in the pen!"

"I am informed that we did," answered Greenbaum defiantly. "That is, I don't *say* we did. Very likely we did. Our books would show. But I repeat—we disavow this circular and we deny any responsibility for this man, Elderberry."

This man, Elderberry, who for twelve long years had writhed under the biting lash of his employer's tongue, hating him with a hatred known only to those in subordinate positions who are bribed to suffer the "whips and scorns of time, the oppressor's wrong, the proud man's contumely," quivered and saw red. He was going to be made the goat! They expected him to take all the responsibility and give them a clean slate! The nerve of it! To hell with them! Suddenly he began to cry, shockingly, with deep stertorous suspirations.

"No—you won't!" he hiccuped. "You shan't lay the blame on me! I'll tell the truth, I will! I won't stand for it! Your Honor, they want to reorganize Horse's Neck because they think there's a vein in Amphalula that crosses one of the old workings and that it'll make the property worth millions and millions."

Utter silence descended upon the court room—silence broken only by the slow ticktack of the self-winding clock on the rear wall and the whine of the electric cars on Park Row. One of the tall hats crept quietly to the door and vanished. The others sat like images.

Then the court said very quietly: "I will adjourn this matter for one week. I need not point out that what has occurred has a very grave interpretation. Adjourn court!"

Old Doc Barrows, the two Tutts and Miss Wiggin were sitting in Mr. Tutt's office an hour later when Willie announced that Mr. Tobias Greenbaum was outside and would like an interview.

"Send him in!" directed Mr. Tutt, winking at Miss Wiggin.

Mr. Greenbaum entered, frowning and without salutation, while Doc partially rose, moved by the acquired instinct of disciplinary politeness, then changed his mind and sat down again.

"See here," snarled Greenbaum. "You sure have made a most awful hash of this business. I don't want to argue about it. We could go ahead and beat you, but Pollak is prejudiced and will probably give you your injunction and appoint a receiver. If he does, that will knock the whole property higher than a kite. Nobody would ever buy stock in it or even finance it. Now how much do you want to call off your suit?"

"Have a stogy?" asked Mr. Tutt politely.

"Nope."

"We want exactly one hundred thousand dollars."

Greenbaum laughed derisively.

"A hundred thousand fiddlesticks! This old jailbird swindled another crook, Bloom—"

"Oh, Bloom was a crook too, was he?" chuckled Mr. Tutt. "He worked for your firm, didn't he?"

"That's nothing to do with it!" retorted Greenbaum angrily. "Your swindling client traded some bum stock in a fake corporation for Bloom's stock, which he received for bona fide services—"

"Like Elderberry's?" inquired Tutt innocently.

"Your man never paid a cent for his holdings. That alone would throw him out of court. The mine isn't worth a cent without the Amphalula vein. We're taking a big chance. You've got us down and we've got to pay; but we'll pay only ten thousand dollars—that's final."

"I ain't any more of a swindler than you be!" said Doc with plaintive indignation.

"What do you wish to do, Mr. Barrows?" asked Mr. Tutt, turning to him deferentially.

"I leave it entirely to you, Mr. Tutt. It's your stock; I gave it all to you months ago."

"Then," answered Mr. Tutt with fine scorn, "I shall tell this miserable cheating rogue and rascal either to pay you a hundred thousand dollars or go to hell."

Mr. Tobias Greenbaum clenched his fists and cast a black glance upon the group.

"You can wreck this corporation if you choose, you bunch of dirty blackmailers, but you'll get not a cent more than ten thousand. For the last time, will you take it or not?"

Mr. Tutt rose and pointed toward the door.

"Kindly remove yourself before I call the police," he said coldly. "I advise the firm of Scherer, Hunn, Greenbaum & Beck to retain criminal counsel. Your ten thousand may come in handy for that purpose."

Mr. Tobias Greenbaum went.

"And now, Miss Wiggin, how about a cup of tea?" said Mr. Tutt.

The firm of Tutt & Tutt claimed to be the only law firm in the city of New York which still maintained the historic English custom of having tea at five o'clock. Whether the claim had any foundation or not the tea was none the less an institution, undoubtedly generating a friendly, sociable atmosphere throughout the office; and now Willie pulled aside the screen in the corner and disclosed the gate-leg table over which Miss Wiggin exercised her daily prerogative. Soon the room was filled with the comfortable odor of Pekoe, of muffins toasted upon an electric heater, of cigarettes and stogies. Yet there was, and had been ever since their conversation about the hat, a certain restraint between Miss Wiggin and Mr. Tutt, rising presumably out of her suggestion that his course savored of blackmail, however justified it had afterward turned out to be.

"My, isn't this nice!" murmured Doc, trying unsuccessfully to eat a muffin, drink his tea and do justice to a stogy at the same time. "It's so homy now, isn't it?"

"Doc," answered Mr. Tutt, "did you really want that ten thousand?"

"Me?" repeated Doc vaguely. "Why, I told you I gave that stock to you long ago. It isn't mine any longer. Besides, I don't want any money. I'm perfectly happy as I am."

Mr. Tutt laughed genially.

"Oh, well," he said, "it's no matter who owns it. Elderberry just telephoned me that he had received a telegram from the Amphalula that the vein had definitely run out. It's all over—including the shouting."

"Elderberry telephone you?" queried Miss Wiggin in astonishment.

"Yes, Elderberry. You see, he's done, he says, with Scherer, Hunn, Greenbaum & Beck. Wants to turn state's evidence and put 'em all in jail. I've said I'd help him."

"Then why didn't you take the ten thousand and call it quits while the getting was good?" demanded his partner icily.

"Because I knew I'd never get the ten anyway," replied Mr. Tutt. "Greenbaum would have learned about the vein on his return to the office."

"Well, I must be getting along back to Pottsville!" mumbled Doc. "This has been a very pleasant trip—very pleasant; and quite—quite—exciting. I—"

"What I'd like to know, Mr. Tutt," interrupted Miss Wiggin, "is how you justify your course in this matter. When you attempted to block this proposed reorganization you knew nothing about the Elderberry circular of 1914 valuing the property at ten million, or of the Amphalula vein. On its face you were attempting to wreck a perfectly honest piece of financiering, and unless it was a strike suit—which I hope and pray it wasn't—"

"Strike suit!" protested Mr. Tutt with a slight twinkle in his eye. "How can you suggest such a thing! Didn't the events demonstrate the wisdom of my judgment?"

"But you didn't know what was going to happen when you began your suit!" she argued firmly. "I hate to say it, but I should think that if everything had not come out just as it has your motives might easily have been misconstrued."

"It was a matter of principle with me, my dear," declared Mr. Tutt solemnly. "Just to show there's no ill feeling, won't you give me another cup of tea?"

BIBLIOBAZAAR

The essential book market!

Did you know that you can get any of our titles in large print?

Did you know that we have an ever-growing collection of books in many languages?

Order online:
www.bibliobazaar.com

Find all of your favorite classic books!

Stay up to date with the latest government reports!

At BiblioBazaar, we aim to make knowledge more accessible by making thousands of titles available to you- *quickly and affordably*.

Contact us:
BiblioBazaar
PO Box 21206
Charleston, SC 29413

LaVergne, TN USA
04 March 2010

174807LV00004BA/108/P